FOR THE RECORD

ALSO BY EMMA LORD

Tweet Cute

You Have a Match

When You Get the Chance

Begin Again

The Getaway List

The Break-Up Pact

The Rival

Emma Lord

FOR THE RECORD

a novel

ST. MARTIN'S GRIFFIN
NEW YORK

First published in the United States by St. Martin's Griffin, an imprint of St. Martin's Publishing Group

EU Representative: Macmillan Publishers Ireland Ltd, 1st Floor, The Liffey Trust Centre, 117–126 Sheriff Street Upper, Dublin 1, DO1 YC43

www.stmartins.com

Designed by Jen Edwards

Record player © GoodStudio/Shutterstock

The Library of Congress Cataloging-in-Publication Data is available upon request.

ISBN 978-1-250-84532-0 (trade paperback)
ISBN 978-1-250-84533-7 (ebook)

Our books may be purchased in bulk for specialty retail/wholesale, literacy, corporate/premium, educational, and subscription box use. Please contact MacmillanSpecialMarkets@macmillan.com.

First Edition: 2025

10 9 8 7 6 5 4 3 2 1

To anyone who's ready for a comeback

PART ONE

"Play You by Heart"

chapter one
MACK

If you think your love life is a disaster, I'm here to make you feel a whole lot better about yourself. Mine wasn't just a disaster, but an international one. As in, anyone on the planet with an internet connection can read up about me and the parade of cliché bad boys, cheating nepo babies, and textbook narcissists I dated while I was touring the world with Thunder Hearts in my early twenties.

Tonight was supposed to be the night I turned the story around. I was already crafting the imaginary headline as I made my way to the bar: MACKENZIE WATERS ON FIRST DATE WITH NICE, SECURE, 401(K)-OWNING MAN WHO TEXTS BACK IN A TIMELY MANNER! I was the kind of proud that bordered on smug.

And now I'm propped up on a magenta barstool in the middle of happy hour at Lightning Strike, panic sweating through my pink satin tank top, and shouting, "Can I borrow literally anybody's phone?"

Nobody can hear me over the chorus of pop sensation Serena's catchy hit, "Kickstart My Heart." I turn to see if one of the bartenders can lend me theirs, only to meet a familiar pair of dark, perfectly winged eyes on the other side of the bar, blinking at me in alarm.

"You good?" asks Hannah, one of my best friends and former bandmate.

Even with the bar half hiding her from the crowd, she's unmissably stunning in a sleek purple slip dress that hugs the pale curves of her body, her glossy black hair catching the sparkles from the disco ball in the dim light. I'm never not happy to see her, but right now I could kiss her on the damn mouth.

"I thought you were uptown!" I say, hopping off the stool.

"I'm about to be," she says. "Why do you look more freaked out than that time we accidentally ate those brownies at Coachella?"

Ah. It was after that particular performance that *Rolling Stone* dubbed Thunder Hearts a "force to be reckoned with," and me specifically a "shiny ball of chaos." The high may have worn off mid-set, but the photo of me singing through a wild tangle of blond hair as I pluck an open bag of Goldfish crackers out of my crop top will last for eternity.

I grab Hannah by the shoulders. "I need your phone."

Hannah doesn't hesitate. "It's charging in the back."

She leads me to the back office, which is littered with pictures of us in our Thunder Hearts prime. The three of us napping on top of each other on a tour bus in our glittery matching unitards. The three of us holding our Grammy Awards with wild grins. The three of us onstage at what would be our last show, huddled reverently around one mic for the final song.

I tear my eyes off them when Hannah puts her phone in my hand. I open her Tick Tune app to see an artist called Seven taking up all the top slots on her daily queue, with ominously sad songs like "Ghosted" and "Cracked."

"It's for the bar," Hannah says gleefully, squeezing my arm. "We're having a Seven night tomorrow. The tickets sold out in five minutes."

Damn. More New Yorkers need therapy than I thought.

"How on earth did you have the time to set that up?" I ask as I tap through the app.

When Thunder Hearts called it quits, Hannah wasted no time pivoting from the stage to running her own small empire. Now Hannah Says includes a size-inclusive, retro-inspired clothing line, a full 1950s-style Target cookware set, and a set of nostalgic coffee table books full of Thai-American-fusion cocktails and dishes she and her sisters grew up with as their parents launched restaurants and bars in every borough in New York City.

On top of all that, she owns this bar. If Hannah sleeps, I sure as hell have never seen it.

"What happened to your phone?" Hannah asks.

"It got into a fight with your floor," I tell her, waiting for the logout page to load. "The screen is more broken than—well, our brains that day at Coachella."

"You dropped it?" asks Hannah.

"Dropped" is an understatement. That thing went down like it was in a damn pinball machine—straight into my cocktail, which then toppled onto the bar, ricocheting the phone in slow motion to the floor like it was going for a dramatic Oscar.

In my defense, I was already on edge. This date Hannah helped set up tonight is my first proper date not just in years, but possibly in my life. Hannah was trying to distract me from my nerves by watching the most recent video I scheduled to put on Tick Tune, where I've been posting songs anonymously as I figure out what to do with the black hole that is my current career.

Turns out Tick Tune is the ideal place to go for that. It's like if

Snapchat and TikTok created a strange little not-for-profit music baby. Musicians post their songs with undownloadable videos that can only be streamed once per day. After that, the song disappears from the user's account for twenty-four hours—which means if you really love an artist and want to listen to the high-quality version of the audio, you better go find other friends who will let you listen with them, stat.

Because it's so fleeting, listening parties are popping up in major cities for popular artists on the app. And because it's so murky in nature, the app has attracted a lot of artists who want to stay anonymous.

But thanks to my idiocy, I might not be anonymous much longer. It took Hannah two seconds to point out that the frame of the video included a tiny edge of the lace dress she gifted me from her line, which she delayed the launch of last week.

In any other universe that wouldn't matter. But we exist in a universe where eagle-eyed fans would make the connection between the unreleased Hannah merch and an anonymous singer and start posting my identity in two seconds flat.

And in the span of those two seconds I'd be professionally, emotionally, and existentially fucked.

The obvious next step was to delete it from my phone as fast as possible. My brain got the "delete" memo and my hands got the "fast as possible" memo, but their wires got crossed, which is how I accidentally smashed my phone screen into smithereens.

"It's seven fifty-six," says Hannah.

The service is so bad that it'll be a miracle if I log into my account by this time next year.

"Shit, shit, shit," I chant.

Hannah raises her eyebrows at me. "What's the actual worst that happens if the video goes live?"

There is such a menagerie of consequences that it's hard to pick just one. The first is, of course, that it would complicate the tentative new contract with the record label. I told them I wanted to launch a solo career a few months back, and they've had me in "former girl band member" purgatory ever since. According to my manager, Isla, they're at odds with how to fit me in the market, but their instructions were explicit: sit tight and don't post anything.

I can't even blame them for the hesitation. My voice changed massively after Thunder Hearts broke up. While Serena immediately vaulted into superstardom and Hannah launched her lifestyle empire, I was holed up in my apartment, trying to relearn an instrument I'd been playing my whole life. The songs I spent the last year posting on Tick Tune—they were never meant to go viral. They were just meant to practice, and to get some less-than-welcome feelings about some less-than-deserving men out of my system.

Which leads me to the next consequence, which is that if anyone knew I was behind these songs, they'd know exactly who I wrote them about. And I'd rather eat my recording mic than let any of those men know they left a mark.

But in some ways neither of those things compares to the worst consequence of my alter ego being revealed to the world tonight. I deflate against the wall of the office, turning my grim gaze from the phone screen to Hannah's expectant face.

"Serena would never forgive me," I say quietly.

Hannah's eyes flicker in confusion. "Serena doesn't know?" Off my wince, she deflates, too. "You two still haven't worked things out."

Not for lack of trying. I have called enough times since Serena left for her tour that "Incoming Call from Mack" might as well be her phone lock screen. The few times I manage to get her on the line she's always rushing off for an interview or a workout or a page spread, talking through her teeth with a steely politeness you'd give a guy who rear-ended you in a grocery store parking lot, not a best friend and former bandmate.

Which is to say, I haven't told her about the Tick Tune videos, or even that I'm trying to start a solo career. I wanted us to be on more solid ground before we talked about it, but we haven't reached it yet.

"Seven fifty-eight," I murmur, my eyes on the still-loading screen.

"Maybe there's better service out back," says Hannah.

I take off like someone just fired off the starting gun at the accidental self-sabotage Olympics, busting out to the back alley. It's a space I'm all too familiar with, since we've been using it as an entrance and exit for years—before Hannah took over Lightning Strike, it was a dive bar so decrepit that none of us could find a sign or a menu to learn its actual name. The kind with drinks so sickly sweet that they might have been watered-down cough syrup, and chairs so unreliable that sitting anywhere was a game of roulette. But it was one of the few places in New York where we could stay out late at the height of our fame without worrying about running into anyone who would post videos of us taking cringeworthy, tipsy selfies after a round of Fireball shots, so it was home away from home.

The service bars on Hannah's phone instantly spike up as I mount the little flight of stairs from the back door to the alley, but not fast enough. The login page only half loads. I hold the phone up to the sky like I'm begging the moon to intervene. When that does nothing, I hike my cowboy boots up the railing of the stairs, so desperate that I'm hoping the extra five inches will be my technological salvation.

Not one second later do I remember why I never wore this particular pair of boots onstage. The pink soles are cute as a button, but have less traction than a waterslide. My foot loses its hold so fast that I don't even have time for my idiocy to settle in before I'm pitching backward.

I scramble to grab the railing, but it's too late. I'm going down and hitting every one of these stairs when I do it. MACKENZIE WATERS COULDN'T EVEN MANAGE FIRST DATE WITH NICE, SECURE, 401(K)-OWNING MAN WITHOUT THOROUGHLY CONCUSSING HERSELF AND BREAKING ALL HER BONES.

Only when I land, it isn't on the cold concrete. It's on the warm, firm plane of someone's chest. Someone whose arms instantly wrap around me, stopping my momentum, and hold me so firmly that my feet don't quite touch the ground.

"Well, look who it is."

It's been ages since I've heard that wry, velvety voice, but its effect on me is immediate. Shock and relief, the kind my body doesn't know what to do with. Like blinding sunshine spilling onto the pavement when I'm still wet from the rain. Like a dislocated joint getting shoved back into place. Like my heart has been slightly off beat and something just slammed into it to knock it back into an old rhythm.

Like turning to stare into the bright hazel eyes of the person who has hurt me more than he'll ever know, but had more of my heart than anyone else ever could.

Samuel Blaze settles both hands on my waist, skimming just under my tank top as he settles me back on the ground with a slow, shameless smirk. "And you said you'd never fall for a guy like me."

chapter two
SAM

Well, shit. If there was a chance I was over Mackenzie Waters, it's shot to hell now.

I knew what I would be in for if I ran into her here tonight, but I was cocky enough to think it wouldn't matter. That time would have dulled the effect of all that wild blond hair flying with each step, all that bare, sun-kissed skin exposed by the thin straps and low plunge of her tank top.

But now she's settled in my arms, her small, panting body an inferno against mine. Now she's tilting her head to look at me, her startling blue eyes flashing under her dark brows.

Now she looks like something about to mess me up all over again, and damn if it doesn't feel good. Apparently two years wasn't near long enough for me to stop wanting something I know I can't have.

She lets out a little gasp against my chest as she pushes herself off me. She's back in my space just as fast, her full, flushed cheeks tilted up to face me. She parts her lips, stares deeply into my eyes, and says, "Give me your phone."

I let out a huff of laughter. "No 'thank you, dashing hero, for saving my life'?"

She's already snaking a hand behind me, reaching into my back pocket for my phone. I snatch it first, unlocking it and holding it up over my head. She's about as tall as Tinker Bell, but she's desperate enough for it that she tries to reach it anyway.

"Someone will be saving *your* life if you don't fork that over," she warns.

I hold it higher, dangling it between two fingers. "At least say 'please.'"

She takes a sharp step closer and lets out a growl through her teeth that I enjoy a little too much for my own good. It's distracting enough that she manages to reach down and tweak my side, making me double over in surprise and drop the phone. She catches it in midair and darts to the wall of the alley before I know what hit me.

A familiar feeling, when it comes to Mackenzie Waters. I saunter in her direction, taking in the rest of her—tight denim jeans hugging the curves of her hips, a pair of cowboy boots I haven't seen before. Nothing like the loud neon getup she and the rest of Thunder Hearts used to wear back on tour, leaving trails of glitter behind them like calling cards.

I told myself if I saw her tonight that it would be enough. That I'd head over to a discreet bar down the street and leave her be. But old habits die hard, and this one has me bracing my hand against the brick wall, leaning over her.

"You clean up well, Sparkles."

She chafes at the old nickname, her eyes still trained on the phone. "Why are you here? Ego too big to fit on the west side?"

My smirk widens. So she knows I'm in the West Village. Guess I'm not the only one who's been keeping tabs.

"I have a meeting with Twyla."

One that I've been dreading all day, even if I've just short of forgotten it now. I crane my neck to glimpse at the phone screen, but she dips under me, her wild hair brushing my arm.

"Lightning Strike is our turf," she says.

She taps something on the phone that makes her go stiller than the walls. Then she blows out a breath and taps it again, exiting out of an app. She knocks the phone into my chest to return it and I let out an exaggerated "oof," then clap my hand on top of hers, holding her there before she can stalk off.

"Turf, huh? I didn't realize we divided up the city." I lean in so the words are closer to her ear. Not as close as I used to, but closer than I should. "What other lines am I not supposed to cross?"

Thing is I swore upside down and backward I wouldn't try to rile this woman tonight. She's doing just fine without me around and I should be glad for it. But I can't help myself. I remember why the second her eyes fly to mine, more paralyzing than any comeback. With looks like the kind she can throw at me, she's always had home court advantage in our little spats, both onstage and off.

She doesn't pull away, but presses her hand harder against my chest. She tilts her head up to better meet my eye, close enough that I can smell the faint fruitiness of her hair.

"I'd make you a whole damn map of lines," she says, "but you'd trip over the beds of half the women in this city before you found them."

The steeliness in her expression cracks just enough that I know something must have cracked in mine first.

Shit. I shouldn't have come here in the first place. The last thing

I need is to kick up another round of this again—letting myself feel too much for this woman I'm no damn good for, who has zero interest in a guy like me. I could blame the circumstances in the past, but now there's nobody to blame but myself.

So before she can soften, I raise my eyebrows, easing myself back. Cocky. Distant. The version of me she loves to hate.

"Ouch," I say. "You think I could only pull half?"

Right on cue she snatches her hand back, rolling her eyes. "Depends on how many are in the mood to make a mistake."

I keep my own hand on my chest, leaning back like I've been wounded. "Aw, c'mon. You're breaking my heart over here."

"You can cut the antics, Blaze," she says, heading for the back door. "Our little sideshow is long over, and the last thing I need is an encore."

She disappears into Lightning Strike, but it's never hard to follow Mackenzie with that curtain of yellow hair in her wake. Still, I stop in my tracks when I reach the main part of the bar. It's unrecognizable from that grimy, tetanus-infected dive bar we used as a hideaway back in the day. Back when I wasn't just Sam, but Samuel Blaze, front man of Candy Shard. Back when I was here with a different woman every month, keeping my distance from the one woman who knew how to get under my skin. Back when I was on the verge of a life unrecognizable from the one I have now.

I skim the braided bracelet tight around my wrist. There are parts of those days I miss like a hole in me, but I'd be a damn fool to take any of what I have now for granted.

The new interiors of the bar are still dark but warm, with Technicolor on the walls and a retro shine on the stools and high-top tables. Mackenzie's hair catches the pink light like a beacon in the back corner.

You're no. Damn. Good for her, I remind myself.

I've seen her. She's alive and well. Time to get back to my own problems.

I turn to look for Twyla, nearly colliding with another man. The haircut-twice-a-month, loafer-wearing kind who clearly just got off work somewhere farther downtown.

He opens his mouth to apologize, then blinks. "Oh," he says. That's how these conversations always start when I get recognized—an *oh*, and then they'll ask for an autograph or a selfie or tell me how Candy Shard's music got them through high school, and I'll be grateful to hear it, even if it makes me feel like the most ancient thirty-one-year-old man alive.

Normally I'm happy to stop, but these days it usually comes with a follow-up of *So what's next for you, man?* And if I knew the answer to that I wouldn't be having this meeting with Twyla tonight.

So I give the stranger a firm, friendly smile I use when I don't feel like chatting. Only he's not looking at me anymore. His eyes are squarely set on the best part of this bar: the pixie of a woman heading toward him, smiling widely, arms outstretched for a hug.

"Grayson!" Mackenzie calls.

It's like watching one of those cute viral videos about unlikely animal friendships. I am so unused to seeing Mackenzie interact with a man who doesn't have "bad news" written all over him that there's no other way for my brain to rationalize it.

Then Mackenzie plants a kiss on his cheek, and the scene is anything but cute. A hot coil of jealousy rises up in me so fast that I take a step back. Both because I am not the *jealous* type and also because it's ridiculous that I'm feeling it at all.

"Hey, you," says Grayson warmly.

Well, I'm officially in need of a drink. It's the only way I'm going to survive glancing up and seeing Mackenzie making doe eyes at a finance bro all night. I'm about to duck out, but Grayson turns back to me.

"You two dated," he says, like he's pleased with himself for remembering.

The instant Mackenzie spots me, her nostrils flare. "Our bands toured together. He's just an old coworker."

"One hell of an office we worked in, if that's the case," I say wryly.

She shoots me a warning look I can't blame her for. I used to mercilessly roast all those idiot "boyfriends" she dragged around our tour buses and hotels—the walking red flags who would make her fall head over her sequined heels by saying all the right things before doing all the wrong ones.

But this guy doesn't look like the type. He looks like he fell out of a nineties rom-com called something cliché like *Mister Right*.

"But that love song you two did. Oh, what was it?" Grayson asks. "It was stuck in my head that whole summer—'Play You by Heart'!"

"That wasn't a love song," says Mackenzie.

"Wasn't the chorus something about your heartstrings being tangled?" Grayson asks.

Mackenzie smiles tightly. "The label made us release it. It was only a big deal because our bands were in a feud."

Understatement of the century. Our rivalry with Thunder Hearts was a mismatch, considering they were a pop girl group and we were a punk rock band, but by the peak it was so notorious that there were internet writers whose entire *jobs* were keeping up with our antics when we were on tour together. Antics that were so well-memorialized that there's a literal "Candy Shards vs. Thunder Hearts" Wikipedia page about it. (One Mackenzie liberally edited to change my name to Asswipe, even if she never copped to it.)

"Oh yeah? I didn't know about the feud." Grayson shrugs affably, turning to me. "I was a big nerd in law school. Hannah had to catch me up on half a decade of pop culture once I started working for her, and Mackenzie's filling in the gaps."

"And she forgot to tell you that Mackenzie and I were in a forbidden, star-crossed romance that spanned continents, years, and dozens of songs?" I ask.

Mackenzie's boot grinds into the toe of my shoe, a clear *Get lost*. And damn it if I'm not trying. But something about seeing the familiar, friendly way Grayson puts a hand on her arm is locking me in place. I've always had a talent for masochism, but if I don't get out of here, I'm about to add assholery to the list.

"They made us pretend there was this whole 'will they, won't they' thing between us when we toured together," she explains to Grayson. "Publicity stunt."

"Aw," says Grayson, laughing in that way that nice guys do. Earnest. Unbothered. It probably doesn't say anything all that good about me that it makes me hate him more than any of Mackenzie's exes combined. "You must have been good at it. Sounded like you two were in love."

I know right then that it's the last time I'm ever going to see Mackenzie Waters. At least, the last time I'll do it on purpose. She's been up-front about what she wanted with every song she's ever written: someone who's in it for the long haul. Looks like she's finally picking the right ones for the job.

Best I can do for her now is stay the hell out of her way.

chapter three
SAM

My manager, Twyla, is easy to spot even in the happy hour crowd, wearing her usual loud uniform of bright colors and a scarf that swallows her whole. She lowers her oversized glasses at me, her dark eyes lined with a punchy blue that matches the streak of it in her graying auburn hair.

"I looked at the menu long and hard, but there wasn't a cocktail I thought you'd like." She casts her eyes at Mackenzie on the other side of the bar before giving me a pointed look. "So I took the liberty of getting you a 'What the Hell Do You Think You're Doing, Sammy Boy' on the rocks."

The glass she offers me is clearly straight whiskey. I raise it to toast with her cocktail, which is just as wild and colorful as her outfit.

"I'm discussing my career prospects with my wonderful, talented, impeccably dressed manager," I say.

"Butter me up any harder and you'll have to put me on a roll."

She tilts her head in Mackenzie's direction again. "And here I was thinking you picked this place because people wouldn't bother us."

New Yorkers are already, on the whole, unfazed by famous people in restaurants and bars. But there are a few spots with enough of them that New Yorkers make a *point* of not noticing famous people in their midst, and I know from my old bandmates—who are far more welcome in here than I am—that this is one of them.

"I thought Mackenzie wasn't in the city," I say, a little too innocently.

Twyla smirks. "Aw. You saw her Instagram go dark."

I take a sip of my drink. Caught red-handed. I can't say I didn't notice she hadn't posted in a while, but I was curious if it was something to worry about or a social media move her agent, Isla, orchestrated. It's safe to say if Twyla knows about it, it must be the latter. The whole reason our bands were in a staged feud in the first place was because our managers are identical twins and set it up from the start.

"What can I say? Life was boring without Mackenzie spicing up my feed," I say breezily.

Twyla lets out a disbelieving hum and says, "Drink that fast, would you? I've got bad news and also bad news."

I knock it back, the dread settling back in faster than the booze can burn it off.

"All right." I set my half-empty glass down. "Hit me with it."

"The bad news is the label said absolutely the fuck not to our proposal."

I blow out a breath, settling my elbows on the table. "Why?" I ask.

Twyla doesn't coddle. She hasn't since the day she plucked me out of the YouTube trenches, where teenage me was angstily posting covers of Linkin Park songs with ten views on them, nine of which were probably my mom.

"You don't have momentum," says Twyla bluntly. "It's all fine and good that you've got a different sound now, but there's jack shit they can do to relaunch you without a tour and with barely any press. It's like shooting a horse before it ever leaves the stable."

"Well, shit." I run a hand through my hair, then pull it out. Compose my face. I can't afford to look upset about anything in public, and besides—this isn't exactly a surprise. "Can we try other labels?"

Twyla nudges my drink closer to me. "That's the other bad news. I asked around. Nobody else wants to touch that plan with a stick, either."

I shouldn't be disappointed. I knew it was a long shot, getting the label on board with turning their former punk rock front man into an acoustic singer after two years off the grid. But I thought maybe if they heard samples of my new work and considered my plan to do smaller, New York–based venues for a more intimate feel, they might take a chance on it.

Twyla snaps a finger in front of my face. "No moping. Game's not over yet. It just means we have to compromise."

I shake my head. There are things I'm willing to bend on, but not this one. "No touring. I won't leave Ben."

I skim the braided bracelet on my wrist again, my touchstone. Finding out I was a dad two years ago was the biggest shock of my life, and now is the best part of it. That kid is my whole world. I miss making music like nobody's business, but if choosing music means losing time with him on the road, I can't do it.

I could never do to him what my own dad did to me.

"If staying home is that important, you have to bring something else to the table here," says Twyla. "Something that draws fans back in. Something that gets their attention."

I wince. That's the other issue. I can't do anything too splashy. Ben's six, so he knows by now that his dad is famous. But his mom, Lizzie, and I have done a pretty good job of shielding him from it, even when the "Samuel Blaze has a secret son!" news blew up every corner of the internet. It's died down since then, but if I do anything that puts too much attention on myself, it could easily put it back on Ben.

"It doesn't have to be *big*," says Twyla, anticipating me. "But it has to be enticing."

Mackenzie lets out a sharp laugh on the other side of the bar. The pang that goes through me is so instant that I'm mad at myself for it, but I can't help it—I want to be the one winding her up. It's a chronic condition. I've had it since the day we met.

"Why did Mackenzie stop posting?" I ask.

Because if it hadn't been for that, I wouldn't have had this ridiculous compulsion to come check on her. I wouldn't have followed it all the way to this bar, watching her fall for Millennial Prince Charming and making this meeting ten times more miserable than it already was.

"If you were so curious you could have just called her," says Twyla, raising her eyebrows at me.

Thing is, though, I didn't know if she'd answer. I didn't even know if she kept my number in her phone. Not after the way we left things. Not after she'd made a point to never call me again after that last time we talked.

Twyla waves a hand in front of my face, blocking my view of Mackenzie. I blink out of my haze.

"Sorry," I mutter, my face hot. I aim the question at my whiskey glass. "Everything's good with her, though?"

Twyla sighs. "If you really want to know, Mackenzie's Instagram was dark because she's trying to—wait. Wait."

She whips her head at Mackenzie, then back at me, her expression shifting like a kaleidoscope—scrutiny to bewilderment to some kind of revelation that has her on her feet faster than a bomb threat.

"Are you—leaving?"

A pointless question, because by the time I finish it, she's halfway to the door. "I'll call you later tonight! Stay put, I ordered apps for the table!"

I am absolutely not *staying put*. I am going to settle our tab and sneak out the back door to nurse my bruised ego with a beer in front of the TV and pretend this entire night didn't happen.

But Twyla isn't the only one headed for the door. Grayson is right behind her, his phone pressed to his ear, turning to wave and mouth an apology.

When I look over, Mackenzie's alone at the back of the bar, waving back with a static smile. She drops the smile when Grayson goes, only to immediately catch my eye. Her face instantly comes back to life—indignant, heated, and aimed right at me.

I use my foot to kick out the empty stool at my table, then lean back and cross my arms in invitation. She rolls her eyes. I roll mine back, overexaggerated and ridiculous. It wrestles the smallest smile out of her—the kind that always feels like a prize, since she tries so hard not to let me earn it.

It's the damn apps that do it, though. The Massaman curry cheese tots and spicy lemongrass popcorn hit the table and the next thing I know, Mackenzie is standing across the table from me, plucking a tot off the plate and saying, "What the hell are you actually doing here?"

chapter four

MACKENZIE

The first thing you need to know about Samuel Blaze is that it's damn near impossible not to fall in love with him.

One of my working theories is that it's because he is so at odds with himself. The sharp, unyielding planes of his face against the smooth tenor of his voice. The mischief in his words against the depth of his hazel eyes. He's a puzzle too damn compelling not to try to solve, and once you think about something too much, you can't help but feel something for it.

I'm embarrassed to admit I was no exception to that rule in the end. But I overcame it. Through practice, time, and a few borderline-unhinged song lyrics, I've beaten it out of my system.

All I'm doing by walking over to him is proving just how effective I was. But then Sam aims one of those shameless smiles at me, and I'm not so sure about that.

"I'll tell you what I'm doing here," he says, "if you tell me what on earth you were doing with my phone."

He tosses a piece of popcorn in the air and catches it in his mouth, the smile blooming into a boyish grin as he gets his first taste of Hannah's inspired fusion menu. I keep my face as neutral as I can, sipping on my cocktail and imagining what his face would do if I told him the truth.

I'm the woman who's been blowing up Tick Tune writing songs about each of her exes one by one, I could say. Or just cut straight to the point with three little syllables: *I'm Seven.*

The song that was supposed to go up tonight is the last one. A song to close out the embarrassment of my old love life once and for all. But now I'm sitting in front of all six feet of the man who inspired that last song and, damn, do I love staring into his fallen-angel eyes.

I settle on the stool across from him. "I asked first," I say coolly.

He doesn't hesitate. "I missed you."

That's a bold-faced lie. We were told to play up the "enemies to lovers" trope onstage with our constant barbs and shenanigans, but the *enemies* part wasn't an act. I couldn't stand being around him and the loud parade of groupies he partied with every night, the women who'd come and go like ice-cream flavors of the month. I steered so clear of him that I didn't realize I was stupidly in love with him until it was too late to do anything to fix it.

"You missed me," I deadpan.

Sam's gaze is so sincere that I almost believe him. Then without warning he reaches for another piece of popcorn and tosses it across the table at me. I tilt my head to catch it in my mouth and he lets out a low whistle, impressed.

"You didn't miss me?" he asks.

"Like a feedbacking amp."

His eyes flicker with mischief. "So," he says. "My phone?"

I skim my tongue over my teeth, swallowing. "I was subscribing you to Aging Punk Rockers Anonymous. Heard it helps with the flannel addiction."

He stares down at the flannel he's got on now, the grin curling wider. Someone else might be tempted to touch the softness of that flannel against the warm planes of his body. Someone else might appreciate the way his lanky frame has filled out enough to see the faint outline of muscle against the worn-out T-shirt he's wearing under it.

Thankfully, I am cured of all of that. It's just hot in here because of the happy hour crowd, is all.

"Is your new boyfriend going to be mad when he comes back and sees an old-timer stole his girl?"

My face flushes. Grayson is the head of Hannah's legal team, and I only met him at one of her launches last week. I ended the cookware demonstration with more sauce on my shirt than the plate, and he valiantly attempted to save it with a Tide-to-go pen. Hannah set up the date a few days after: *If you're serious about dating good guys, Grayson's one of the best.*

But that's none of Sam's business.

"We rescheduled," I tell him. "His mom locked herself out of her apartment and he's got her spare key."

I brace myself. This was one of Sam's favorite bits during rehearsals, when we were forced to share space—finding little things to mock about the guys I was all starry-eyed over, smirking like a cat just before he did it.

Babe. Babe. *Baaaabe!* he would call in a hazy voice, making fun of the startup guy who was always blitzed out of his mind. Or he'd put a finger up to his bandmates and say, *Shhh. You're interrupting my process*, roasting that trust funder I brought around a few times who called himself a "sculptor" and clearly had never so much as touched Play-Doh in his life.

I hated him for it then, but hated him even more for it later. He saw through all those jerks long before I did.

This time, though, Sam just nods. "Good on him."

There's a beat of quiet, so I decide it will be the last one. I passed the test. I faced off with the final boss. I am over Sam Blaze once and for all, and can move on with my life.

I slide off the stool.

"Wait."

Sam's hand wraps around my wrist, stopping my momentum. My breath stalls, at first in surprise, and then something else entirely. A feeling that doesn't creep in, but floods. It's all over me before I can stop it—every nerve in my body is humming to the point of screaming, wanting to get closer, let the flood in until it drowns me.

It's the warmth of his grip. It's the unexpected need in his eyes. It's the way I feel, irrationally, like every place in New York is the wrong place to be except right here.

Fuck the test. I'm still failing the pop quiz.

Sam eases his grip but doesn't let go. "This is one of her best," he says.

An unexpected hush has fallen over the bar, so I can hear the verse of the soft, acoustic song playing through the speakers, with a low, slightly raspy voice.

I only make it through one verse. I can't bear it another moment. The rest of the bar is still at half volume, a few even singing along, but I clear my throat.

"Sounds like she could use one of these cocktails," I say.

Sam blinks. "Tell me you've heard of Seven." When I don't answer, Sam is downright incredulous. "She blew up a few months ago on Tick Tune."

He clearly has more to say, but I cut him off. "Maybe I'll check her out."

His hand is still around my wrist. He slowly lets it go, and his warmth is immediately replaced by an ache. I'm dizzy with it, and the impossibility of this whole moment—his eyes on me as he listens to words he has no idea I'm the one singing.

I pull in a breath, avoiding his gaze. "This is new," I say, gesturing at the braided bracelet around his wrist.

Sam's entire face softens in a way I've never seen. "Ben made it for me."

I nod. "Your son."

Sam was a magnet for wild antics back in the day, but the grand finale was the wildest of all—on the last night of our final joint tour, Sam discovered he had a four-year-old son. In the brief conversation we had in the aftermath, he said he was doing everything he could to keep it quiet for Ben's sake, but it was splashed all over social media within days.

There were so many times I almost called. But checking in felt too self-serving. By then I knew I'd always want something more than he could offer, and would always be looking for it. It was better to have a clean break, and besides—I had problems of my own to deal with. Big ones.

Still, I couldn't help but worry. It's a relief to see the ease in his posture, to see the quiet pride in his smile.

"He's the best," says Sam.

My throat goes thick. "Proud Dad" looks good on him, the same way everything does. Which means I better get the hell out of here before it starts looking *too* good.

"I've got to go," I say, knocking back the rest of my drink. "Maybe I'll see you in another two years."

Sam stands, too, and for a moment I think he's offering to leave with me. He surprises me by wrapping me up in a hug, the full-body kind that's impossible to resist. Just like that, my arms are sliding up the sinewy muscles of his shoulders, my head settling in the tempting crook of his neck. He smells sweet; he always has. Sweetness with a depth to it. Like browned butter. Like a lazy sunset.

God dammit if I'm not already drafting more lyrics about this man as I let him go.

"Take care of yourself, Sparkles."

And I do. I go home and edit the video on my laptop so it's just the window curtains fluttering, no telltale unreleased merch in sight. Then I open the desktop version of Tick Tune and upload the new draft of the song—the last song the anonymous singer known as Seven will ever publish. The song I'll sing to finally let Samuel Blaze go.

I take a breath, and another, and another. But my thumb doesn't press "Post" just yet. The story between us may not have had a good ending, but that doesn't mean it won't hurt, closing the book.

Just as I'm hovering over the button, an incoming text from Hannah pops up on my laptop screen:

Excuse you?? What happened to the perfectly
nice lawyer I set you up with?????

I open the link she sent. At the top of the article is an image of me and Sam hugging in the bar. You can tell it's me because of the trademark messy blond curls down to my waist, but Sam's face is in full view of the lens. His eyes are crushed shut. It looks like he's in pain.

It looks like a feeling I know too well.

Waters set ablaze once more? it reads, with the teaser, *"Smack" spotted together for the first time since steamy awards show.*

The comment section of the article is already on fire, but I don't let myself read it. I close the tab. I close my eyes. It doesn't work—I'm still stuck on the expression on his face, stricken by the recognition of it. By the way it wraps around my heart and *tugs* with a pull he's had on me since before we even met.

I toss the laptop on my bed. "God *dammit*."

Because despite everything, the story isn't over. Or rather—for some reason, I still can't let it end.

chapter five
SAM

Lizzie Ford is a lot of things. The mother of our son. The co-owner of New York City's most delicious bakery. My best friend.

But right now, she is primarily a pain in my ass.

"Nope!" she says, swatting my hand before it lands on one of the milk tarts on a back counter. Her thick pepper-brown braid swings over her shoulder as she turns back to her cake batter. "No dessert until you see reason."

Little does the world know, this is how "punk rock" my life is now. When Ben is in school, I spend most of my days in the back of Sugar Harmony getting bossed around by Lizzie and her wife, Kara, who opened this hybrid Scandinavian and West African bakery based on their grandmothers' recipes just before Ben was born. It's my favorite place on earth, even if I have to check most of my free will at the door.

"I helped make them," I protest.

Lizzie raises her brows at me. "Licking the emptied-out bowl does not qualify as 'helping.' Now give me one good reason why you won't hear Twyla out on this."

By "this," Lizzie means the call from Twyla that I was dumb enough to take on speaker in front of her after I got home from Lightning Strike last night. If I had any idea that Twyla had spent the evening conspiring with Isla, I might have changed my damn number before I heard her say, "Good news! We're pitching you and Mackenzie to the label as a duet."

The call was over too fast for me to protest, but lasted just long enough for Lizzie to latch onto the idea like a dog with a bone.

"If you'd seen Mackenzie last night, you'd know she would sooner strangle me with a guitar string than work with me again," I tell Lizzie.

She tightens the strings on her bright blue Sugar Harmony apron. "Are you saying that because it's true, or because you're secretly chickenshit?"

"Hey," I protest. "I play all the time."

New York is a city full of "if you know, you know" places, and one of them is the back room at Sugar Harmony. At night we convert it into a speakeasy where I started holding open mic nights a few days a week, no phones allowed. My old bandmates Divya and Rob started inviting friends, who invited friends of friends, and now it's a mix of newbies and regulars every week.

Lizzie smirks from under the brim of her baseball cap. "I meant about getting Mackenzie on board."

Fun fact: Lizzie only got half a psychology degree before she quit for culinary school, but will never let me, Kara, or any of our friends forget it.

Fortunately, I am spared any more of her cross-analysis by someone opening the back door. Unfortunately, it's Twyla herself.

"Don't worry," she tells me, sweeping in with a loud orange-

and-red ensemble, complete with a giant butterfly brooch. "I'm too magnanimous for an 'I told you the fuck so.'"

"Told me the fuck about what?" I ask.

"Don't be coy," she says, flashing her phone screen at me.

Sam Blaze not so Waters-proof after all?

Mackenzie and I generated enough headlines in our rivalry to paper-mache the Empire State Building, so the terrible pun is no surprise. The image just under it is another story. Someone caught us mid-embrace. Her face is mostly concealed by my shoulder, but there's a little crease between her brows—one I only ever saw a handful of times.

"Oh," I manage.

Twyla lets out a disbelieving snort. "Look at you pretending you don't have internet."

Lizzie winces on my behalf. "We blocked Sam's name on our phones and all the laptops. Little eyes and ears."

Little eyes and ears that didn't need to be reading headlines about the dad they didn't even know about for the first four years of their life. Particularly headlines like BLAZE RUMORED TO HAVE *DOZENS* OF OTHER SECRET KIDS!! and Lizzie's personal favorite, AN ANALYSIS OF THIS DECADE'S LINGERIE TRENDS, BASED ON UNDERWEAR THROWN AT SAMUEL BLAZE ONSTAGE.

"Did you come all the way downtown to torture me with this?" I ask Twyla.

"That's just a bonus. I came here to take a look at the cupcakes. Or did you forget that your favorite manager is turning fifty?"

I doubt there's a soul in Manhattan who doesn't know about Twyla and Isla's joint fiftieth birthday party this weekend. Not only did they rent out several floors of a building for the night, but the invitations were sent with massive masquerade masks that were "required dress." Half the music industry was Instagramming about it before they could type out an RSVP.

"I heard a rumor," I say.

Lizzie heads back to grab the cupcake design sampler book. My hand is halfway to the counter when she calls from the office, "No treats for Sam!"

I grab a milk tart that's too ugly for the display case, breaking it in half and winking at Twyla. "I won't tell if you won't."

Twyla takes her half. "Only if you care to explain the origins of this . . . Doritos muffin?"

"Ben special," I explain, lifting one of them up from the experimental batch for her inspection.

A "Ben special" is really just shorthand for "somehow Lizzie and I created a kid who hates sweets." Every week he comes up with a different "dessert" we help him make—pepperoni cinnamon rolls, mac and cheese scones, even an ill-fated lasagna cake. We've gathered that he doesn't like to eat these "specials" of his half as much as he loves to watch customers react to them on the shelf.

"Horrifying," Twyla declares. "I must have one."

I grab one from the pan and hand it to her, cutting right to the chase. "If you think an article is going to sway me on this, you're wrong. Stunning as ever, but wrong."

Twyla flips her hair appreciatively, but doubles down. "That's because you haven't read the comment section. Fans think you're up to something. They *want* you to be up to something." She taps the phone adamantly. "The draw the label wanted—it just got handed to us on a silver platter."

I occupy myself with taking the now-empty batter bowls to the sink.

"Mackenzie hasn't performed in two years," I point out. "The last thing that's going to get her on a stage is me."

Twyla's lips thin smugly. "So you *do* want to perform with her."

Of course I do. Nobody in their right mind would pass up the chance to perform with Mackenzie. But performing with Mackenzie comes with a price, and that just might be my damn sanity.

But Twyla's playing hardball. She reaches over and shuts off the sink before I can start scrubbing.

"I'll cut right to the chase here," she says. "The label thinks you're both a risk on your own. It's why they haven't relaunched Mackenzie yet, either. But this—this has potential. This has people talking."

She's got my attention now. I know why they'd consider me a risk—I've made it very clear that I have no interest in touring the way I did before. But Mackenzie was born for the stage. She's as sure a bet as they come.

I open my mouth to protest, but Twyla puts a hand up and walks back over to the counter.

"You have exactly the amount of time it will take me to finish this unholy muffin to try to tell me I'm wrong."

It's a damn good muffin, so I don't have a second to lose. I lean against the sink and face her.

"Reason one: I don't want to leave the city. We could never go on tour."

Twyla waves me off. "Mackenzie's not interested in touring."

That's hard to believe about a girl who took Instagrams on the international legs of our tours like it was her second full-time job, but I've got more in my arsenal.

"Reason two—our styles won't match."

The new music I've been playing at the open mic nights is much calmer. More acoustic than punk rock. The command Mackenzie has onstage is anything other than quiet, and only a fool would ask her to be.

"It's been two years," says Twyla. "You're not the only one who's changed their style. I think they'll be a perfect match."

Damn it. I don't want to hear that. Because if it's true, it's going to make this whole thing even more tempting.

Thankfully, it doesn't change my ace in the hole.

"Reason three," I say, making sure to hold her gaze. "Mackenzie Waters hates my guts."

Twyla's lips thin. "Well," she concedes. "There is that."

In my defense, Mackenzie hated me before I did anything to deserve it. Before the rivalry started, even. The day we first met Thunder Hearts was coming off a set at a music festival. I hadn't meant to watch, but Mackenzie was impossible to look away from. All sweet-faced and sharp-eyed, delicate and wild-haired, tearing up and down the stage like it was a playground and shouting some of the most beautiful lyrics I'd ever heard at the top of her lungs.

At the end Mackenzie stuck her tongue out at the crowd and tossed her mic to a stagehand, the screams pitching to impossible volumes as she and the band ran off the stage.

I should have been threatened. Candy Shard was losing momentum just as Thunder Hearts was headed for the moon. But I was every bit as riveted as the crowd.

"Go wait outside the Thunder Hearts trailer, will you?" Twyla asked me. "I'll get the rest of the band."

I knew the plan. Twyla and Isla decided it was best for the bands to meet and come up with a few ideas for how to stoke the fire on the "rivalry" that fans were starting to buzz about after some interviews we'd given. It's why we were closing the festival even though Candy Shard hadn't performed in it for years.

Despite taking my sweet time, I somehow beat everyone to the trailer. I leaned lazily against the door with a cigarette in hand, knowing full well what I looked like—not just self-assured, but cocky. A little too at ease.

But Mackenzie wasn't even looking at me, focused on Isla, who handed her a water bottle and a half-open Take 5 bar. "Did you hear that fucking *riff* Serena did, holy *shit*," Mackenzie was crowing. "We've got to get into the studio and rerecord with that."

Isla didn't answer, her lips curled into a smirk at the sight of me. "Mackenzie, you know Sam," she said.

The moment Mackenzie turned to see me, her face fell so flat someone might have pressed it like a penny. But it did nothing to dull the blue flame of her eyes. It was clear in an instant—she didn't just hate me. She *despised* me.

"I've heard of him," she said coolly.

Right from the start that anger in her eyes felt like an electric spark. I wanted to test the current.

"I didn't realize Taylor Swift had a tiny feral cousin," I said.

She looked me up and down slowly. "I didn't realize you'd look like a knock-off of yourself up close."

A grin split across my face. It was rare anyone mouthed off at me in those days.

"Heard we're going on tour together, Sparkles." Her face stayed hard at the nickname, but I didn't miss the quick twitch of her nose. "First time for you, huh? Maybe you'll learn a thing or two from this knock-off."

Mackenzie pressed her pointer finger into my shoulder, nudging me out of the way of her door. She leaned in so I could feel the heat of her sweat, smell the citrus of her shampoo.

"Oh, buddy," she said. "*I'm* going on tour. You're just old news coming along for the ride."

A few hours later Thunder Hearts joined us onstage for our last number, a cover of "Should I Stay or Should I Go." The plan was simple: the bands would sling a few choice insults back and forth before the performance and between verses. Divya and Serena riled the crowd with dueling guitar riffs. Rob and Hannah battled over the drum kit, each taking turns showing the other one up.

But Mackenzie avoided me like the plague. I was irritated. She was disrupting the plan.

Then the last chords of the song played. I lifted the mic back to my mouth to announce our joint tour, but she ran up from behind me, launched herself onto my back, and yelled into my mic, "Our label is making us tour together against our will! Tickets went on sale five minutes ago! Anyone using the code 'Candy Shard Sucks' gets entered for a VIP package contest!"

The crowd roared. Mackenzie shifted to slide off me, but by then my arms were hooked around her legs, holding tight. I felt her tense in surprise, her breath hitching but her arms tightening around my shoulders.

"Candy Shard's new single is also dropping tonight," I said into the mic. "A portion of the proceeds will go to teaching these newbies how to keep up with a *real* band."

Mackenzie let out a sharp cackle into my ear. "We've got nothing to learn from a has-been like you."

It was innate, what happened next. I tilted my head toward hers, looking right into her waiting eyes. A hush fell over the crowd.

"Don't you?" I asked lowly.

Our lips were inches apart, but neither of us moved. She smelled like sweet chocolate and salty sweat, the heat of her pressing so tight against my back I could swear I felt her heart picking up speed.

But her lips curled into a wolfish smirk. She spoke into my ear instead of the mic, so only I could hear.

"Oh, it's going to drive you nuts, isn't it?" she said. "That I want nothing to do with a guy like you?"

I have no idea what kind of expression I made. Only that people were screaming the word "kiss" before the words were fully out of her mouth. The bands may have been in a rivalry, but it was our heat that fueled its fire. People loved to watch us hate each other. It was the greatest un-love story ever told.

"Dad Dad Dad Dad!" I hear a voice calling from the front.

A grin splits across my face. Hearing those words never gets old. Ben darts into the back a moment later, abruptly dropping his Brooklyn Cyclones backpack on a small table, which means Kara must not be far behind. Whenever one of us picks Ben up from school we let him sprint ahead into the bakery once he hits our block.

I reach out to ruffle his hair, Lizzie's curls in the same dark shade as mine, but he grabs the top of my hand, pressing it to his head and staring up at me accusatorily.

"You didn't tell me you know Mackenzie Waters."

Well, that's it. I will never know peace.

"Oh boy," says Twyla, entirely too entertained.

Ben scoots out from under me to grab my phone off the counter and type his birthday in the passcode, opening Spotify to one of the playlists we made for him. It's almost all Thunder Hearts. If this has bruised both my ego and every punk rock bone in my body, I have kept it to myself.

"I saw a picture of you hugging Mackenzie Waters at recess, and when Hunter got time-out for having his phone, our teacher said there's a whole *song* you two wrote together," says Ben in an indignant rush.

He taps the button to play it. The sweet bite of Mackenzie's voice fills the space, so satisfying that it sneaks up on me, hearing my own voice join in on the chorus.

Ben taps the phone to pause the song, staring at me expectantly.

"I know Mackenzie Waters," I concede.

Ben's eyes widen. "Why didn't you tell me?" he demands. "You know she's my favorite."

That's right. Somehow Lizzie and I not only created a tiny jock who insists on a "birthday pizza" every year instead of cake, but one whose favorite singer once taped a fake tarantula to my water bottle in the middle of a show.

"I hadn't talked to her in a long time," I say.

Ben raises his brows in an uncannily Lizzie-esque manner. "You're in a fight with Mackenzie Waters?"

Twyla cackles. I keep my face as even as possible. "Nah. We're just—not that close."

Ben pulls in a breath to ask more, but then Kara finally catches up to him. She's as unmissable as Twyla, wearing her usual outfit of neon leggings and a Sugar Harmony T-shirt, her box braids pulled back in a giant scrunchie. She gives my back a quick scratch of hello and nods at Twyla, then says to Ben, "Got any idea where your cleats are, champ? We're going to be late for practice."

Ben perks up. "They're on Mom Side." He slides off his seat, then points a finger at me. "I have lots more questions."

"Fair enough," I say, saluting him.

Kara leans in. "Meant to warn you an interrogation was coming, but the kid went supersonic. You're set with the open mic tonight?"

Usually, Kara helps me with sound check and moving the tables around, but once a month she performs one of her own spoken-word poems and uses the prep time to make last-minute adjustments.

"Rocket can help if I need it," I tell her.

A lot of businesses in the city have cats, but Sugar Harmony has an overemployed, underpaid twenty-year-old skateboarder. Rocket sits at the front table of the bakery chugging coffee and working his freelance internet jobs during the day, then performs his offbeat songs in our open mics at night. Even if we didn't love him, he's good for business—he's got that "everybody's little brother" vibe that has all the regulars charmed.

Kara nods. "Also, the Go-Gurts are on Dad Side, right?"

"Top left drawer," I confirm.

She follows Ben to the side door behind the bakery counter, which leads upstairs to Mom Side and Dad Side—Ben's words for our adjoining apartments. I live in one apartment on my own, and Kara and Lizzie live in the larger one beside it, but only on paper. We installed a wide door between the apartments that stays open all day, so Ben just dashes back and forth between either side before he goes to bed on "Mom Side" in the room closest to "Dad Side."

Dad. The word still hits me in the solar plexus. The way Ben says it as easily as he calls Lizzie "Mommy" and Kara "Mom." No matter how Ben feels, I'll always feel like I'm making up for lost time. I'll always worry I might fail him the same way my own dad failed me.

The guilt of that goes deeper than anyone knows. I've kept it to myself, but after the news about Ben blew up two years ago, my dad tried to get in touch. I never knew him growing up—or at least I thought I didn't. Turns out I know his name the same way half the country does. He's even more famous than I am. *Caspar* is such a prolific rock star that I've never heard anyone bother to use his last name.

So prolific that when he got my mom pregnant, he chose music over me before I was even born.

My stomach sinks as I watch Ben tear off for practice, nearly knocking into Lizzie as she walks back in with the lookbook.

"Maybe I could just do something low-key. Anonymous, even."
I reach for my phone. "Like what Seven does."

Twyla yanks the phone out of my hand before I can pull up the
Tick Tune app. "Absolutely not. First of all, that app is setting any
career-minded musicians up to fail," she says. "And I know you,
Sammy boy. You can't work in a vacuum anymore. You've been
running this open mic, but that's not going to scratch your itch
forever. It's time to get back out there."

I can't deny it. Only it's less of an itch now and more of an ache.
I miss being part of a team. I miss the exhilaration of a crowd. I
miss that magic of noise coming together, and everyone being a
part of it.

I miss performing with Mackenzie.

But that doesn't change a damn thing.

"These articles popping up make me think working with Mackenzie might make too big of a stir," I say.

Twyla shakes her head. "That's exactly why this is your best bet.
We give the people what they want. We keep the focus on the two
of you, and off your private life." She grabs the cupcake lookbook
from the table. "So get to my party on time for once and use that
handsome mug of yours to get her on board."

The idea still feels like too much to absorb, but not because it's
complicated. Because it's simple. Because Twyla is right.

"You're going to regret this when she maims me in front of all
your friends," I say.

Twyla beams as if I've just agreed to the whole thing. "I'll start
thinking up album concepts."

After Twyla leaves, I walk over to the bowls, hoping for a distraction. But Lizzie grabs a drying towel and gets to work right
beside me.

"I think we all know the media focus is well off Ben by now," she says carefully. "So if you're really thinking about Ben in all this—what he needs is for *all* of his parents to be happy."

I set the bowl down, startled. "I am happy," I tell her. "You know that, right? Ben is the best thing that ever happened to me. I wouldn't trade this for the world."

This isn't a life I ever imagined, but it's more than I ever deserved. My days are a blur of baked goods and soccer games, music and mayhem. All these little, quiet moments of my life that did one thing the big, loud ones never did, and built me a home.

Lizzie nods. "What I mean is—Kara and I are living our dream. You're allowed to go back to yours." She tilts her head at me, searching my face. "Maybe Mackenzie's a part of it."

The duet is tempting. All of it. Especially for the fourth reason I didn't say out loud—one that I *can't* say out loud. One that's every bit as much a reason to do it as a reason to stay away.

I'll never be over Mackenzie. It's a problem I learned to live with. But if I'm not careful, I might fuck up and make it her problem, too.

Lizzie pulls me out of my self-pity before I can indulge in it, tweaking my arm on her way to the front of the bakery. "If that's not enough motivation to get her on board, well—consider that Ben might run away from home, get a Thunder Hearts tattoo on his forehead, and disown you if you don't."

I sit with it the rest of the day, going around in circles in my mind. One of them leads me right back to that crease in her brow. The thing is, I only ever saw that crease when she was writing a new song. I only ever saw that crease when she was thinking about something that broke her heart.

I know better than to think I could ever be a reason. The best I could ever do with Mackenzie's heart was rile it a few hours at a

time when we were on tour. But that never stopped me from wanting to know the shape of it—apparently not even now.

"Damn it," I mutter to myself.

They say the definition of stupidity is making the same mistakes
twice. But they don't say anything about how good it feels when
Mackenzie Waters is one of them.

chapter six
MACKENZIE

"I had a crush on Tuxedo Mask as a kid and a bigger one on the Phantom as an adult. You're going to need to watch me like a hawk around all these masked men tonight," Hannah warns me, using the selfie mode on her phone to touch up her lipstick under the giant royal-blue and green feathered mask covering the rest of her face.

We're a few blocks out from the historic building in FiDi that Twyla and Isla rented for their birthday masquerade, watching the historic churches and buildings of earlier versions of New York fly by from the back of Hannah's hired car.

"I will be encouraging any and all shenanigans," I say. "You work hard and you deserve to have a masked man in a cape rock your world."

Hannah's dating life hasn't exactly been smooth, either. The kind of success we had in Thunder Hearts is enough to bring out the insecurity in any potential partner, but becoming the face of a successful brand took that to another level. The way Hannah put it, she had enough challenges with executing her vision for Hannah Says both as an Asian woman and a former popstar in lifestyle industries run by men who didn't take her seriously. But Hannah Says is her true love. She isn't about to deal with stroking some guy's ego while she's building it, so she's spared herself the trouble by swearing off dating until her forties.

But even if Hannah doesn't plan to flirt with anyone here, the rules baked into this thing might be too sexy to avoid it. First of all, you can't tell anyone your name. You can't give anyone identifying information about yourself. And you absolutely can't take off your own mask before the stroke of midnight—unless someone else takes it off for you.

There are caveats to that, too. You can only ask to take off one person's mask the whole night, and only if you agree to pay the price they set for you, capped at a thousand dollars. All the proceeds from unmasking and other activities tonight go to the at-risk-youth music foundation that Twyla and Isla have been involved in for years.

Which is to say, any and all flirting tonight is for a good cause.

"Speaking of masked men—are you going to let America's favorite bad boy take off yours?" Hannah asks.

Leave it to Sam Blaze to kill my party buzz before I've even arrived.

"Not if he knows what's good for him." I touch the short-cropped pale pink wig on my head, fashioned to match the magenta feathers on the mask that came with my invite. My hair is too distinctive to go incognito, so I took an extra step to commit to the bit. "Even if he's on board with this duet nonsense, he's not going to know me from Strawberry Shortcake."

"The way that man looks at you, I think he'd know you under a pile of bricks," says Hannah.

I roll my eyes. "Ah, right. That old 'star-crossed lovers' smolder. Wonder if he'll whip it out for old times' sake."

Old times that Isla is doing her best to convince me to relive, despite the lengths I've gone to get Sam out of my system. "Ignore him for two years" lengths. Just short of "hire an exorcist to erase any thoughts of him from my brain" lengths. And now here she is insisting that I don't just let Sam back into my life, but inextricably tie him to it all over again.

It's not that I don't see her logic. It makes an infuriating amount of sense to launch us as a duet. There's the hype and the history. The palpable, ridiculous chemistry between us. And the most damning piece of evidence of all: we wrote "Play You by Heart" in less than an hour and it topped more charts than any song either of us wrote in our entire careers.

"Speaking of star-crossed lovers, I noticed Seven never uploaded that last song of hers this week."

Hannah has hinted a few times that she thinks Sam will be one of the subjects of a song, but I've always played coy. It's not that I don't trust her to know. I just think the less I talk about any of the men the songs are about, the easier it will be to forget them.

"I resent what that segue of yours is implying," I say lightly.

"Please," she says. "Your lyrics wax poetic about enough 'embers' and 'burning' to start a damn forest fire."

Yikes. That was part of the gimmick, back in the day—the label and the media playing on our last names being Blaze and Waters. I didn't mean to play into it, too, but I guess the lyrics of the last song snuck up on me the same way my feelings for Sam did.

The difference is I didn't write them to stoke a flame. I wrote them to burn one out.

"Seven is just for me," I hedge. "And I had—technical difficulties. I'll post the last song next week."

Hannah hums knowingly, but lets it go. I busy myself with

patting another layer of foundation on my neck, just over the faded scar that runs horizontally at the base of my throat.

"You can hardly see it anymore," says Hannah, tilting her head at it.

Two years ago, when I first had surgery to remove the growth in my thyroid, the scar looked *Game of Thrones* ghastly. Anytime I left the apartment it was with a strategic ascot, turtleneck, or scarf in tow. But these days it's so faded I almost forget it's there.

"Old habit," I say. That, and you never know where the photographs from a Twyla and Isla bash will end up the next morning. The last thing I want is for someone to notice the scar in a weirdly lit image and start asking questions.

And if I have to start answering questions, it will lead to the inevitable one: *Weren't you worried the surgery might affect your voice?*

Which, of course, I was. Especially when it did.

The car rolls to a stop outside a stately three-story building with large, round arches at the entrance and upper windows, tucked so neatly into the chaos of Manhattan that you might blink and miss it.

"If we see Sam, the code word is 'Oh no, oh no, oh no.'"

Hannah laughs. "I'll sweep you uptown to my loft. Maybe we'll even run into my neighbor Grayson. Rumor has it the two of you were hitting it off at Lightning Strike."

I feel a twinge of guilt. Grayson and I have plans to get dinner this week after his rain check, but I've been so busy worrying about Sam that I've barely thought about the date. That will have to be my guiding light: there are nice, emotionally available men in New York if you squint, and after my bad luck I'm not going to take one for granted.

Hannah's driver opens the door and it feels like we aren't just stepping out of the car, but out of time. Hannah is a vision in an emerald off-the-shoulder, deep-V-neck gown with sky-high bedazzled gem heels; she steps back on them to admire me in the magenta, backless gown with a pale-pink flowing tulle skirt she paired with my white boots, a style I dubbed "yeehaw *Bridgerton*."

"Flawless," she declares.

Two ushers come to take our phones from us to lock up for the night. Once we're free of them, Hannah reaches out to squeeze my hand.

"For what it's worth," she says, "you could just say screw Sam, screw the label, and keep going as Seven. Maybe even go public with it one day."

I smirk, imagining all the execs panic-dropping their Aperol Spritzes in their Hamptons rentals at that particular reveal. It would serve them right for leaving me on the hook for so long.

But Seven isn't my new beginning. It's a quiet ending—after this, she won't have anything else to say. I won't ever let my heart break over people who don't deserve it again.

"Seven was just me messing around with my new voice," I say. "And besides, people like her to be a secret. It's easier to project on a shadow."

She squeezes my hand once more before letting it go. "If you say so," she says, leading us inside.

The interior of the building is even grander than the outside, moodily lit with high vaulted ceilings, a winding front staircase, and a massive ballroom on the first floor that showcases a glittering bar where a party is already in full swing. Guests in ornate masks of all colors dance in spellbinding ballroom dresses and sharp suits to a string quartet playing covers of songs by Twyla's and Isla's clients. Masked servers mill around holding appetizers and mini cocktails that gleam in the soft gold light. It's impossible to know what to look at, the people or the space.

We make our way through the clusters of bodies, thrilling at the anonymity of it all. Of being able to look wherever I want without it looking back. It feels like recording as Seven—the way being nobody frees me up to be anybody, without worrying about what a single person wants or expects.

I'm grinning ear to ear as Hannah grabs us both a dark, glittering shot that someone calls a Teeny Mystery Tini. When I knock it back it's somehow rich, bitter, sweet, and briny all at the same time, and so strong that the *zing!* immediately hits my spine and starts trickling down.

"Yowza," I say with a happy shudder. "Keep me away from Isla. A few of these and I won't just agree to relaunch as a duet, but I'll sign the contracts hanging from the chandelier."

A teeny tini drops to the floor at our feet, splashing on my boot. I glance up into wide green eyes watering behind a bejeweled marigold mask. The eyes of one of my best friends, blinking at me in disbelief and hurt.

"Serena," I gasp.

She stiffens. I wasn't supposed to say her name. But nobody turns to look at us—at least, they don't until I step in to hug her and she steps back abruptly enough to nearly knock a tray of drinks out of a server's hands.

I try to steady her, but it's Hannah's hand she takes. The hurt is immediate, but I'm too thrown off to fully feel it.

"I thought you were adding two weeks on the tour," I say.

I've had the day marked for ages. Hannah and I were planning to spruce up her apartment with flowers and fill up the pantry and fridge with all her favorite snacks to surprise her, and do welcome-home drinks at Lightning Strike.

And privately, I've been waiting for her to come back so we can talk things out. I thought we were in a good place before she left for her tour, but it's clear from the way she's been dodging my calls and the way she's looking at me right now that we weren't.

"You're doing a duet?" Serena asks quietly.

My stomach plummets. "Who said that?" I ask.

"You did," says Serena, her voice tight. "Just now. After everything you said last year you're just—doing it with someone else?"

"I'm not," I say adamantly. "Why are you back early? Is everything okay?"

Her eyes flood with tears so fast that the party feels even more like a strange fever dream. Serena doesn't cry. She is the picture of control. From the first day Isla threw us together for our sound test when we were all twenty years old and naive as shiny pennies, she's been the unyielding backbone of the group—the oldest of six kids and as "Eldest Daughter" as they come.

Sure enough, Serena blinks it back with such brutal, practiced efficiency that it's more startling to watch it stop than start. I turn to Hannah.

"Can you give us a sec?" I ask.

Hannah nods, reaching out to squeeze both our arms. "Love you both."

Serena softens, but only for a moment. She does a quick scan of the room. "Upstairs," she says.

I follow her up the staircase, trailing behind her sweeping golden gown with its thin, dainty straps and corseted waist. We weave past rows of rooms and attractions—a library stacked with old books and ornate pieces; a series of small rooms with fortune-tellers, magicians, and temporary tattoo artists; another ballroom on the second floor with aerial hoop acrobats and silent dancers. There's nowhere to sit privately, so Serena stops at the next best thing—the small landing between the second and third floor where nobody's gathered yet.

"Is everything okay?" I ask, leaning in close. "Isla said you were adding extra shows in London and Paris these next few weeks."

Serena isn't looking at me, eyes set on the stairs. "I will," she says, voice clipped. "I just need a few weeks to focus on other things."

Well, that's a worryingly empty explanation. But I tread with caution. Serena may have ice shields thicker than Elsa's, but Hannah and I are well-practiced in thawing her.

I rest my hand on her arm. "You didn't tell me you were back," I say.

Her eyes fly to mine then, with a bite. "You didn't tell me you were going to be in a duet."

I shake my head. "Isla's trying to pitch me on it again, is all," I explain. "I wouldn't just—do that without saying anything to you."

My throat tightens around those last few words. For months now I've been waiting for the right time to tell her about Seven. This is clearly not that moment, but it adds a ripple of guilt that she doesn't already know.

A ripple that's already riding a wave. The duet with Sam isn't happening, but Serena would have every right to be pissed if it did. Before she took off as a solo artist, she asked me to do a duet with her. When I said no, she kept asking. When I told her my voice was too messed up for it, she offered to do whatever it took—she'd wait until it was better. She'd adjust our sound. Every time I said no, she dug in harder, as unyielding as she'd always been.

I was grieving a voice I'd never get back. Serena wouldn't let up. I'm not proud of the things I said when I exploded at her, but at the time it felt like there was no other way to make her stop.

"You should do it," Serena says now. "The duet, I mean. If it makes you happy."

I'm too distracted to give her a proper answer. Her words are sincere, but her voice is flat. Nothing like the force she usually is, onstage and off.

I lean back to take her in, but it's hard to read her under the mask. Instead, I touch the edge of her new red bob, tilting my head. It was her idea for all three of us to keep our hair long to match in our Thunder Hearts days—Hannah's dark, sleek hair against Serena's wavy red locks against my wild blond curls. I've kept up with all the posts from her tour stops, so if she cut it, it must have been in the past few days. But she won't meet my eyes again.

"Don't worry about that. Let's get out of here," I say. "Go back to my place or Hannah's. Catch up."

Serena pulls back from my hand. "I've got plans. I was already on my way out," she says. "I only came so they can bundle our dresses in the charity auction as part of a Thunder Hearts thing."

I know better than to try to convince her to stay, but if I can get her to ease up, she might stay on her own.

I keep my voice light. "But nobody's taken your mask off yet."

Serena lets out a bitter laugh. "That's not happening tonight."

I cup my hands around my mouth, doing the "paparazzi voice" we would pretend to use when we got famous enough to start making headlines.

"Pop sensation Serena universally canceled after refusing to partici-pate in good cause, and also not doing a round of glitter shots with her best friends in a ball gown after."

She almost cracks a smile. I knock my shoulder into hers until it becomes a real one. Then I reach into my top and hand her my ticket—the one we were given to exchange with whoever's mask we took.

She shakes her head. "Keep it," she says. "I'll use my own ticket on myself."

It would feel like a dig, but I know Serena's hang-ups too well. She's never been able to sit with the feeling of owing anybody anything. Hannah and I figured that out the hard way after the band's rocky start, when Serena insisted on calling all the big shots herself—it's not that she doesn't trust us. She just doesn't want to depend on anyone.

I used to envy her for it. She was the picture of independence, and I was so desperate chasing love in all the wrong places that I was the butt of dating jokes on *SNL*. But I'm not so certain if either of us were better off.

Especially now that I can see under her mask. Serena is the kind of beautiful that makes strangers do comic strip–worthy spit takes—full-lipped, keen-eyed, with high cheekbones that make her look like she fell out of an Old Hollywood film—but she looks like two dimensions of herself right now. Her eyes are red-rimmed, her skin pale, her expression wavering. It's like someone smothered her shine.

Something in my face must shift, because her own hardens.

"Something's going on," I say. Not a question, but as close to one as I can ask without her throwing the ice shield back up.

She juts out her jaw. "Nothing's going on."

I take her mask from her, clasping her hand in mine. "Then tell me about the nothing. About anything. I want to know."

She's quiet for a moment. Then she meets my eye, aiming the words carefully. "I wouldn't want to be *needy*."

Ah, shit. I deserved that, and we both know it. That's the word I threw out when I got her to drop the duet idea—it was the most hurtful one I had in my arsenal, and I knew better than anyone how damn fast it would work:

Stop asking me. You're the one the label wants. Can't you do something on your own for once instead of being so needy?

Serena trusted us. It took years, but Hannah and I were two of the very few people in the world she let herself rely on. And I went and threw it in her face.

"You know I didn't mean that," I tell her. "I'm sorry I ever said it."

It's not the first time I've apologized, but it was clear the first time didn't stick. It's why I've called so many times. Why I considered just hopping on a plane and cornering her after one of her shows. But Serena has never wanted to hear it, and when she speaks again, I know why.

"Don't be," she says bitterly. "It was the damn truth."

It's not me she's angry with—it's herself. And that makes it a hundred times worse.

"And I mean it about the duet," says Serena, before I can recover. "I overheard Isla in a meeting. The label won't risk backing another Thunder Hearts member on their own. So just—do it, okay?"

Make that a thousand times worse.

"That's the last thing I'm worried about right now," I start, and then—

And then a goddamn camera flashes right in our faces.

"*Shit*," Serena blurts.

It's only an event photographer, but Serena goes from zero to "this just got uploaded to DeuxMoi" before I can blink. She yanks her mask from me and shoves it back on, flying up the stairs.

"Hold up!" I call.

"Do *not* follow me," she calls back, the words throaty with tears.

Serena's exercise regimen for the tour is no joke, because I feel like a baby horse trying to keep up with a cheetah. A door slams, and when I reach the third-floor landing I can't for the life of me figure out which one. There's a strip of light visible under one of the doorframes, so I chance it, swinging it open and pushing it shut behind me in case anyone followed.

"Don't let the—"

Slam.

"Door close behind you," says Sam.

Sam.

Not Serena, but Sam fucking Blaze. He's in a black mask with faint gray edges like smoke against the night sky, hiding more of his face than any other guest here. What a joke—I'd know that voice if I was hearing it from my damn grave.

Even if I didn't, there's that telltale stubble at his jawline he always got when we were on the road, and his line tattoos peeking out from under the tailored sleeves of his cream-colored suit. Fallen angel: Reformed Punk Rocker edition. The look is lethal and there's no way he doesn't know it. It only gets worse when he scratches the back of his neck, lifting his shirt up just enough to reveal a sliver of his toned stomach.

"Door locks from the inside," he says.

No. Absolutely not. I refuse to be in this genre of waking nightmare. I turn and yank the doorknob with all my might. When it doesn't budge, I lean my head against the doorframe and mouth the words Hannah will never hear: "*Oh no, oh no, oh no.*"

chapter seven

MACKENZIE

One time, when all three Thunder Hearts girls were considerably tipsy, we decided to look up each other's names on Tumblr. It only took one extra click to find rows and rows of self-insert fan fiction about Sam—*POV: you're stuck in an elevator with Sam Blaze and you KISS. POV: you and Sam Blaze are trapped in a storm cellar and have to huddle for warmth.*

POV: you're locked in a glorified supply closet with Sam Blaze and realizing you're the universe's favorite joke.

Sam observes me from the wall he's leaning against, arms crossed and irritatingly at ease.

"Don't worry," he says. "I don't bite."

Oh, dear god. Did *Sam* read the self-insert fan fictions? I turn to him, incredulous, and realize—he didn't call me Sparkles. He might not even know it's me. I don't have my signature hair, and the one lightbulb in here is so dim that I wouldn't be surprised if it clocked out on us.

And I know my voice is different, even if he didn't notice back at the bar.

"I might," I say, without doing anything to hide the slight rasp.

Sam's lips are barely visible under the mask, but I can feel the ripple of warmth radiating off him. He definitely doesn't know it's me. The thing about Sam is that he'd flirt with me within an inch of our damn lives onstage, but he'd either avoid me or tease me from a distance when we were off of it.

"Is that so?" He pushes off the wall. The one step he takes is all he needs to bridge the gap between us. "Well, there's plenty on the menu up here. You want to try?"

He plucks one of the cupcakes lined on the tower that's taking up most of the space and saunters over to me. I feel the heat of his eyes even under the mask, and then the heat of his body as he stops just short of me and dips his finger in the thick frosting.

"Open," he says.

There is some higher part of my brain that says, *Absofucking-lutely not.*

If I'm never going to see him again after tonight, why shouldn't I have a taste of this, even just for a moment? Of that curiosity I used to have, wondering what it would be like to be one of the dazed, blissed-out women who flitted in and out of Sam's trailers. A curiosity that snuck up on me when it hardened into pure, undiluted *want.*

My lips part. His thumb is inches from me, salty and sweet and close enough that I'm already salivating.

"Uh-uh," he says, pulling his hand back. "I have a condition."

I swallow hard.

"You have to hear me out about this duet."

My face sears. It's more of the same, then. Sam only ever seemed to be flirting with me when it was part of a *bit*, teasing me or disappearing so fast after it happened that it felt like he was trying to put me in my place.

No need. I already know my place, and it's anywhere far from him.

"Help!" I yell, kicking the back of my boot into the door. "I'm stuck in here with a man who is *absolutely delusional.*"

Sam licks the frosting off his own finger, watching me with amusement. "Pounding on the door and yelling. Why didn't I think of that?"

A few seconds pass. Serena might be a dozen kinds of pissed off, but if she could hear me, we'd be out of here by now.

"*Help!*" I try one more time.

"Yeesh," says Sam, pressing his hand to his chest in that "pretend wounded" way of his. "Am I really that bad?"

"To be clear, *you're* the one I'm calling for," I tell him. "If we don't get out soon someone's going to find you smothered to death with cupcake frosting."

He leans against the wall beside me, that faint smoky sweet smell of his too close to ignore. "You'd have to take off my mask first."

"I'll get creative."

He offers me the rest of the cupcake. "Is that a promise or a threat?"

It's clearly got peanut butter frosting with caramel and pretzels smashed into it. A Take 5 bar in cake form. Damn it if my taste buds are louder than my pride.

"A reminder," I tell him. I take a bite of the cupcake, sinking my teeth into salty sweetness. "Unlike whatever's in this, you and I don't mix well. I'm just fine on my own."

A lie and a half, but if there was ever a time to take a page out of Serena's book, it's right now.

But Sam just tilts his head at me, dipping his finger back into the frosting of the cupcake in my hand. "Since when did you settle for 'just fine'?" he asks, licking it off again. "Doesn't sound like the Sparkles I know."

I can't decide what's worse, looking away from Sam's lips so he thinks it has an effect on me, or stubbornly watching and *letting* it have an effect on me. I'm salivating all over again, for something other than frosting.

And that's just the problem, isn't it? We could never keep the music separate from whatever this push-and-pull is between us.

"The Sparkles you know doesn't want her success to hinge on a bunch of strangers wanting us to fuck," I tell him.

It's rare that I ever catch Sam off guard, but he goes satisfyingly still. He knocks the back of his head lightly on the wall, setting the cupcake down.

"Well, shit," he says.

Nobody could claim we weren't famous in our own rights before we were thrown together, but there's no denying what catapulted that fame. When you're teetering on the edge of something—even a *staged* something—for as long as we were, people get invested. They want catharsis. They want release.

And nothing holds their attention more than giving them everything just short of it. Our near kisses that never landed. Bridges with harmonies that never fully resolved. A *what if?* so sexy and compelling that our careers depended on it not having an end.

"Yeah. Shit," I agree. "Half of our sales relied on all the teasing and tricking and touching onstage."

I'm expecting him to pick one of the above to barb me with, but he's quiet. Thoughtful, even. I'm so unused to it that I can't help but fill up the silence, fast.

"Speaking of, what the hell are you doing up here? Planning on meeting someone for a pastry tryst?"

"Tempting. Lizzie asked me to check and make sure all her desserts were delivered." He turns his head toward me. "Is that what *you* were hoping for when you followed me up here?"

I shudder. "No. I can only assume I'm here to pay some kind of karmic debt."

I can hear the grin in his voice. "So you're saying it was fate."

A split second later I'm pitching backward, the door abruptly opening behind me. Sam moves with lightning speed, grabbing me by the forearms before I topple backward into an incredibly surprised server.

Sam holds me there for a suspended moment. My heart is pounding from the near drop, is all. Not from the heat of his hands on my bare skin. Not from the way the light from the hall is casting gold against the hazel in his eyes.

"I'm thinking," he says. As if it's his fault we haven't moved.

I blink, pulling myself away. "Don't hurt yourself."

The third floor is so small that it only takes a few moments for me to try all the doors. Every one of them is open, and every one of them is empty of Serena. I sweep my gown up to make my way back down the stairs when Sam grabs me by the crook of my elbow, stopping my momentum.

"We both have different sounds now," he says.

Isla sent me samples of the kind of music Sam has been working on the past few months. Now the upsettingly hot videos of Sam in worn-out button-downs singing low, acoustic love songs at Sugar Harmony get to live rent-free in my brain forever.

"So?" I ask, without pulling away.

"So, we can tell a different story," Sam proposes. "This time as— mature, mutually supportive friends."

My brain doesn't even bother with the mental gymnastics of imagining that. "Elaborate," I demand instead.

"We'd focus on the music," he says easily. "No teasing. No tricks. No touching."

I narrow my eyes up at him. I played into our dynamic as much as he did, but Sam was always the one who improvised to wind up the crowd. He'd take off a belt and put it around my waist to pull me in. He'd press his forehead into mine so I'd rise up to meet him until we were near bruising. He'd initiate every "almost" kiss.

I may have rolled with it, but he *thrived* on it. Enough that by the end even I was convinced it was real.

So I lean in and say, "If those are the rules, then I give you five minutes before you fuck them up."

His eyes flicker at the challenge, sliding his hand on my forearm as he releases me. I feel oddly cold when he lets me go, his eyes still steady on mine.

"I don't even need all five to convince you," he says. "But I'll take whatever you're offering."

As if to emphasize how committed he is to the bit, he puts his hands up, sliding past me on the wide staircase close enough for me to feel the warmth radiating off his body. I roll my eyes and surge ahead of him, but within a few steps it's clear we're entering a very different party from the one we left. Half of the crowd is unmasked, laughing loudly over flutes of champagne and starting to mill up the stairs to the themed rooms on the second floor. I spot Hannah unmasked on the landing between floors, looking worried until she spots me.

"There you are," she says.

"Serena?" I ask quietly.

Hannah shakes her head, leaning in. "She had a car waiting. I couldn't catch her." Her eyes snag on the space just behind me, and she leans in. "Also—who's your tall friend?"

I follow her gaze to the person in the smoky black mask standing next to me. "Please tell me you're kidding."

Sam lets out a breathy chuckle, and even then, Hannah's expression is blank. Turns out a nice suit and some low lighting is all it takes for a former punk rocker to disappear.

Someone calls Hannah's name up the stairs. She starts heading back up, but not without a warning. "Well, whoever you are, beware. New rules. Anyone can take off your mask if they double their donation."

I haven't even processed the words before Sam takes a large step to crowd in front of me. There's no intimacy or teasing in it—it's quick and protective, with an edge.

"That's enough," says Sam.

There's a man who must have come up from the side of me, his hands still extended toward my face. Sam steps again, fully blocking him from me.

"If I have the money to take off her mask, I can," the man says obstinately.

I hold in a snort, but Sam's voice has no humor in it. "Excuse you?" he demands.

"Rules are rules," says the guy, trying to skirt past Sam and reaching for me again. "Don't go turning this into some dumb fight."

Sam catches him by the arm, his entire body rigid. "Then don't give me a reason to."

An embarrassing thrill goes up my spine. I've never needed anyone to fight my battles, and even calling this one is a stretch. But damn if Sam doesn't look good doing it.

I cancel that thought on arrival, because the last thing I need tonight is a full-fledged fistfight on my hands. Both because I don't want to wreck Isla and Twyla's party, and also because I'm worried about what that tingle in my spine might turn into if I saw any more of this particular show.

"Sam," I say, quietly enough that only he can hear it.

He doesn't loosen a single degree, but he goes still. It doesn't matter—whatever that guy sees in Sam's eyes intimidates him enough for him to stumble away and head up the stairs without looking back.

"My hero," I say wryly.

But Sam doesn't turn back with the smugness I'm expecting. Instead, he shakes his head sharply. "I don't like this."

"It's only a game," I laugh.

Even with a mask covering most of his jaw, I can see it twitch. "Reminds me too much of those jackasses trying to grab you on-stage," he says.

I blink. Sam used to have a "bit" sometimes where he'd scoop me up and cart me to another part of the stage if anyone in the audience got too close. But it was just part of the show. Sam acting all protective, but also annoying the hell out of me while he was doing it—it made perfect fodder for the crowd.

Only now that I'm seeing it tighten up every inch of him do I realize that he was actually, legitimately pissed.

I take a step down the stairs, distancing myself from him. I am no mathematician, but an angry Sam and an inconveniently hot and bothered Mackenzie will likely not add up to a productive conversation tonight.

"Rain check on the five minutes," I offer. "Besides, if people see us together, they're going to think we're up to something."

He clears his throat, rolling his shoulders. By the time he's turned back to me, all his usual cockiness has been knocked right back into him.

"Oh, make no mistake. I'm up to something." He extends a

hand to me, nudging his head playfully toward the dance floor. "And they can't get our masks if they can't catch us. May I have this dance?"

I cross my arms, staring at his hand pointedly.

"Come on, Sparkles. We'll break one little rule." Even a damn mask isn't enough to stop a trademark Sam Blaze wink. "Consider it my reward for a full minute of good behavior."

As much as I hate myself for it, I want to hear him out. I roll my eyes, but I take his hand. It's warm and firm as he leads me to the main floor.

"You wouldn't know 'good behavior' if it bit you in the ass."

"That's just one more thing we can work on while we're reviving our careers."

I stop just short of the dance floor, forcing Sam to stop abruptly, too. I wait until his eyes are set on mine to speak.

"Make no mistake," I tell him. "I don't need you to swoop in and save my career."

Sam almost blows our cover, the way he throws his head back and laughs. His laugh, just like the rest of him, is distinct—warm and loud and bright, pitching over the music and the crowd like its own song.

"I'm the one who needs *you*," he says.

I let out a huff, about to draw my hand away, but Sam doubles down on the rule he's breaking and squeezes lightly. His voice is so low and sincere I barely hear it over the music.

"I'll never be half as good a writer as you. We both know it."

The words pull up a hurt so ancient that I have to look down at my boots before he can see it.

"You write just fine without me," I counter.

"Bullshit," says Sam candidly. "I'm the sound guy, but you're the lyrics girl. Don't go getting all modest on me now."

But Sam's got it all wrong. *Now* isn't the issue. The issue started before Sam and I even met.

There were a lot of things to be grateful for the year I turned twenty-one—I was traveling the country in an old bright pink van with my two best friends, playing to crowds who sang my own lyrics back at me, fueled off sour candy and applause. But best of all was that for the first time, our band was going to get featured by the legendary music YouTube channel Noted Scene.

What I didn't know was that Sam would be their guest that day.

I must have watched the full episode where he trashed us, but I don't remember that. All I remember is Serena abandoning her road snacks to scoop me up into her arms, letting me cry into her shoulder. All I remember is Serena balling her fists into the back of my glittery dress and saying through her teeth, *Oh, I'll kill him for this.*

By the time Sam introduced himself, I didn't have to pretend to hate him. I already did.

Sam tilts his head at me now, his concern so immediate and clear that I feel strangely naked. Like he isn't just seeing under our masks, but under something else.

"You're all right?" he asks.

An unmasked, tipsy guest in a ball gown is coming up behind him, clearly trying to take his mask. I pull Sam by the arm and take the lead, spinning him outward just fast enough for her to miss him.

"Careful there," I say.

His grin is back, wide with mischief as he lets me use the momentum to tug him deeper onto the dance floor. "See what I mean? We've got each other's backs."

One song ends, and a familiar one starts—a ballad version of "Play You by Heart." Twyla and Isla's doing, no doubt. Sam hums along cheekily as he draws in close.

"You're enjoying this too much," I accuse.

Sam stops to take my waist, his touch gentle but his words wicked. "No rules against that."

He eases us into a rhythm, so light and electric that I'm tempted to lose myself in it. But I know better than to do that with Sam Blaze.

I breathe in, grounding myself. "Don't forget you're on the clock here. Five minutes are ticking."

"I told you I don't need them all," he says, all bravado again. "I'm taking my time."

He slows our pace then, steady and lulling, and—oh, fuck it. I'll take my time, too. I'll let myself imagine we're in another time and place. One where we met at school or work or a coffee shop. One where nobody knows our names. One where I'm tempted to do something worse than kiss him—something like rest my head on his shoulder and breathe more of him in, like I could if he were mine.

"Listen," says Sam, voice so low that it does nothing to break the spell. "You could strike out on your own. I thought about it, too. Be a ghost like those artists on Tick Tune, even."

Thank god for the mask, or he'd see the truth burning in my cheeks.

"Yeah," I say after a moment. "I suppose."

Sam's grip tightens so lightly on my waist that I'm not sure he's aware of it. "But we're the same way, you and me," he says, just above a whisper. "We're better when we're working with other people. When we're getting *challenged* by other people. And who the hell does that better than you and me?"

My throat feels thick when I swallow. "We do have an unfortunate knack for it."

"Sparkles. We're *exceptional* at it," he says. "We wrote this ridiculous song in a half an hour by accident. Imagine what we could do if we did it on purpose."

My skin is tingling, the pull of his words too strong to resist. "Maybe we just got lucky."

"Or maybe we just know how to handle each other."

He dips me so low and so suddenly that I let out a gasp of surprise. He leans down to meet me, his grip so solid and firm that I can't chalk any of the fluttering in my stomach up to fear.

"That little stunt just cost you one of your minutes," I tell him.

"Another mask vulture," he says innocently, snapping us both back up to face each other with a gleam in his eye. "We have to stay close."

Funny. I don't see a single person near us. In fact, the dance floor is considerably more bare than it was when we started. The eyes that were on us before are all watching from the edges of the room. Even in disguise, it seems, we can't help but make a spectacle of ourselves.

I let him draw me in tighter. It's not that I can't resist him. It's that—this is another test. It's okay for me to be attracted to Sam. So normal it's downright cliché. But if I can prove that it's only in my body now—that it doesn't do anything to my heart—then maybe we can make this work.

"So, what else do you get out of this?" I ask him. "Aside from my dazzling presence."

"Well—we both get a chance to explore a new sound."

He leans his head in closer to mine. I brace myself, certain it's to say something maddening right into my ear to try to rile me up again.

"And I get a chance to stay close to home without leaving Ben," he says instead. "The kind of music we're writing doesn't ask for as much production or touring. And the speculation about us—it would keep the attention off Ben."

I can't see his face, but his voice is as vulnerable as I've ever heard it. It softens me instantly. I may not know Ben, but I feel a strange protectiveness of him. The same protectiveness I've felt for Sam, even when I was trying to write him out of my heart.

I squeeze his arm so he knows I understand. We wouldn't feed into the speculation. But if it already exists, we might as well take advantage of it.

"But the most important thing I get out of this?" says Sam. "I get to work with the best damn songwriter I know again."

All these years later and here I am, finally getting the validation I wanted then. But it doesn't ease the old hurt; it reminds me how fast it could come back. If I let him in, he could let me down again.

I could let *him* down.

Dammit. This is why Seven existed in the first place. An attempt to get all the men who let me down out of my system. To cure myself of feelings like the ones I had for Sam once and for all. It shouldn't matter what he thinks, or what he wants.

What matters is what I want. What I want is another shot at this. What I want is to make music I'm not using to destroy something in me, but build something new.

I wasn't ready two years ago when Serena asked. I wasn't ready a year ago, when I could only trust myself to sing behind a fake name. Hell—I wasn't ready a half hour ago, when I was determined to cut and run before Sam had a chance to speak.

But now I feel it spitting like a spark under my ribs. It's fanning into a flame so fast that it's burning the past away, burning everything away aside from one damning truth: I need this.

I need this more than I need to get over him.

"My voice sounds different now," I tell him.

Sam's grip tightens as he spins me suddenly and triumphantly, as if just by mentioning this, I've acknowledged the duo is happening.

"Twyla told me," he says. She must have also told him not to dig, because he doesn't miss a beat. "Everything about this is new. If anything, that's a damn boon."

This seems like a cavalier thing for him to say, considering what's on the line. Which is why I have to ask my next question, for his sake as much as mine.

"If we go through with this, it might be our last shot. You're not worried we'd fuck it all up?"

The question is as sincere as I've ever been with Sam. Our little show may have all been a game to him, but I'm all too aware of how fragile that line between real and pretend was, in the end. How many times I told myself I'd never trip on it, only to realize I was tied up in knots.

His grin softens, but his resolve firms. Enough that he pulls me in again, and we're just barely swaying to the music. Enough that I forget people are watching, and that this is a performance of sorts, too.

"I'd rather chance fucking up a great thing with you than settle for a good one on my own," he says into my ear.

It's coming back together now—not the line between real and pretend I caught myself in, but the loose threads of a story that I know isn't over yet. A story I can't end on my own, or I would have posted Seven's last song by now.

There are lyrics humming under my skin again. They don't have the angst of Seven's. But something hopeful and nostalgic, brimming and sweet.

I press them down into myself, clearing my throat. Maybe we bring out each other's best, but he also brought out my worst. If this is happening, I have to protect myself.

"I have another condition," I tell him. "No more love songs."

His eyes flicker in momentary surprise, and then mischief. "I thought you said ours wasn't."

"It's not."

His jaw ticks, but his eyes are steady on mine. "No love songs," he agrees.

I hold his gaze. For once, neither of us is playing at anything. The cards are already on the table, and we both have a lot at stake.

He squeezes my waist lightly, his voice barely above a whisper. "Say you'll give it a shot, Sparkles."

It's near impossible to resist the *yes* on the tip of my tongue, but it's dizzying, how fast it's happening. I've let myself get caught up in the moment too many times to know whether to trust my instincts.

"Say you'll stop calling me Sparkles," I say instead.

"But I'm a man of my word," Sam protests. "I only make promises I can keep."

I tilt my head at him gamely. "Then what are you promising?"

His answer is so immediate that it's as if he was waiting for me to ask all night. "We decide everything together. Not as rivals or lovers or puppets for some sideshow. But as a team."

The final notes to "Play You by Heart" draw to a slow, satisfying end, filling every corner of the ballroom with a sweet warmth. In the quiet that follows I can't hear it, but I can feel it—lyrics I've never written. Feelings I could never capture with words. It felt like they were running from me, but maybe they were only waiting. They needed someone who could understand the shape of them. Someone who would make them shine.

They needed Sam.

I draw in a breath, and even then, I don't know how I'll use it. A *snap!* echoes through the room before I get the chance.

It's the strap on Sam's mask, which falls to the floor. There's a hushed murmur in the crowd, the flash of an event photographer. I'm just as stunned as the rest of the room, swept up in the planes of his face—how earnest and boyish he looks, when he's caught by surprise. How unexpectedly sweet he is when he isn't posturing.

All traces of it are gone in a flash as he scans the room and firmly spins me away from him and into the crowd. No—into Hannah, who is watching on the edge of the dance floor. He's giving me an out. He releases me so that I'll spin right into her arms, where she'll no doubt conceal me for at least as long as it takes for Sam to get off the floor.

People will speculate, of course. But there won't be clear images of us together to give the speculation much weight. I can easily leave this party and pretend this conversation never happened at all.

It's that thought that stops me on a dime, breathless in the middle of the dance floor. It's empty now of everyone but the two of us. It only takes a quick sweep to understand why—midnight came and went. Everyone else's masks are off.

I take deliberate steps toward Sam, watching his expression shift from confusion to surprise to something I haven't seen in ages. It's the *what if?* at the heart of everything we pretended to be onstage. I haven't seen it in so long that I forgot the full impact of it. The way it feels when Sam Blaze is looking at you like he doesn't know how to look anywhere else.

Nothing could prepare me for the impact of the way he's looking at me now—not as a rival, not as a lover. Not even as a teammate. But as some untapped energy, where we could be all of those things or none of them. Where we could push each other to be something we haven't thought to dream up yet.

Sam reaches out not to take my mask, but my hands. He lifts them up to the edge of my mask.

My heart is in chaos, but my voice is calm. "I'd rather fuck up a great thing."

We take off the mask together. I don't know what Sam sees in my face, but his grin is brighter than every flashing bulb in the room.

PART TWO

"Out of the Water"

chapter eight
SAM

"Well now," I say, looking Mackenzie up and down as she crosses the bike path to meet me outside the Central Park Boathouse. "The walk of shame sure gets interesting when you spend the night with a . . . radioactive dairy farmer?"

Mackenzie glares from under the fuzzy neon-pink cow print bucket hat she is rocking outside in the eighty-five-degree early August heat. I will myself not to stare at the rest of her, but in my defense, she's in denim shorts and one of those tight sporty black crop tops that make it damn near impossible to look anywhere else.

"It has a twin with your name on it."

She reaches into a tote bag and, sure enough, out comes a second one. That can only mean it was one of the pieces Thunder Hearts was styled in, their neon and glitz loud against Candy Shard's matte blacks and leather.

"Ah, sorry," I say. "I have a chronic condition called 'self-respect' that makes me allergic to that hat."

"Hope you brought an EpiPen, then," she says, getting on her tiptoes to put it on my head.

I dodge by ducking to the side and then down low, so our eyes are level. It's been two weeks of nonstop meetings with Mackenzie and the label trying to firm up the direction for the demo we're working on. You'd think I'd get used to the *zap* of those blue eyes crackling on mine by now. No such luck.

"Not on your life," I tell her. "I'm still cleaning your glitter out of my ears from the last tour. I draw the line at neon."

Mackenzie holds her ground inches from my face, putting her hands on her hips. "You want us to keep a low profile? Then we're not broadcasting all . . ." She makes a sweeping gesture over me. "*This* in broad daylight."

She has a point. It's New York, where nothing makes people more determined to not pay attention to you than looking like you want attention.

Still, I can't help it. "All *this*, hm?" I ask, also gesturing at myself.

She rolls her eyes as she sets the hat back in her bag. "For what it's worth, you're more ridiculous than this hat could ever be."

I slide on my sunglasses as we walk over to the line for the rowboats, but it turns out we don't have to worry about anyone recognizing us. The only other people here on a hot weekday are a group of older European tourists and some junior high kids distracted by a video about hypnotizing squirrels.

I pick up the pace so I'm right beside her. "Careful there. You almost broke a rule," I say.

Not that I'll ever enforce them. The whole "no teasing, no tricks, no touching" thing seems about as realistic for us as a "no shoes, no shirt, no service" sign at a boardwalk pizza joint at the height of summer. But I won't be any less smug when she breaks them first.

Mackenzie answers without missing a beat. "I'll preemptively add one, then: the rules don't count if you're being a dope."

Interesting development. The kind that makes me wonder if she's also spent the last few weeks thinking not just about our rules, but how satisfying it would be to break them.

"This tall lug and I would like to rent two boats for an hour," Mackenzie tells the rowboat attendant.

The attendant's eyes shift from Mackenzie to me to both of our hats back to Mackenzie. "Two separate boats?" she asks.

"One boat," I counter. "What are we gonna do, shout lyrics at each other across the water?"

"It was two last time," Mackenzie points out.

Last time was over two years ago, when we weren't surrounded by teens and tourists, but a film crew and makeup team and a buzzing camera drone capturing all the angles of the two of us as they filmed the music video for "Play You by Heart."

"Eh. They told us to revisit it, not re-create it." I put my hands up lazily. "And I can't man those oars alone. I'm counting on you to be the muscle here, Sparkles."

Mackenzie eyes the water without answering. The sun pokes out from behind a cloud, gleaming against the loose strands of her hair, the shine of her full lips. Leave it to Mackenzie to look like a damn museum portrait even in the ugliest hat I've ever seen.

I have to shake the thought fast, and there's one surefire way to do it—piss her off.

"Unless you're afraid you won't be able to resist me," I say, tilting my gaze at her from under my sunglasses.

Mackenzie lets out a snort, turning to the attendant. "If I bring back a boat and he's not on it anymore, you've got my back, right?"

The attendant laughs and pulls up one boat with two life jackets inside. Mackenzie watches it bob without getting in. I make a show of offering her my hand and she blinks at it in surprise, then rolls her eyes.

"We are *not* going fast," she tells me pointedly, easing herself into the boat.

"Why's that?" I ask as I follow.

The attendant interrupts before she can answer, leaning in to push us off the dock. "Wait, so—*are* you guys dating?" she asks.

"Oh, sure," says Mackenzie breezily. "Just not each other."

The boat attendant's eyes widen, looking over at me. I shoot her a wink. "One of these days she'll admit she's wildly in love with me."

Funny how Mackenzie and I say we're not doing the "will they, won't they" bit anymore, but even now we can't help but fall into it. Only this time it feels like a buffer. I can't deny the way I feel about Mackenzie, but at least this helps keep it at bay.

But damn, this isn't helping. Once we get on the lake it's the kind of beautiful that looks like we were dropped into a rom-com set. I take the oars and row us toward the sweeping bridge that cuts across the middle of the lake, but no matter where I look, the awe on Mackenzie's face is the best part of the view.

It would be downright romantic, if I weren't sitting across from someone who just threatened to dump my body into the lake.

"So the dating thing," I say. "Does that mean Corporate Ken got a date number two?"

I've resisted the urge to ask for days. Apparently, all it took was one offhand comment from a stranger for all that resolve to disappear.

Mackenzie pushes a stray curl back into her bucket hat. "His name is Grayson," she reminds me. "And yes. Well—as soon as things calm down."

Fair enough. The last two weeks have been so busy that I'm mostly running on fumes and leftover cake batter. The label didn't just bite on the idea of us as a duo, but latched on and sprinted with it. We've spent so many hours pitching concepts with the marketing team that we might be common-law married to all of them now.

Some meetings ran smoother than others. We all agreed on an alternative/indie sound off the bat. But then they kept showing us mock-ups of album covers with enough sexual tension that they were a shade away from making *me* blush.

In the end we compromised. Instead of reviving our not-quite-romance, we'd retrace our steps. Each song would be centered around some place of significance to us, whether we were there together or on our own. Now *Haunts* is a work-in-progress concept—hers, mine, and ours.

The kicker? They want a demo from us within the month, followed by a showcase with a hand-selected audience from the label. It should be top of mind, but I'm still stuck on the Grayson thing.

"He's not your regular type," I remark.

Mackenzie doesn't take the bait.

"Four o'clock," she says instead. She tilts her head toward a couple on a rowboat not far from us, who are very unsubtly taking our picture with a camera phone.

I wave and they draw back, embarrassed. But not nearly as much as they are when Mackenzie does her usual schtick, which is whip out a camera and take a picture of them right back. Only this time it isn't with her phone, but with a bright pink Polaroid camera I remember her tossing around backstage between Serena and Hannah and Divya on our joint tour.

"Sorry!" one of the girls calls.

Mackenzie just tugs the picture out of the camera and waves her off with it. "We're even!" she calls back.

Then she turns to me, camera up to her eye again. "Do something interesting."

I raise my eyebrows at her. "I'm boring you already?"

"Isla said they want pictures of us writing in each of the haunts for the album art," she says, taking a shot. "Let's get it over with while we can still tolerate each other."

I glance at the interior of the boat. The benches are wide enough for two people, but the fit would be snug.

"Only way we're going to be able to get in the frame without touching is if one of us sits below the other," I say, not-so-innocently.

The last thing I'm expecting is for Mackenzie to spread her legs out. "Go on, then," she says, gesturing that I should lower myself to sit between them.

I raise my eyebrows. She raises hers back.

All right, then—guess I asked for this.

I secure the oars and slide off my seat, settling into the hot metal of the bottom of the boat. Not one part of us is touching as she backs up on the seat, but if anything, it only makes the closeness more pronounced. To feel the heat of her legs on either side of me. To hear her voice just above my ear.

Masochism is my middle name.

"You take it," she says, handing me the camera and pulling off her hat. Her hair tumbles down so far that it brushes my arms. "You've got the better angle."

She leans down for me to take the photo, but she's got me so distracted that the odds of us both being in the frame are anybody's guess.

"Let's get some shots on our phones for insurance," I suggest.

I reach for the phone in my back pocket, and it rocks us just enough that when she pulls the phone from her tote bag, she loses her grip on it. I lunge before it hits the water, jostling the boat so that Mackenzie is knocked over to the side.

The next thing I know Mackenzie is literally hitting the deck, dropping until she's on top of me, her eyes crushed shut.

"Shit shit fuck mother*fucker*," she bites out, in a string of curses so impressive even seasoned New Yorkers double take. The boat rights itself, but she's not done. "Fucking *fuck*."

"Fucking fuck?" I say with a surprised laugh. But when her eyes fly to meet mine, they're full of the kind of embarrassment that has an edge, like she's mad that I saw it. Or maybe just mad that my arms are around her, securing us both in the bottom of the boat.

Still, she doesn't pull away. "I can't swim," she says through her teeth.

The words are so unexpected that all I can think to say is, "But I've seen you in a swimsuit."

Correction: I've seen her in *many* swimsuits. A plunging retro one at Hannah's annual "end of the summer" lake party that had necks cracking. A neon-green one at my old high school pool that Candy Shard and Thunder Hearts broke into one night with cutouts that made no sense, but perfect sense at the same time. I have embarrassing recall for things that have been on Mackenzie's body.

The boat rocks slightly again and she stiffens. "Turns out you can buy those without flashing your swimming license at the cashier!" she says, voice pitched with panic.

"I've got you," I tell her, and I do. My arms are still braced around her shoulders to steady her. The temptation to pull her into me is almost too strong to resist, but I don't have to—she settles her weight into me, pulling in long, hard breaths.

I stay perfectly still as her breaths even out against my chest, as her heart stops hammering against my arms.

"Thanks," she says quietly, her face already a passive mask.

I clear my throat. "You never took swim lessons?" I ask.

She shrugs, repositioning herself on the seat. "My parents were busy. I think they just never thought of it."

I frown. "Were you just scared shitless the whole time we were filming that music video?"

"I wasn't scared," she says, without meeting my eye.

There's no way in hell she wasn't. We were on the water the entire day. At some point they had the boats rigged so they were getting pulled along, for a whole scene where she and I were racing each other in the boats.

"We said no teasing," I remind her. "I'm not going to make fun of you for being scared."

"I wasn't," she insists again. She's looking at me now, a faint smirk on her face. "Never had the time to be, back then. I was always too busy trying to show you up to be afraid."

The words catch me by surprise. Partly because Mackenzie rarely admits I'm worth trying to keep up with at all. But also because that's not how I remember it.

"Nah," I say. "I was the one using *you* for that."

My first few years in Candy Shard felt like being in a pressure cooker. I was young and careless and all too aware how much of the band's success depended on its front man being young and careless. I was never allowed to lose my cool, even when we rose to fame fast enough that it felt like whiplash.

It snuck up on me, the way the big things got easier with Mackenzie around. I was so much calmer on the road after Thunder Hearts came along for the ride that Divya used to call Mackenzie my "emotional support enemy."

But now Mackenzie shakes her head. "You were smooth sailing by the time I showed up. It was just my job to blow you out of the water."

Our eyes connect the instant that last phrase comes out of her mouth. It's the same crackling feeling we had two years ago in the back of that bar, when she first uttered the words *Play you by heart.* After years of never knowing where we stood, we'd stumbled on an idea compelling enough to put us on common ground.

Mackenzie does the same thing she did then, and pulls a notebook out of her bag, starting to scribble. I catch the words *Out of the water,* but then she tilts it away from me.

I wait until she pauses to reread her work. "Gonna share with the class?" I ask.

She shakes her head without looking up. "It's not there yet."

"Damn," I say idly. "If only you had a cowriter who might be able to help."

I lean forward to peek, tilting the boat enough that Mackenzie lets out a quick yelp. "Sorry," she blurts, snapping the notebook shut. "Fuck. Sorry."

"Don't steal my sorry," I say. "I'm the jerk who rocked the boat."

She still won't look at me. I reach for one of the life jackets and fan it over her shoulders. After a moment she bends her arms, letting me ease it onto her.

Even when I reach forward to tighten the straps on it, her eyes are cast toward the bottom of the boat. "Sparkles." I snap the front buckle and hold my hand there, giving it a light tug so she looks up. "You're stuck with me now. I'm not gonna let you drown."

She stares at me for a beat, looking almost startled. Then she lets out a breathy laugh and pulls her eyes off mine.

"No more photos," she says. "This thing makes me look ridiculous."

I let her go, then pull one of the ugly hats out of her bag and stick it on my head. "Now we both do."

When she looks up again, she lets out a real laugh. The kind so unexpected that she has to clap a hand over her mouth to keep it from echoing across the water.

"You look like an unhinged Muppet," she cackles.

Her laugh is such a relief that I'd put ten of these monstrosities on my head to hear it again.

"Joke's on you," I say, easing back and grabbing the oars. "As a dad I now hold all the Muppets in great esteem."

Her laugh tapers as I use the oars to turn the boat.

"Wait, what are you doing?" she asks.

I tilt my head toward the boathouse. "Taking us back."

"No, no, I'm fine," she says, with a sharp shake of her head. She shoves the notebook back in her bag. "Just, uh—consider this a PSA to put Ben in swim lessons."

I still haven't seen a single new word she's written, but I let it go. She's shaking so hard that she can't hide it. Which is saying something for a woman who has headlined entire stadiums without breaking a sweat.

So I pull up the oars again and keep moving, this time toward the edge of the tree-filled Ramble that borders the water.

"Ben could probably go for a refresher," I say. "Not that he'll mind. Kid's a jock through and through."

Mackenzie's death grip on her bag straps loosens by a degree. "Is he now?" she asks. "How exactly did you manage that?"

"Recessive genes," I crack.

Mackenzie's eyes are back on me in full force. There's no panic in them this time. Just curiosity.

"I know when you found out about Ben," she says. "But—how? How did Lizzie figure it out?"

It's easy to forget that Mackenzie knows Lizzie. Of all the women I saw casually while we were touring, Lizzie was the only one who introduced herself to the rest of the crew. We knew each other from high school, so there was enough of a history that on the weekends when she flew in for some fun, she felt fine to wander around and chat people up, rival band members included.

"Well—Lizzie thought Ben was her ex's kid. He was never involved, but his mom came by once," I say, pushing the oars along. "It was pretty anticlimactic. They were looking at Ben's baby book. She saw that he has type O blood. Which I guess would be impossible, because Lizzie's ex is AB."

It was something Lizzie's ex didn't know, but his mom did. Not that her ex had ever stuck around long enough to find anything out about Ben in the first place.

"She got in touch with me that night," I say. "I was on the next plane out of LA."

Mackenzie nods slowly. "We all woke up and you were just—gone."

She doesn't sound hurt, but bewildered. The way she sounded in that last conversation we had before we lost touch, when she called me to check in and I told her about Ben.

Truth be told, I try not to remember that call. I'm not proud of it. A lot of the specifics are lost on me, but the feeling isn't—whatever I said, it was to push her away.

It felt like the only move. I'd spent years steering clear of her. She wanted a big romance, the kind of guy who was in it for the long haul. She didn't just talk about it, but sang her heart out about it. I wasn't that guy when we met, so for years I shoved all the feelings I had for her so far down that I nearly choked on them.

But there was this moment, the night before I found out about Ben. We accidentally crossed a line.

We kissed.

When I realized it wasn't accidental at all—that Mackenzie felt something, too—that's all it took. Just like that, I was ready. As ready as I've ever been.

And then there was Ben. Suddenly there was this tidal wave of love and shame, of wanting the world for him and feeling like an alien invader in it. There was no room for anything else, and even if there had been, I couldn't put that on Mackenzie. I'd never forgive myself for holding her back.

"It's weird," says Mackenzie. "Twyla said it was a family thing, so I thought your dad had gotten in touch."

My brows lift in surprise. I don't talk much about my dad. "You did?"

"You mentioned him once," says Mackenzie.

My face burns at the memory. It slipped out the night we were writing "Play You by Heart." Booze and sleep deprivation and the adrenaline high of writing will do that to a guy. Before I knew it, I was admitting to Mackenzie something I'd barely admitted to myself—that some part of me had always wondered if he'd see me in Candy Shard, and try to get in touch.

I could tell her right now. He did, in the end. And not only does she know who he is, but she probably knows all his hits, the same way half the world does.

But if someone else knows about Caspar—hell, if *Mackenzie* knows—I'll have to own up to being a damn coward about it.

"Nah," I say. The grin on my face feels stretched. "Just got a surprise preschooler."

Mackenzie watches me carefully, like she can see a hole in what I just told her but doesn't know where to dig.

"Is that why Candy Shard broke up?" she asks. "I never knew because we ended up calling it quits around the same time."

I shake my head. "Divya wanted to go back to school; Rob

wanted to settle down. It was a good time for us all to bow out," I tell her.

Mackenzie nods. "We were more or less the same. Hannah wanted to start her line. Serena was ready to try something new."

Now Mackenzie's the one leaving something out. It's in her face, even if it isn't in her words—in that distinctive pucker between her brows. The heartbreak one.

"What did you want?" I ask.

She blinks back to herself, lips twisting to the side. "Some peace and quiet from all your punk rock racket."

I lower the oars and let us coast. It's quiet here. Just distant sounds of kids playing in the park and birds chirping in the woods.

"Really, though," I say. "You fell off the map for a bit."

Enough that she must not have been singing much. Twyla said not to ask about it, but I had enough vocal instruction on the road to know that your voice changes when it's out of practice.

Which makes me wonder what on earth could happen to make a woman so stubbornly, unrepentantly full of love songs stop singing altogether.

"Well, we're back on the map now." She eyes the water, then looks back at me. "And—you're right. We should head back. Get some writing done on solid ground."

She's clearly putting me off, but I let her for now. I don't like the idea of us being in the boat if it scares her.

After we drop off the boat, we wander to find a place to sit, and Mackenzie spots the couple who took our photo by an ice-cream truck. "I actually got a really cute shot," she calls over to them, pulling out the photo she took. After the girl who took the picture of us recovers from her absolute mortification and some clear hero worship of Mackenzie, she offers to AirDrop her picture in return.

"I'm so glad you guys are finally together," she says to us, waiting for the photo to send.

Mackenzie puts up a hand. "Oh, we're not—"

"You deserve it after that parade of losers," the girl insists. "I mean, damn. Talk about kissing frogs."

Mackenzie laughs, entirely unfazed, but my jaw drops. The girl turns to me sharply, pointing a finger at me.

"Do not fuck this up," she says. "Our girl can't take another hit."

Ah. No need to ask which side of the Thunder Hearts versus Candy Shard divide she was on. "Wouldn't dream of it," I say.

But they've already moved on, chatting Mackenzie up about Hannah's latest clothing drop while they wait for their ice cream. I'm still dumbfounded as Mackenzie lingers to buy two Powerpuff Girl ice pops, one of which she hands to me.

"For your valiant rescue earlier," she says wryly.

She's letting me milk that for all it's worth, but I'm not in the mood. "I forgot how weird people were about your exes," I say.

"Funny, isn't it?" she says, unwrapping her ice pop. "You dated like it was a damn charcuterie board, but I'm the one who has 'dating timelines' on all the major new outlets. Scam."

I consider it, leading us up to a spot in the Ramble with enough tree cover that nobody will bug us. "I guess everyone expected me to be the way I was. But you were America's sweetheart. People got mad whenever someone broke your heart."

She snorts. "Well, we don't have to worry about that anymore."

"Bad-boy phase officially over?" I ask.

Mackenzie bites off a hunk of Bubbles' head and chews thoughtfully.

"I don't think it was the 'bad-boy' thing that was the problem. I think I just fell for guys who came on strong. But in the end, they all just got insecure or intimidated. Like anytime I got too happy or too comfortable they had to put me in my place. They were all so damn predictable that it's more boring than sad, looking back on it now."

She says it all so frankly that I know she means it, but my chest still aches. Some of it is guilt. I resented all those relationships, and was secretly relieved when they crashed and burned.

But the rest of it is for her sake. Mackenzie earned the name Sparkles for a reason. She was always looking on the bright side, even when she loved so hard that the internet wanted to make a fool out of her for it. I hate the idea that something finally took her shine.

"So cynical now," I say. "Did Candy Shard's angst rub off on you?"

She shakes her head. "It's been good for me, being single awhile. Gave me some clarity on what I want."

"And what's that?" I ask, half-teasing, half-curious.

She shrugs. "I'll let you know when I finish figuring it out."

We've reached a quiet spot. Mackenzie unceremoniously plants herself in the grass, glancing up at me to follow. Her lips are slick from the ice cream, the sun casting shadows from the trees against her face. Not for the first time, I wonder who would be enough of a fool to win over this stunning, funny, ridiculously talented woman and let her go.

But I guess I'm not one to talk.

"For the record," I say, bumping my shoulder into hers, "anyone who *isn't* intimidated by you is an idiot."

Mackenzie bites down a smile, tucking her legs to her chest. "Rules," she says, with zero conviction.

I don't bother hiding my own smile, using my free hand to root through her bag and pull out her notebook. "You said it yourself. They don't count if you're being a dope."

She lightly smacks my hand, grabbing the notebook from me. "Quit being nice to me."

"Why should I?" I ask, still going through the bag to find her pen.

"Because then I'll have to be nice back."

"Oh no," I say, biting a chunk off my ice pop's head. "Almost like we're friends."

Mackenzie kicks off her shoes, settling in with the notebook on her lap. "We were never friends."

Can't argue with that. "Yeah. You really committed to the bit," I say, as if impressed. "You were meaner to me than you were to *any* of those bad boys."

She raises her eyebrows at me, the faint smirk returning before she casts her gaze back at the trees. "You were the original bad boy. Gateway Bad Boy, if you will."

I keep my eyes on her. "You're saying I broke your heart?"

"Worse," she says plainly.

Well, shit. That's not how this back-and-forth usually goes. Somehow that one word lands harder than anything she's thrown at me today.

"Oh, don't get your Ray-Bans in a twist. I don't mean *romantically*." She clears her throat. "I just mean—that Noted Scene episode."

"Sparkles, not to flex, but there were at least five of those."

She sighs. *"They're too green. If that counts as good music these days then I hope we get some stiffer competition soon."*

She's directly quoting me. Or at least, I think she is. It was so long ago that I'm not even sure if I'm the one who said it.

"Okay," I say, prompting her to go on.

She shakes her head, exasperated. "You don't remember."

I tilt my body toward hers. "Then tell me."

After a moment she lets out yet another sigh. "Break Out *is so unoriginal I feel myself losing brain cells every time I hear it.*"

I laugh because, damn, do I remember now. That comment got me roasted within an inch of my life. *Break Out* was a wildly catchy debut album of breakup songs and power ballads, and my twenty-something self was nothing short of an ass about it. Here I was finally getting featured on Noted Scene, and all the hosts wanted to do was talk about some brand-new sparkly pop group that took over the world in one summer.

"Joke's on you, buddy," Mackenzie deadpans. "You're stuck with the album writer now."

Well, that shuts me up. I turn to her, incredulous.

"You're not telling me you wrote that whole album."

I feel stupid for asking before I even finish. Of course she did. It's probably right on the album credits, too. I was just so petty and focused on my own shit at the time that I refused to even google Thunder Hearts, or I would have thought twice before going after an all-girl group.

Still, I should have figured it out by now. The lyrics have Mackenzie's style all over them—deceptively simple, but impossible to forget. I could write myself in circles without writing a hook as catchy as one of hers.

"Damn, Sparkles," I say, impressed. "You never said."

By the time the rivalry kicked off, Thunder Hearts had enough recognition that pop writers and DJs were knocking themselves over to collaborate with them. But Mackenzie's style was so distinct that people always knew which songs were hers, and had endless theories about which of her terrible boyfriends they were about.

Mackenzie shrugs. "I was embarrassed."

"Yeah, bet those royalty checks were mortifying," I crack.

Mackenzie's smile is rueful. "I didn't want to look like my love life was a mess," she says. "If I'd known it was going to be a public train wreck, I'd have leaned into it from the start."

That brings the conversation to a halt. Mackenzie bunches up grass in her fist and lets it go. I watch the blades crumple, my throat thick. I was so damn furious at all those guys for hurting Mackenzie. So careful never to be one of them myself. But it turns out I hurt her just the same.

"Well, I was young and stupid and petty as hell," I tell her. "And *wrong*. You saw the way the internet ate me alive for it."

Mackenzie doesn't bother trying to hide her smirk, even as she shakes her head. "You hated my lyrics. It's fine. Ancient history."

"You know that's not true. I mean, shit," I say. "Whatever you scribbled in a few minutes on the boat is better than anything most people could come up with in their lives."

I mean it, but Mackenzie just looks amused.

"All right, that's enough groveling for one afternoon."

"Too bad," I say. "Already hired the apology skywriter. He charged extra to spell out 'Sparkles.'"

She laughs, turning her attention to the gumballs on her ice pop. I stare at my own, trying to wrap my head around Mackenzie penning all those hits herself and never saying a word. It's a reminder that for all the years we spent in each other's orbit, there's so much of Mackenzie I don't know. So much I *want* to know.

"Do you ever wonder what might have happened if we'd written more back then?" I ask. "If the bands hadn't broken up."

I'm not one to linger on the past. My mom is a firm believer that everything happens for a reason, and with every unexpected thing that has happened in my life—Ben chief among them—I have to believe it, too.

But nobody could have predicted what happened with that song we never meant to write. It wasn't the song of the summer, but the song of the damn century. I couldn't walk into a grocery store, a bar, or even the damn dentist's office without hearing us.

Within a week of its release the entire atmosphere started to shift. When we looked out into the crowd at concerts, there were fewer TEAM THUNDER HEARTS and CANDY SHARD SUPREMACY posters, and more that said things like JUST FUCKING KISS.

Two years and I'm still stuck on the one time we did.

"I don't have to wonder," says Mackenzie, polishing off her ice pop with a blue-dripping bite. "I already know what would have happened."

"What's that?"

"You and I would have messed around and fucked everything up."

I nearly choke on my last bite. Mackenzie is unfazed, like she's reading out loud from a familiar book.

"I was falling for guys who didn't want to commit; you were the ultimate commitment phobe. Basic relationship math says we were only ever going to hook up eventually, even though we were doomed from the start."

It should be a relief that we were on the same page all those years. That I was right to steer clear of her. But despite everything, there's some part of me that wants to be proven wrong.

I ease back on my palm, trying to seem casual. "You seem to have thought this through, so I gotta ask—was it good? The part where we messed everything up?"

Her eyes meet mine, but only for a moment. Next thing I know she's taking in the rest of my face, lingering on my mouth, on my jaw. She's never looked at me this long or this unapologetically. She's never looked at me with a quick skim of her tongue over her bottom lip.

"Guess we'll never know," she says, opening her notebook. "Now that we're *mature, mutually supportive friends*, and all."

She's already looking away, so she doesn't see the flash of disappointment on my face.

"Well then," I say, recovering. "So you *do* admit we're friends."

"On a trial basis," she says. "We'll see how long we can be nice to each other before we make anything permanent."

"Sure. But to be clear, I wasn't being nice before," I tell her. "Just honest."

Her cheeks flush faintly. "Careful there, or my ego's gonna get big enough to match yours."

"Damn, I hope so," I say. "Better that than these god-awful matching hats."

This time she puts the notebook between us so I can watch her write. I pull out my phone to record, experimentally humming a few melodies to her words. She goes perfectly still a few times, nodding her approval. I repeat those lines, waiting for her to add a harmony, a sweet bite against my mellow tone.

Only this time Mackenzie doesn't sing along. She just murmurs the words to herself and occasionally looks up at me for approval, scribbling down what we silently agree on.

We're secluded, but enough people pass by that I figure she doesn't want to call attention to us. "We could go somewhere else to write," I offer.

She shakes her head, then closes her notebook abruptly. "I'll, uh—type up the lyrics and send them over."

I tilt my head at her. "This isn't my first cowriting rodeo. That's not how this works."

Mackenzie's already got her bag packed, easing herself up from the grass. "Sure it is. I'll still be doing lyrics, and you'll still do the melody. And we'll just keep it like that."

It's surprisingly hard to keep up as she heads for the main path, despite the foot of height I've got on her. "We'll both be singing on the tracks, though," I remind her.

"Let's just try it this way once," she says, waving me off.

I stop just before we hit the main path. "I'm not letting you off that easy, Sparkles."

She comes to a reluctant stop, too, shifting her weight uneasily. "I don't know how I'll sound yet," she says quietly. "So I'll sing it on my own. Then try it with you."

When she looks at me, all the usual crackle in her eyes is gone. There's only uncertainty, the kind I'm so unused to seeing in her that it stops me on a dime.

"It's just me," I tell her.

She's still watching me. "I know," she says, giving the words weight.

That's just it, then. Whether we're friends or rivals or something in between—it matters, what we think of each other. It always has.

It hurts to think she doesn't fully trust me with hearing her new voice. But if I said anything in the past to break her trust, then this time around I'll have to earn it.

"Once," I relent. "I'll send you some recordings by tonight."

Mackenzie nods, relieved. Then she lifts herself on the tips of her toes and hugs me, hard and fast.

"Thank you," she says.

My arms are wrapped around her before I can even remember our rules. Turns out I can't be smug that she's breaking them first. That's the problem with Mackenzie Waters—whether she's breaking rules or breaking my heart, I'll never get enough.

chapter nine

MACKENZIE

sardineprincess92: knock knock seven????? is anyone home???????? my sad girl playlist needs you

Sevenpalooza: She was supposed to post last WEEK did someone kidnap her

AYCMUAJTBMLAP: seven if you can see this we are so hungry for your despair

I groan, resting my forehead into my guitar to get all the Tick Tune comments on my phone out of my line of sight. I'm used to struggling with my voice. But until now, I was lucky enough to never understand the concept of "writer's block."

Zero out of five stars, would not recommend.

The thing is, it was easy to write Seven's song about Sam when he wasn't in my life. It's another thing entirely to be seeing him every other day. Watching his lean frame stretch when he tips his chair back in meetings. Watching his jaw flex when he's lost in a thought. I keep observing him like an anthropologist, trying to understand what's so damn compelling about him, only to get hit with one of those cheeky Sam Blaze winks when he catches me staring.

I keep reworking Seven's last song so I can recapture that closure I thought I had. But after a week of fruitless writing and countless comments from impatient Seven listeners, I know that whatever it is I need to write, it's a different song entirely.

The worst part is, it's just as bad when he's not around. The man has a damn superpower for uncanny timing. He's sending me potential harmonies at midnight when I'm in a hot bath. He's sending me a chord pattern for the bridge when I'm half-naked in my room trying on Hannah's new designs. It's like he has a sixth sense for when I'm going to get irrationally hot and bothered by listening to him pick a few strings and quietly say things like, "How does that feel, Sparkles?" and, "Let me know if that's building right for you."

My phone buzzes, making me gasp. Damn it. Leave it to Sam to make me daydream about a damn *voice memo*.

Mercifully, the text is from Hannah: You mind getting here a bit early?

I'm so relieved for an excuse to quit writing that I all but leap from my couch to get to Lightning Strike, where Hannah is hosting her loungewear launch event. By the time I reach the bar, it's been converted into a makeshift runway, the low lights brought up for a poppier, daytime feel to match the aesthetic of her latest loungewear release. Her family is already there, her parents taking pictures of anything and everything and her sisters helping the caterers arrange the mango sticky rice–inspired mini cocktails and the mini Thai chili sliders Hannah just added to Lightning Strike's menu. I give them all a quick hug and hello as I pass, grateful for the way her parents hug me for an extra beat the way they always do with me and Serena.

Even with the quick stop I end up beating all the other friends Hannah has modeling for the show to the back office, so I find the pale pink scalloped pajama set she set aside for me and pull it on.

"I didn't know Grayson might be headed to the North Pole," says Hannah wickedly.

I follow her gaze to my Rudolph-emblazoned granny panties. Yikes. I almost forgot I'd chosen today to run my trademark Christmas Underwear Test.

The test is simple to execute. One: purchase the most outlandish, holiday-themed underwear that the internet can offer. Two: identify That Date. The "you can take a joke and if you've murdered anyone, at least you were discreet—should I bring you home?" date. Three: don the underwear for That Date.

Four: well. Step four really depends on him.

"We got drinks the other night," I tell Hannah.

"Just drinks again?" she says, handing me the evening's call sheet.

"I was sabotaged."

It was meant to be dinner, but we were interrupted by a call from Isla. It turns out that the couple on the boat weren't the only ones who spotted me and Sam the other day. Someone got a video of us just after I lost my balance and practically clobbered Sam.

It was bad enough to look so "damsel in distress" that the internet was swooning over how Sam pulled me into him. But it also inspired enough fans to play Sherlock Holmes that they discovered some truly cringeworthy trademarks had been taken out by the label for us, like "Thunder Shard" and "Candy Hearts." The leak generated enough hype that the label decided to just cop to us working together.

"I hope you weren't planning on sleeping anytime soon," said Isla to me over the phone, "because now they want the six songs by the end of the month, and they want them all showcase-ready."

At that point I ducked my head and walked toward the bathrooms so Grayson wouldn't hear. "That will put me well above my 'time spent in the same room as Sam Blaze' threshold," I reminded her.

"Think of it like—ripping off a Band-Aid," said Isla. "A really hot, tall, edgy Band-Aid that you have excellent chemistry with. And need to get a photo with tonight, because they're going live with the announcement tomorrow."

"I'm on a *date*," I protested.

"I know. A fan tweeted the restaurant. I already sent a car. Chop-chop, girly pop!"

Between Grayson's long hours and my newly chaotic ones, we haven't seen each other since.

"We're going to hang out after the show," I tell Hannah. Grayson has to regroup with the rest of Hannah's team when we wrap up, but then we're going to pick a place and sit over an actual meal.

Hannah peers at herself in the mirror, adjusting the soft high bun she always pairs with a classic black minidress at smaller launch events. "Is that going to be weird with Sam here?"

I nearly trip pulling on the pretty pink sweatpants.

"Repeat the words that just came out of your mouth."

Hannah casts her eyes at the office door. "Sam's here."

"You invited *Sam*?" I ask.

She shakes her head, as confused as I am. "I thought you did. Twyla had me put him on the guest list. Something about this being one of the 'haunts' for your songs?"

We talked about the bar being one of the places we wrote about, but didn't lock down a day yet. I know we're on a time crunch here, but what would possess Sam to attend what is basically a boozy corporate pajama party is beyond me. If he thinks I'm going to ditch a date to write a song with him tonight, he's got another thing coming.

"Oh. Hey?"

I startle at the sight of Serena in the door. Her red bob is blown out with voluminous curls, and she's looking effortlessly cool as ever in a pair of ankle jeans and a sleek white corset-style top. She doesn't look fragile like she did last week at the ball, but her expression is utterly bewildered.

"Serena," I say, as surprised as she is. I've been calling and texting her nearly every day, only to get curt responses assuring me that she's fine, or sent straight to voicemail. Never once did she mention she'd be on the runway today, too.

I take a step to hug her, but Serena's too disoriented to notice, taking a step back.

"Wait," she says, looking at Hannah and then back at me. "I thought you had to drop out. Do I not need to fill in?"

"No?" I say.

Hannah smiles sheepishly. "Sorry, hon. I knew I could only get you here if it looked like an emergency. You were dodging too many of my calls."

Serena's face burns red enough to match her hair. "Yeah," she says, closing the door and lowering her voice. "Because I'm busy. Just like you two are."

Whatever Serena's been busy with, Hannah and I aren't the only ones speculating. A quick search of her name is all it takes to see that her fans were just as stunned by her disappearing before a rumored tour extension as we were.

"We've been worried about you," says Hannah. "I figured it was time to pull out the big guns."

Hannah pulled out even more than that, since her whole family is here. With Serena's family so complicated and mine so distant, we always drifted toward Hannah's as the grounding force when we were on the road. It was Hannah's mom who gave us business savvy and money talks we needed during our quick ascent, and Hannah's dad who kept the mood light with bad puns and double-checked all the reservations to make sure we'd be safe. If there's a chance Serena will lower her guard, having them nearby can only help.

But Serena crosses her arms, the pointed look she aims in my direction a whole lot less subtle this time. "As far as I can see, I'm not the one we should be worried about."

Anytime Serena's having a hard time, she'll deflect like it's her second job, but it's never targeted at someone. Especially not me.

"What do you mean?" I ask.

She pulls out her phone. It's already open to Instagram, where the label just launched a new account for Mack & Sam. There's only one post so far. We're sitting back-to-back on separate barstools, Sam tilting back to look at me while I avoid his eyes with an exasperated smile. It was only a candid test shot, but it was the only one that captured the new dynamic—not rivals, not friends, but something compelling in between.

"When I told you to go for the duet, you didn't tell me it was with *him*."

My stomach drops. I wasn't going to fully commit to the duet with Sam, but the day after the masquerade ball was the one and only time Serena texted me without prompting. She told me she meant what she said—that if I wanted to team up with someone, I should do it while the label was on board.

I didn't anticipate there were exceptions, or that Sam would be one of them.

"You left pretty fast that night," I say carefully. "And I haven't gotten to talk with you since."

Serena shoves her phone back into her purse. "You couldn't drop it in a text?"

It didn't even occur to me. I've been so focused on trying to talk to Serena about why she left the tour early that the Sam news fell to the wayside.

"I'm sorry," I start. Hannah's about to interject, too, but Serena beats her to it.

"I understood that the timing was bad when I asked. I get it." Her face isn't just indignant, but incredulous. "But to pass on me and end up with *him*? A guy who's been nothing short of an asshole to you since the day you met?"

I'm not exactly on the Sam Blaze Defense Squad here, but even I can admit that he wasn't an asshole. He avoided me on tour and baited me onstage, but if that made him an asshole, then I was every bit as much of one to him.

"It's going to be different from what we were doing before," I say. "We're not playing up the rivalry anymore."

"And I suppose we're just playing down the times he made you cry like a baby while we're at it," Serena snaps back.

She knows the instant she says it that she's gone too far. Serena may keep her guard up, but so do I. I'm not a crier. With a dating life as public and disastrous as mine, I couldn't afford to be.

So I only ever cried about Sam twice—once over that interview before we met, and once after that last phone call we had. When the heartbreak was so stark and mortifying that Serena and Hannah were the only ones I could trust with it.

Maybe it's for the best, that Serena's throwing it in my face now. Maybe this will finally settle the score between us—calling me out on a moment of weakness the same way I did to her.

"That wasn't his fault," I say.

Serena draws in a sharp breath, but Hannah cuts her off. "Maybe we should take this to the Hole."

She's referring to the only part of the old bar that remains, a cramped, likely haunted space that smells like dust older than we are. Back in our younger days, the Hole was where you went to cry, hook up, duke it out, or, on particularly messy nights, do all three.

But Serena shakes her head, her curls shaking a beat behind. "I'm just going to go. I have a recording session tomorrow. I don't want to mess up my vocal cords."

"Well, the good news is you don't need to say a word to walk that runway," says Hannah. She holds up her own phone, flashing a text message thread. "And another model *did* just drop out, so either you put this on or I go out and start taking crowd volunteers."

"Just have Mackenzie go twice," says Serena. "She never had any trouble hamming it up onstage."

Hannah frowns, jumping in to defend me. "What's that supposed to mean?"

But Hannah's phone starts to ring, so when Serena answers the question, she turns to me.

"We'd rehearse within an inch of our lives, but what did it matter? You and Sam stole the show every time. It's like you were allergic to sticking to the plan."

The last thing I want to do is kick up a fight with Serena, but that isn't fair. A huge part of those long rehearsals was the choreographers giving us specific moments they *wanted* us to throw new antics into the mix. Choreographers Serena helped handpick and spent hours talking to, because she had to have a hand in every little thing. We didn't make a single move without Serena's sign-off.

I turn back to Hannah, but she's distracted, murmuring something into her phone.

"We were doing what we were told," I say.

I'm expecting Serena to drop it, but she doubles down.

"And how do you think the rest of us felt about it?" she demands. "You got to be the fun, messy one that everyone loved. Mackenzie can do no wrong! If she goes off script, it's adorable! If any of us did half the shit you got away with onstage or in interviews, we'd be hung out to dry."

Serena's breathing hard, and now so am I. It's true that I was never as polished as she was—always making herself scripts and practicing the tiniest of gestures and expressions in the mirror. But working the crowd was my role in the band long before Sam was ever a part of the act. The same way Serena thrived on order, I thrived on chaos—with Hannah splitting the middle, it was the perfect combination of hitting our usual marks and surprising people with new ones.

But when it came to any maneuvers that all three of us were involved in, I never once did anything to throw Serena or Hannah off. I was even more careful reading their energy than I was the crowd's. She knows that. She wouldn't have asked me to keep performing with her if she didn't.

Maybe Serena is only doing this to keep the focus off whatever is going on with her. But that doesn't mean I have to take it.

"Well, what a relief that you don't have to worry about it anymore," I say.

Serena's expression hardens. "Yeah. What a relief."

Hannah hangs up the phone, then puts a firm hand on both our shoulders, hustling us out. "Sorry, sorry, but we have to pause on this—we need to go over the new show order."

Next thing I know we're all lined up by the back entrance in our pajamas for the start of the show, Serena burying her face in her phone so she doesn't have to talk to anybody. She only looks up when the music starts, cueing her to kick us off. It's "Hype Girl," one of Thunder Hearts' earliest hits, and of course it starts out with the two of us locked in a powerful, belted harmony.

Serena straightens her shoulders, locks on her "I ate sunshine for breakfast" grin, and struts onto the runway cutting through the middle of Lightning Strike, hair bouncing and hips swishing in the nightdress. The small audience cheers as Serena twists this way and that, gracefully showing off the matching scrunchie hidden in a slim pocket under the dress's ruffles.

Despite all the tension, I can't help but admire her. She never makes one wrong move. She may resent the way my antics worked the crowds we used to play, but it was her polish that launched her to superstardom.

"Girl, you're up," says one of the models, nudging me toward the catwalk.

Shit. The song changed to cue me while I was lost in thought. I stumble onto the catwalk, pulling a sheepish look as the light hits me. A few people in the audience laugh just as Serena passes me, rolling her eyes at me as if to say, *See?*

I collect myself, grinning with my head held high. But within a second I realize I'm not just walking on the runway, but straight into an early 2000s YA novel love triangle. Sitting right next to each other directly on the far edge of the catwalk, eyes locked on me, are none other than Grayson and Sam.

I glance at Hannah. Hannah raises her eyebrows gleefully. "This next look is one of my favorites, because with the reversible fabric, it's *double* the fun."

That's one way of putting it. Another quick glance tells me that Grayson is leaning forward and smiling encouragingly in a clean-cut navy-blue suit and Sam is fully leaned back in his seat and smirking in a beaten-up leather jacket like this is a closed show just for him.

New nightmare unlocked: standing backlit from all sides in

slumber party pajamas in the middle of a bar while my potential new boyfriend and past heartbreak sit shoulder to shoulder looking hotter than either of them has any right to, both of them clearly waiting for me to meet their gaze.

There's a low, catcalling whistle I recognize too well not to scowl at it, which means Sam and his smug eyes win.

My fist curls in my sweatpant pocket. Not for long.

"As Mackenzie will demonstrate, these are deep, deep pockets, providing a cavernous hole for snacks."

On cue I pull out a bag of Sour Patch Kids, Cheez-Its, and Milk Duds from the pocket the way Thunder Hearts used to do onstage during our longer sets. Hannah holds out her hand expectantly without so much as turning around, and I dispense a Milk Dud for her, getting a cheer out of the crowd as she seamlessly tosses it into her mouth.

"For anyone who wants to snooze in style, there's also a matching eye mask," she adds.

I pull it out from my other pocket and hook my finger around it, spinning it mock seductively and earning a few more laughs.

"This isn't just any sleep mask, though—it's contoured so it won't put pressure on the eyes, and made with a ridiculously soft memory foam for the most satisfying sleep of your life."

At this point Hannah instructed me to offer it to any random person in the front row to feel. I usually make Isla or one of Hannah's sisters my victim in this kind of fashion shenanigan. But today I lock eyes with Grayson, deliberately walk to the edge of the catwalk, and lean down to his level. He's watching me gamely, but Sam's eyes on me from beside him burn hot enough to sear.

I slide the sleep mask over Grayson's head and cover his eyes, then lean in and press a finger to the top of his nose.

"What do you think?" I ask, loud enough for the crowd to hear me, but low enough that it sounds intimate. "Is it as . . . *satisfying* as she says?"

"Sure," he answers. "But the last thing I want to do now is sleep."

The few people close enough to hear it let out a laugh, save Sam, who's gone very still next to Grayson. Serves him right, showing up here out of the blue. I pull the sleep mask off Grayson's eyes and blow him a kiss before heading back over to Hannah.

"And if your mood changes in the middle of the night—well," says Hannah, gesturing for me to proceed.

I lift the shirt up just enough to flip it over and show the pale blue fabric on the other side of it. I turn with every intention of giving Grayson a pointed wink, but my eyes snag on Sam's first. They're bright even in the low light of the audience, his whole body tilted toward the edge of the stage now, watching me as if in challenge. As if to say, *Go ahead. Do it.*

God dammit. I don't.

Instead, I spin on my heel, giving the shirt a little flourish while Hannah explains how stain-resistant the fabric is, and manage to avoid both his and Grayson's eyes for the rest of my time on the runway.

When I slip back to change into my next outfit, Serena's in the middle of changing into a lilac robe, her back pointedly turned to me. That doesn't stop me from seeing her reflection in the mirror—how tired her face is when it's in neutral. How it doesn't age her, but makes her look younger than she has in years.

How her chest is covered in stress hives.

"Oh, shit," I blurt.

Serena's eyes snap to meet mine in the mirror, then follow my gaze down to her chest. "Great," she mutters dully.

I cross the room to examine her, yanking the robe open before she can pull it away from me. She's covered in red splotches from her collarbone down into the camisole she's wearing. "Has it ever been this bad?" I ask worriedly.

Serena is unfazed, already in damage-control mode. "I'll tighten the robe. Do you have concealer?"

I shake my head. We both know it won't be enough. "Just switch with me," I say, handing her the hanger with my hoodie and leggings.

She hesitates, but only for a beat. "Fine."

"Does this happen a lot?" I ask as she wriggles into the leggings. She used to get hives on the road before, but I can't remember a time it was this extreme.

Serena doesn't answer, looking over the call sheet for our cues. "Should I go out first anyway?" she asks.

I nod. Hannah will be surprised by the outfit switch for a fraction of a second before rolling with it. Serena finishes yanking on the hoodie and heads back into the hall so fast that I just barely manage to kick off my sweatpants and secure the robe as I follow her.

"Are you okay?" I ask.

"Did you put anything weird in the pockets on this one?" she asks back.

I grab her by the wrist. "Seriously, Serena. Can we just—talk after this?"

She grits her teeth, then sags a bit. "I really do have to record in the morning."

I let her go. "Right," I say, my throat tight.

She opens her mouth like she's going to say something else, but the song is coming to an end. Serena lines herself up at the edge of the door to walk on and I duck behind her, fiddling with the robe to get the straps tied on right.

We both freeze when we hear it. The opening chords to "Play You by Heart."

"You're up," says the last model to Serena.

But Serena shakes her head, her jaw tight. "You go," she says without looking at me.

I'm still fiddling with the robe straps. "What? We said same order."

Serena pushes me forward. "Go. Your little boyfriend will eat it up."

My cheeks burn. "Don't be ridiculous," I protest. "We're just working together; we're not—"

I don't know what terrible thing I did in a past life, but it must have followed me through the time, space, adorable loungewear continuum. What happens after Serena nudges me onto the runway can only be the universe coming back to collect: I am standing in a massive spotlight in nothing but a white tank top and none other than my drooping Christmas underwear.

Not only that, but I appear to have tripped on the power cord to the speaker. The place is dead silent, save for Serena's quiet, "*Shit.*"

I look down just to confirm my situation, and yes. A bedazzled Rudolph is still perched over my nether regions on full display. I close my eyes. Maybe it's a dream. A holly jolly nightmare.

One that can only get worse, because a quick glance back at Serena tells me that she has the tie to the robe in her hands, but the wind machine has fluttered the robe away.

I'm frozen until I hear it. The noise is faint, but it's undeniably the opening to "Jingle Bell Rock." When I look up, Sam is grinning wickedly, his phone held up in his hand.

Damn it. How many damn times is this man going to rescue me this week? It's like the universe heard my resolution not to fall for him and is testing me with everything it's got.

But when I meet his eye, there's that same quick, conspiratorial beat we'd have onstage just before we did something wild. This isn't just a rescue. It's an inside joke that we haven't gotten to tell in a long, long time. So I roll with it, doing an exaggerated shimmy before launching into an approximation of the dance from *Mean Girls*. Hannah doesn't miss a beat before joining in, much to the very loud delight of our audience.

"Ah, yes," Hannah says into her mic, half wheezing with laughter. "Our unsubtle but effective reminder that everything in this collection will be available in time for this holiday season."

Someone tosses the robe up to us then, and I catch it and spin it around our heads for a bit more of the song before Hannah offers a hand to help slide my arms into it. At some point someone hops up and fixes the speaker, transitioning back into "Play You by Heart," and the rest of the demonstration goes on without a hitch.

"A round of applause for Mackenzie and her robe, which I think we all can agree are 'so fetch'!" Hannah calls out as Serena and I swap places on the runway, Serena steadfastly avoiding my eye.

I take a deep breath. I know Serena. She is a master of self-control. If she's acting this impulsively, then Hannah and I were right to think something is up.

"Okay," I say, keeping my voice light. "I think I'm owed some Serena time after that debacle."

Serena's cheeks are flushed, but she doesn't apologize. "Oh, come on. They loved it, same as they always do. Another messy Mackenzie moment for the books."

It cuts deeper than it should, but I'm exhausted. I know she needs us right now, but I've been trying. It was one thing when she was avoiding us, but another to get pushed away.

"Maybe you wouldn't be so unhappy if you loosened up every now and then, too," I say back.

"I am perfectly happy," says Serena through her teeth. "I do everything I'm supposed to do. I never give anything less than my best. Why is everyone jumping down my throat over a damn tour delay?"

I reach for her hand. She lets me take it, too stunned to pull away. She wants me to be angry, I realize. She wants me to fight. She wants to goad me so she can justify walking away, and protect whatever it is she doesn't want me to see.

We've pulled each other through so much worse than this. I can't let her.

"I'm not worried about your career," I say quietly. "I'm worried about *you*. This doesn't look like happy to me."

Serena yanks her hand out of mine. "Says someone making the dumbest move of their life."

I ask it, then. The question that's been on the tip of my tongue all night. The one that started to form long before it, back when Serena took one look at me and Hannah at the start of Thunder Hearts and decided she was the one calling the shots.

"Are you upset because it's a dumb move, or because you're not in charge of me anymore?"

Serena reels back. Turns out being someone's best friend is a blessing and a curse—she knows where to cut me deep, and so do I.

Maybe I should apologize. But there's some unsettled part of me that knows it won't do any good. I've been apologizing and apologizing, and it hasn't gotten me anywhere at all. Serena's impenetrable now, her walls so thick that even I can't see inside.

Her face hardens as she turns to leave, but not before I see the crack in it. She got what she wanted. Both of us still lose.

chapter ten
MACKENZIE

The same way I never understood writer's block, I never understood stage fright, either. Even when I was a little kid hamming it up in school talent shows, the stage felt like an escape. The one place I could throw my limbs and pitch my voice and let my heart tip over without my parents telling me I was *too much*. If I earned a reputation for being chaotic onstage, it was because I laid my whole self out and didn't leave a shred behind.

I almost dropped in the wings after a few encores in our early days, before Isla started shoving Take 5s and Gatorades down my throat. But at the tail end of our last tour, that trick stopped working. All of a sudden, I wasn't just exhausted at the end of shows, but practically catatonic.

Only later did I put two and two together on my thyroid being completely out of whack.

But those symptoms are regulated with meds now. The exhaustion I feel coming off Hannah's fashion show is nothing unusual—

just the kind that comes with putting on a show and fighting yet another round with Serena, without making a shred of progress.

That said, nothing wakes me up faster than walking out to the sight of Sam and Grayson chatting each other up at the bar. They both spot me at the same time, Grayson waving, Sam tipping his head.

This is fine. Good, in fact. It will be easier to shake Sam off for my date if Grayson's already here.

Still, Sam's smirk is a bit too suspicious for my taste.

"The first one of you to make a Christmas pun gets banned from this bar for life," I say, eyes aimed at him.

Sam only leans back on the bar with his usual cocky ease. Still, I don't miss the quick twitch of his jaw when Grayson leans in to kiss me on the cheek.

"Sleigh it ain't so," Grayson jokes.

I squeeze an arm around him. "I'm only letting that slide so Hannah can put that on the holiday cocktail menu."

"Speaking of," Grayson says, holding out a deep red spice-rimmed cocktail with three glitter-infused cherries perched over it. "Figured you earned one after putting on quite a show."

It's a Shiny Ball of Chaos, a spicy cherry martini that Hannah put on the menu in honor of *Rolling Stone* dubbing me one. Before I can thank Grayson for it, someone calls his name from the front, and he offers me an apologetic smile.

"Is it okay if I meet you outside in a bit?" he asks. "The team wants to debrief at the cafe across the street while we're all together."

So much for pushing Sam out the door. "Sure thing. I'll see you then."

In the meantime, Sam takes a seat at the bar next to my usual stool, hooking his foot around the legs of it to beckon me to join him. I set my drink on the bar but don't sit, watching him watching me.

"Here, Sparkles." Sam pulls a Take 5 bar from his coat pocket and tosses it to me. "Trade you."

It's only a two-dollar candy bar. But it's also evidence that Sam was paying attention back in the old days, even when he was pulling out every stop to make me think he wasn't. Paying enough attention that he knows I don't like to drink right after shows, either.

I don't know what to make of it. More importantly, I don't like not knowing what to make of it.

"What did I say about being nice to me?" I ask.

Sam liberates the cocktail from my hand. "Trust me, Sparkles. I'm being nice to *me*." He takes a long sip. "This is your cocktail, right?" he asks, lips lingering on the spiced rim. "You taste delicious."

Damn him. It's stunts like this that are going to make it near impossible to write Seven's last song.

"You think flattery is going to distract me from asking what on earth you're doing here?"

Sam sets the cocktail on the bar, looking me up and down. "Aside from saving your Christmas-clad ass?" he asks. "Twyla and Isla said this was the best time for us to meet up here, if we were going to make it one of the haunts."

"Did they, now?"

Sam raises his eyebrows, amused. "Don't tell me they didn't warn you I'd be here."

This is classic Isla and Twyla. They love and support us, but also have no problem playing God when it suits them. Maybe they thought the surprise would make for a better song.

"Must have slipped their minds," I say, finally taking the stool next to his.

Sam lets out one of those bright laughs of his. "They're evil."

"Devious," I agree, ripping open the Take 5 bar with my teeth. "But I do owe you a thank-you for the assist earlier."

Sam shakes his head, eyes bright with mischief. "Don't thank me yet. Turns out you can play music and record video on your phone at the same time."

"If you know what's good for you, you'll burn that." But the instant I bite into the bar, the salty, crunchy sweetness makes me forget my last shred of dignity. I close my eyes and sink my elbows into the bar, moaning. "Fuck, that hits the spot."

Sam's lip curls, undeniably smug. "I bet it does," he says. He lifts his cocktail up for inspection. "And this is certainly a step up from—what did Serena call the old bar's 'house cocktail'?"

"Cough syrup," I recall.

Sam makes a show of craning his head toward the back of the bar.

"Speaking of Serena," he says out of the side of his mouth, "I assume she's going to pop out to bite my head off any moment now."

I set the chocolate down on the bar. "She left."

"What a shame," says Sam. "I miss fearing for my mortal soul."

My eyes linger on the door as if Serena will magically reappear through it. Sam nudges my boot with his sneaker. "Still in there?"

Maybe I'm just tired, or the chocolate has loosened up my guard. But instead of brushing it off, I tell Sam the truth.

"Serena's not happy about this," I say. "Mack & Sam, I mean."

"Neither am I," says Sam somberly. "'Sam & Mack' has a *much* better ring to it."

I pluck the umbrella perched on his drink between my fingers, spinning it. "After Thunder Hearts broke up, she wanted us to team up," I tell him.

Sam's expression loses its teasing edge. "Damn," he says. "Why didn't you?"

I didn't mean to keep the thyroid situation from Sam. In fact, I almost told him on that last phone call we had, just before the surgery to remove the growth they found. But it felt like a clear line had been drawn. I asked him if there was anything I could do to help with Ben, and he said no. Kindly, but firmly. It defined what we were by defining what we weren't—if he wouldn't let me take on any of his burdens, I didn't want to put any of mine on him, either.

Then so much time passed. Enough that I never imagined seeing Sam again, let alone telling him what happened to my voice.

Let alone worrying the instant he heard it, he'd recognize it as Seven.

It's that quick lurch of unease that makes me brush the whole thing aside. "There were a few reasons," I say. "But I could have handled it better at the time."

Sam watches me carefully. When I don't elaborate, he gives me one of those easy, confident shrugs. "You'll work it out."

I raise my eyebrows at him. "Not all of us can rely on our 'bad-boy charm' to win people over."

"Aw. You think I'm charming?"

"Did you conveniently miss the part where I called you bad?"

Sam lightly kicks my stool, and surprises me with the sincerity in his voice. "Serena loves you. Anyone can see that. Hell, she was in full guard dog mode with you whenever I was around."

My head tilts at that. Serena was certainly not Sam's biggest fan after that episode of Noted Scene had me spiraling, but he never came up much, outside of rehearsals and shows. "She was not."

Sam raises a finger, a quiet *Just you wait.*

"Unlike you, I actually *did* some homework for our assignment for today." He reaches back into his bag and out come a bunch of Polaroids, these ones with kitschy flowers on the borders. They must be the ones Divya took. We all used my camera with different film borders, so we'd know whose photos were whose. It's oddly sweet, imagining Sam tracking her down in the city to collect them.

"See for yourself," he says, putting one of them on the top of the pile.

In the photo I'm teetering on my stool, leaning into Hannah and looking self-satisfied. Sam is just barely in the frame, a blur poised to stick a plastic fork in the slice of cake I had on the bar only to be stopped in his tracks by Serena, who is standing in front of him brandishing a plastic knife.

I throw my head back laughing. It's the best I've felt all day.

"By all means, have a laugh at my near murder."

"'Candy Shard Front Man Killed in Cake-Related Manslaughter,'" I say, gesturing in front of me like I'm reading the headline. "You could have been a legend."

Sam hums regretfully. "Guess I'll have to settle for all those Billboard 100 hits."

I reach for the rest of the photos. Rob trying to nap in the corner of the bar with a baseball cap over his head as Divya and Serena shake glitter all over him. One of me and Hannah trying to tip drinks into each other's mouths. One of Divya, Sam, and Hannah huddled over a phone screen trying to get tickets for a late-night showing of some indie movie playing at the Times Square AMC.

The truth is that for everyone else, the rivalry between our bands *was* just an act. This bar was one of the few places we could safely shake it.

"The worst part was it was my slice," says Sam about the photo. "You stole it."

"Excuse you," I say. I hold up another Polaroid, where I am standing beside him, triumphant, with his sleeve yanked up to show a lopsided temporary tattoo. "I won it fair and square."

"You cheated," Sam accuses.

"There's no cheating in Sweet Spot. Just winning and losing. *Sore* losing, apparently."

Sweet Spot was a game Rob made up that quicky devolved into madness. It started when he ordered dozens of temporary tattoos that were supposed to look like Candy Shard's broken-candy logo, and instead looked like they'd been drawn by a drunk toddler. Every week he'd choose one of us at random to hide a tattoo on their person, and choose—within reason—where they put it. He'd announce the start of the game, and each of us would have one guess as to who it was and where the tattoo was hidden.

There were rules: You could only guess once, and you could tell your guess to Rob. Most importantly, if you were the one with the Sweet Spot on you, you had to lie and pretend you were in the game, too.

Those rules aside, it was straight-up chaos. We were accidentally-on-purpose barging into each other's dressing rooms to see if we could spot tattoos, hiking each other's shirts up between songs, just short of using interrogation tactics we'd seen in crime procedural dramas to trick the Sweet Spotter into confessing.

"How'd you even figure out it was me that time?" Sam asks.

I prop my elbows on the bar, making a show of examining his face. "You've got a tell."

Sam's eyes are both amused and disbelieving. "I do not."

"You do," I say, leaning in. He raises his eyebrows as if to challenge me, and I raise mine right back. "For instance. Remember when Divya's puppy interrupted a live broadcast at the Moonbeam Awards?"

Sam lifts the rim of his cocktail to his mouth, betraying nothing. "It rings a bell."

"You wouldn't happen to have been the one who snuck him backstage in that giant emo leather jacket of yours, right?"

There it is. Whenever he's trying to pull a fast one, he has this little corner of his mouth that turns down like he's trying not to smile. All I had ever had to do was loudly mention Sweet Spot within earshot of him and he'd give himself away just like he is right now.

"I knew it," I say.

"Know what?" Sam's brow furrows as it hits him. "Wait—did I do it right then? The 'tell'?"

"Maybe. Maybe not," I say.

Sam sets his cocktail down, laughably indignant. "You have to tell me what it is," he insists.

"And lose my one advantage over you?" I say, tapping the photo. "Not a chance."

"From where I'm sitting, you've already got plenty."

When I look up, our faces are close enough that I almost startle. Not at the distance, but how natural it feels to want to lean in and close it.

"For instance," he says, "it's one thing that you knew when I had the Sweet Spot. But you always had an uncanny way knowing *where*."

My cheeks flush. I may have sworn upside down and backward I was immune to Sam back in the day, but it sure never stopped me from glimpsing him all sweat-soaked and throwing clothes off himself on the way to his dressing room to make sure.

"Can't give away all my secrets," I say, lifting my chin.

"Secrets plural, huh?" he asks. "Wouldn't have expected that from a goody-goody pop princess."

Little does he know the biggest secret of all is looming in the air right now—the bartender is using Tick Tune to play a Seven song over the speakers.

"I'm full of surprises," I say.

Sam grins. Our faces are still close enough that we're suspended in a wordless challenge. Like if one of us moved, we'd be acknowledging that we're too close for *friends*.

Sam really does catch me off guard then, leaning in so sharply that for a split, wild second I think he might try to kiss me. Instead, he reaches over and grabs my Take 5 bar, not breaking eye contact as he takes a smug bite, fully aware of what he just did.

"I'll get them out of you eventually," he says, tongue skimming over his teeth. "But first I'm getting my tax for that cake slice you stole."

I lean back against the bar, feeling my heart pound where my elbows meet the cool surface. "Don't you live on top of a literal bakery?" I ask.

"Not just any bakery, but the best in the city," says Sam. "Play nice long enough, Sparkles, and I might convince Lizzie to give you a discount."

The pride in his voice is unmistakable, the same way it is when he talks about Ben, or when he talked about his mom when we were on tour.

"You love her," I say about Lizzie.

"Course," says Sam, without missing a beat.

"So why weren't you guys ever serious?"

I've always been curious. Even before I realized I'd fallen head over sparkly boots for Sam, I couldn't understand it—not just how Sam wasn't interested in relationships with the women he was "having fun" with, but one he seemed to be good friends with.

Sam seems mildly surprised by the question, but answers it just the same. "Neither of us wanted to be. Especially back then. I was on the road and Lizzie was backpacking."

I nod, but there's still an itch here that I can't ignore. One that I've been trying to scratch by writing Seven's song. One that makes me keep digging now, to see if he might say something that makes it stop.

"Why weren't you serious with anyone?"

It's a question that felt impossible to ask back then. Like it would give him some power over me, even acknowledging that I was curious. He'd file it away and know that I lied when we first met—that he had an effect on me after all.

But Sam ducks his gaze like I'm the one with the upper hand. "Aw, c'mon. We were in a punk rock band. Where would the fun have been in that?" he asks.

My arms stiffen against the bar. "Sure."

Sam must clock my disappointment in his answer, because he rubs the back of his neck sheepishly and tries again.

"Honestly, I just knew there was no room for it. When I do something, I do it all the way," he says. "So I couldn't be a relationship guy."

It's a strange, belated relief to hear him say that. Maybe because it makes more sense than any of the reasons I thought up at the time—that Sam was just a player, or incapable of that kind of love. It didn't seem in line with the rest of him, but this does.

My next question is treading into unfamiliar territory. Maybe even dangerous. But if I don't ask it now, that itch is going to linger the same way it has for the past two years. Not just the *what if?* we had onstage, but the *what if?* we briefly had off of it.

"Do you think that'll ever change for you?"

He's not fully meeting my eye, torn between me and the last bit of his drink. "Yeah," he says, after a moment. "But it just—depends."

"On what?" I press.

Sam still won't look at me, but he doesn't shy from the question, either. Just considers it for a moment.

"You know when it feels right," he says. "The whole 'lock, click' thing."

"Lock, click," I repeat.

Sam nods, his eyes distant but his words firm. "Maybe you don't know what you're walking into, but the key goes in so easily that it's like you're already home. So you just know."

Neither of us speaks for a long beat. I'm not worried about the itch anymore. It's something else that makes me keep digging— something I thought I'd buried, but might be pressing against new ground, starting to bloom.

"And you've had that feeling before?"

Sam's eyes meet mine then. There is none of the usual heat in them, no bite. Like he isn't just looking at me but letting me look, too.

"Yeah," he says. "I have."

We are both very still as the words settle between us with an un-expected weight. It's nothing I don't already know. Sam is perfectly capable of falling in love. Just not with me.

My eyes sting, but it's my heart that spills over. Lyrics are start-ing to form on some invisible page. Not the kind Mack & Sam would write, but the kind Seven would.

I clear my throat, tucking it away for later. Sam's watching me until he isn't, turning back to his drink and clearing his throat, too.

"Well, now that we're getting all deep here, I need to ask you a very serious, personal question," he says. "You know—friend to friend."

I pull in a breath to collect myself, then turn so I can narrow my eyes at him. "All right, *friend*."

He's back in full mischief mode again. "This unexpected writing session. Your date with Grayson later." He gestures to my under-wear, his lips curling into a smirk. "Are we both sabotaging you in a highly concentrated effort to seduce Santa Claus tonight?"

My laugh is so unexpected it borders on a cackle. "Can't a girl bastardize the Christmas spirit without having an agenda?" I ask.

"Sure," he says, far too pleased with himself for getting a reaction out of me. "But if there's a better story, then I want to hear it."

I consider saying, *Laundry day*, and leaving it at that. But we're friends now, according to Sam. And what's a mildly risqué underwear explanation between friends?

"All right," I say, straightening up. "It's called—trademark pending—the Christmas Underwear Test."

Sam leans in, eyes flickering with amusement. "Oh, this is gonna be good."

"Good? You mean genius," I correct him. "The underwear acts as a buffer. It's not that it's *stopping* me from hooking up with anyone—it just stops me from hooking up with anyone who isn't right for me."

Sam opens his mouth like he has a dozen questions, but nods. "Christmas cockblock," he repeats, putting a finger to his temple. "Got it."

"If I'm too embarrassed to let them see the underwear, then they are not worthy of rocking around my Christmas tree. But if I decide I'm comfortable enough for them to see me cosplaying as Mrs. Claus? *Then* I know it's time to find out who's on the naughty list."

Sam is doing such a terrible job of not laughing that he has to put down his drink instead of sipping it. "And you have to resort to this particular brand of nonsense because . . ."

"You saw what happened to all my relationships," I say. "I fell madly in love with any guy who knew the right things to say. My inner compass was like a damn pinwheel."

Sam shrugs. "Or maybe you just believe the best in people. Nothing wrong with that."

He says it so casually that I'm not expecting it to hit as deeply as it does. People have called me a lot of things over the years. Foolish. Naive. Slutty, even, when they were being particularly vile.

But the way Sam puts it feels like it isn't a weakness, but a strength.

I swallow hard. "Well, that's rich, coming from the one person I didn't," I joke, so I don't bring down the mood.

He uses his foot to spin the bottom of my stool so I'm directly facing him. "But I'm growing on you now."

He is, dammit. But maybe that's a good thing. I have thought myself in circles about the way we ended before we began, but I never once considered a friendship on the other side.

"Trial basis," I remind him just the same. No matter what we are to each other, I can't help but want to keep him on his toes.

But Sam is unperturbed. So much so that he's leaning back and smirking pointedly at me.

"What?" I ask, at my own peril.

He shrugs innocently. "There's just one factor you're not considering here."

"Which is?"

He takes his time leaning back in, like he's relishing what he's going to say before he says it. "You just explained the whole thing to me. So wouldn't that make me a man who passes your little test?"

Well, shit. I cross my legs and lean back, trying to seem like someone who isn't simmering from the heat in his eyes.

"Aw. Don't tell me my sagging Christmas underwear got you all hot and bothered."

So much for catching him off guard. As usual, he's living for it.

"Giddyup, jingle horse," he says, the words patently absurd but his voice hypnotically low.

This is circling the drain on that whole "no teasing" rule we had in place. Then Sam's teeth graze his lower lip, as he watches me watch him, and suddenly we're not breaking the no teasing rule at all. This feels like something else. Something that has my blood rushing and my cheeks burning and my eyes lingering on his lips, stained red from my cocktail like I branded him.

"Sweet Spot," he says, his voice so low it rasps. "If we're going to write a song about this place, that should be it. That's the memory that sticks out to me the most."

"Me too," I say.

Maybe it's just because Sweet Spot was fun. But maybe it's because even when Sam and I barely ever acknowledged each other, Sweet Spot was the one exception to the rule.

My phone buzzes with a text. Neither of us moves. When it buzzes again, my eyes skim the screen.

"It's Grayson," I say. "They'll be wrapped up in ten. Shit."

Sam waves me off. "Ten minutes to write a three-minute song?" he says. "We've pulled some crazier stunts than that."

He reaches over the bar to grab a receipt pen and a cocktail napkin, writing the words *"SWEET SPOT"* in all caps before handing the pen over to me, like he's issuing a challenge. It's our old dynamic, but with a new twist—not wanting to prove him wrong, but to prove him right.

The next ten minutes slip out from under us in a blur. Like we're suspended together in this place's past and present—the bright camera flashes and syrup-sweet drinks and late nights that shifted into moments like these, where the lights don't burn and the drinks don't sting and a new sweetness lingers.

Sam hums. I write. I don't know who breaks the rule first, but when my phone goes off again, we're hovered over the napkin so close that the back of my shoulder is pressed against his chest.

"Shit," I mutter, but don't move away.

Sam doesn't, either. "You can't go until we get a picture."

"Of what?" I ask.

He takes the pen out of my hand. "Hold still."

He leans in, gently setting the tip of the pen on my arm and slowly, carefully drawing a lopsided candy in the same spot his temporary tattoo was when I caught him years ago. When I shiver it doesn't have anything to do with the sensation of the pen on my skin.

"There," he says. "Now you're the one with the Sweet Spot."

We get the bartender to quickly snap a picture of us, re-creating the old one from the bar. Just after she snaps it my phone buzzes again, letting me know Grayson is waiting outside.

"I'll type up what we've got later tonight," I tell Sam.

He hands me the napkin with our lyrics on it. "You might be a little busy there, Rudolph."

I brace myself for him to follow it up with some choice remark about Grayson the way he always did about guys I was with, but he's got nothing. He just meets my eyes with a smile that doesn't reach his own.

"Might be," I say lightly.

Turns out I'm fresh out of remarks, too. It feels off-kilter for us. But maybe that's part of this new chapter of "mature, mutually supportive friends."

And that should be a relief. My arm is still tingling where Sam drew the Sweet Spot on me, but his words left a more permanent mark. Whatever it is I needed to finish that last song from Seven, I should have it now. A clear answer. A tidy end. We got caught up in the heat of the moment during that kiss, but we were never going to be anything more.

No—that's not true. We're a team now. And despite everything, I *like* working with Sam. This is the best-case scenario.

And that's what I tell myself as I leave the bar and meet Grayson in the early evening light. That's what I tell myself as I politely kiss Grayson goodbye outside my building at the end of the date, and walk back in alone. That's what I tell myself as I start another draft of Seven's final song, and the melody takes on a new feeling entirely—one that chases the edge of every lyric, like a song I haven't written yet, but know better than any I've ever heard.

A song that sounds an awful lot like *lock, click*.

chapter eleven
SAM

"Pizza muffins," Ben declares, all toothy-grinned and wet-haired from the pool.

"I dunno, small fry." I nudge open the door to Sugar Harmony. "That might just throw the city's pizza industry into chaos."

Ben laughs as he zips into the bakery, just barely dodging Rocket, who is walking back from the counter balancing his laptop and a cold brew.

"I thought I heard a tiny dessert anarchist outside," he says.

I catch up to Ben, lifting his backpack off his shoulders and opening it on the table behind the register. Inside it are his homework packet and some loose drawings of what appears to be a pizza croissant, complete with stick figure people reacting to it in horror.

"Music day or capitalism day?" I ask Rocket.

Rocket winces, running a hand through his neon-blond curls. "Capitalism all the way down, man," he says, flashing his laptop screen at me.

Poor Rocket. He got tangled in music industry drama before

he could even get his foot in the door. Before we met, he was one of the first breakout artists on Tick Tune, anonymously playing offbeat, earworm songs that blew up on the app. It all happened fast, and the wrong people noticed first and offered him a record deal. I didn't know him at the time, but I got my lawyer on the scam of a contract he signed when we did. Too little, too late— the kid's locked into it, and so are a bunch of his friends. They still can't release any music until the terms run out at the end of the year.

In the meantime, Rocket's been working on new music in the open mic night and surviving off freelance gigs, which is how he ended up in Sugar Harmony. The way Lizzie and Kara tell it, he showed up in one of his comically oversized all-black outfits the day of the bakery's soft launch, asked if there was Wi-Fi, said, *Cool*, and planted himself there. By the time I showed up he was working for the bakery part-time and doing freelance work on his laptop from a corner for the rest of it. If anyone tries to mess with him again, they'll have us and a whole army of Sugar Harmony customers to fight first.

Ben spreads his homework on the table next to Rocket. "Mom says if I'm going to do pizza muffins, I can only pick three toppings to stuff it with or it'll *explode*."

"Oh snap," says Rocket. "What are you thinking, little dude?"

Ben's lips press into an impish smile. "Anchovies."

I love this kid to death, but god only knows where he came from. "Homework first, then abominations," I remind him.

Ben nods. "I'm gonna get the fun pen from the office," he says.

He dips into the back just as the front door jingles, and Rocket blurts out, "No freaking *way*."

It's Mackenzie, her yellow hair a wild curtain from the humidity like it was during our outdoor shows. She's wearing an old pair of overall shorts over a tight tank top and a beaten-up pair of combat boots, her eyes bright and her face flushed from the heat.

Damn. I've been telling myself it's a good thing, the two of us being friends. But the more I have to look at her the harder it gets to look away. The only reason I don't get caught this time is because something else catches Mackenzie's eye.

"Rocket?"

Rocket nearly trips on his own gangly limbs getting up. I just barely catch his cold brew before it makes friends with his laptop.

"Mack Attack!" he exclaims, hugging her with enough force to pull her boots up from the floor.

You'd think I'd be used to plot twists by now, but I can't wrap my head around this one.

"You two know each other?" I ask.

As Rocket sets her down, Mackenzie nods, then puts her hands on his shoulders and rattles him. "Congrats," she says. "Serena's a tough act to open for, but if anyone's up for it, it's you."

Apparently, the whiplash today knows no end.

"You're opening for Serena?" I ask Rocket.

His cheeks go wildly pink against his pale skin. "I found out right before the tour got delayed," he says, apologetic. "It's just a week. And I can only sing covers."

Shit. I didn't mean to make him feel bad. I clap a hand on his shoulder and rattle him, too. "You gotta tell us stuff like this, kid. You know we love an excuse to celebrate."

But Rocket shakes his head. "It's not announced yet. I don't wanna jinx it."

Mackenzie's smile dims. "Rocket was going to do a remix of a Thunder Hearts song a few years back," she explains. "He was even set to open for us. That's how we met. But then that contract screwed him over."

Rocket nods, head bobbing like a goth Labrador retriever.

"It was fun to chill with you guys. Snack game was nuts." He deflates. "I'm psyched about Serena, but I gotta be careful. She could swap me out in a snap. That Seven chick is eating us all for breakfast and she's only got like, three songs."

"Six songs," I say.

Then Mackenzie's eyes finally land on me, crackling blue. Maybe she's right about my ego. There's no place I like her eyes better than when they're right on mine.

She turns back to Rocket. "You're phenomenal onstage," she says. "People are gonna go nuts. Nobody's even *seen* Seven."

Rocket grins bashfully. "Low-key, though, Serena brings her up all the time. I think she thinks I know her, like there's some secret underground Tick Tune club."

Mackenzie ducks her head. "Serena listens to her?"

Rocket's computer pings. "Ah, sorry. My overlords are summoning me," he says, saluting us both.

I lean on one of the empty tables next to Mackenzie, looking her up and down as she lifts her head to take in the bakery. "Damn," I say. "You must have missed me real bad if you couldn't wait a few hours."

Twyla and Isla are still pulling strings, but at least telling us about them. We both got calendar invites to the third "haunt" where we're writing a song from tonight—of all places, my old high school's pool.

Mackenzie rolls her eyes. "I was in the neighborhood. Figured I'd pop in so we can finish 'Sweet Spot' before you drove me up the wall with a fifteenth voice note."

I grin. I needed to send those, sure. But it wasn't strictly necessary to send them while she was on her little date with Grayson.

"Better pick a wall then, Sparkles," I say. "I've got more ideas where those came from."

The truth is that the issue isn't my melodies. The issue is that Mackenzie still hasn't sung any of them. It's impossible to know if I've got the right sound for her if I can't hear it in her voice, so she picks and chooses from them herself.

I'm about to bring it up when she tilts her head toward my neck. "You already smell chlorine-y."

I turn to face her, close enough that I can smell the flowery shampoo in her curls. "Ben heard we were going to the pool later and wanted me to take him, too."

We're interrupted by the telltale squeak of his light-up sneakers from the back office, and then nothing. When I check behind me, I have to stifle a laugh.

A few months ago, we took Ben to one of those wax museums. He spent half the time trying to prank us by pretending to be a wax statue, too, but he couldn't stop laughing. He's got the look down pat now—wide-eyed and so perfectly still that it looks like someone cast a spell on him.

I walk over and put a hand on his shoulder, pulling him against me. "Ben," I say, "this is my friend Mackenzie."

Mackenzie looks as stunned as Ben, looking at him and then back at me. Her eyes mist up just before she blinks, hard, and smiles.

"Well, look at that," she marvels. "We've got ourselves a tiny Sam."

Ben shakes his head, indignant. "No," he says, pointing up at me. "*He's* a big Ben."

Mackenzie and I both laugh and Ben reddens, embarrassed and pleased with himself. He's still clinging to me like a koala. Mackenzie sits on a chair so she's level with him, her eyes conspiratorial. Next thing I know her pinky is hooking under the braided bracelet around my wrist.

"You're the one who made this, right?" she asks Ben.

Ben nods, his eyes like moons.

She leans in closer. "Well, it's my favorite thing I've ever seen him wear," she says. "Pretty cool that you used Candy Shard's colors."

"Thunder Hearts' colors are cooler," Ben blurts.

Mackenzie's eyebrows rise in surprise and delight. "You think so?" she says, the question for Ben but aimed in my direction.

"I know all your songs," Ben says excitedly. His hand shoots up at me, all traces of temporary shyness gone. "Dad, give me your phone."

I pull it out of my pocket. "Only if you leave me one shred of my dignity."

"No thanks," says Ben, pulling up Spotify and thrusting the phone into Mackenzie's eyeline. "Look."

Under the playlist "Ben's Jams" is all of Thunder Hearts' discography, remixes and live versions included.

"He's your biggest fan," I tell her.

Mackenzie's face is Christmas levels of gleeful. "Funny how that's never come up."

"My favorite is 'Heart Crash,'" says Ben. "I get it stuck in my moms' heads all the time."

"I bet your dad *loves* that," says Mackenzie.

Damn. This is as humbling as when Rocket and I first met and he had no idea who I was, even *with* all the news blowing up about me having a secret kid.

"No comment," I say wryly.

"Dad's stuff is cool, too," Ben says. "Just really loud and sad."

"You'll appreciate that when you're a teenager," I tell him.

Ben sticks out his tongue like the thought tastes bad.

Mackenzie leans down and says, "Can I tell you a secret?"

Ben nods. Mackenzie grins and cups her hand close to Ben's ear, saying something in a low tone. Ben looks at her incredulously.

"*Really?*" He turns from her to look directly at me. "My dad?"

"Your dad," Mackenzie confirms.

"His dad what?" I ask.

"Wouldn't you like to know," Mackenzie singsongs.

Ben jolts with excitement, eyes wide on Mackenzie's. "What would you say if I told you we had salt and vinegar chip blondies?"

"I'd say bring it on," says Mackenzie, without missing a beat.

I point toward the pastry display. "I'd stop you, but after what-ever that was, I think you might deserve it."

Rocket pulls off his headphones. "Those blondies are the tops."

Ben wrinkles his nose. "You say that about *everything*," he says.

Rocket puts his hand up like a Boy Scout. "Never met a Ben creation I didn't like," he says, getting up to grab one of the blondies.

Ben hands me back my phone. "Someone's texting you."

I tap it, opening a text from an unknown number:

Hey, Sam. Your mom gave me your number. If you're open to meeting, I'm happy to come to New York. My door is wide open anytime you're in Boston.

There's no name attached to it, but of course there isn't. Famous as Caspar is, he probably hasn't had to say it in years.

"All good?" Mackenzie asks.

I tuck the phone into my front pocket, too stunned to process it. So far, he's only ever been in touch through my mom. I thought we were keeping it that way, but I guess I've put off dealing with him long enough that she must have changed her mind.

I nod and ask, "How's that blondie treating you?"

Mackenzie narrows her eyes at me, but doesn't press. "The cream cheese frosting is a nice touch."

I take a seat at the table with them, pressing a hand to the top of Ben's head to ground myself. Ben tilts his head into it, flashing me an impish grin as he chatters away, soaking up Mackenzie's shock and delight as he lists the other concoctions he wants to make.

Soon enough Lizzie shows up to collect a reluctant Ben for soccer. It's raining now, so the bakery is unusually quiet after they go. When I finish looking the place over, Mackenzie is leaning against the register, watching me with a close-lipped smile.

"Hate to break it to you, but your kid's way cooler than you," she says.

I settle in the space next to her. "Must be, if he won you over that fast. Took me years."

Mackenzie's smile is wry, but her voice is sincere. "He's pretty great."

My throat goes tight. It's funny. I never thought of myself as all that emotional of a guy before Ben. Now all it takes is someone saying one nice thing about him for the pride to swell up all at once, like I've got no filter when it comes to him.

"Yeah," I say. "We're pretty lucky."

Mackenzie doesn't hesitate. "So is he."

Mackenzie politely ignores the way I have to clear my throat. She only has an hour to spare, so we head to the back office, where I keep the guitar I use at open mic nights. I've gotten ahold of myself by the time I pull out my phone to get the recordings, only to open it to Caspar's text. I close out of it fast, but Mackenzie's gaze lingers the same way it did when I first read it.

For once I avoid her eyes, for the same reason I'm always tempted by them—she's been able to see right through me from the start.

"All right," I say. "Neither of us are leaving his room until I hear you sing."

Mackenzie goes still on the plush green couch she settled herself on. "Play a melody that works and I will," she says lightly.

I raise my eyebrows at her. "Challenge accepted."

I play back some of the melodies I already sent her, riffing off the ones we like. Mackenzie manages to firm up the lyrics, but we're still stuck on how we want the bridge to build. This time it's got nothing to do with her not singing. I keep stopping just short of a resolution, not sure where I want it to go.

After too many tries that sound off, I set the guitar down on the couch. "Damn. Must be off my game today."

Mackenzie doesn't waste time denying it. "You've been distracted ever since you got that text."

"Not enough to realize you haven't sung yet," I say right back.

But she doesn't bite, staring at the phone and then back at me. "You want to tell me what it said?" she asks.

Our eyes meet. There's no denying we've got each other in a bind here. There's some reason Mackenzie hasn't sung yet, something more than just her voice sounding different. But whatever it is she's not saying, this stalemate is making me understand why—she still doesn't trust me.

I don't blame her. We spent years trying to one-up each other. The last thing we were going to do was show even a shred of weakness. Trust is something you earn from someone, and we never gave each other a chance.

"I do," I say.

The words surprise me as much as they surprise Mackenzie. But I mean them. I want Mackenzie to know about Caspar. She's the lyric girl, after all—she has an uncanny way of putting complicated feelings into words.

She has an uncanny way of making me see the truth of what I feel, even when I'm trying my best to avoid it.

"I will," I correct myself, picking up my phone. "But you've got to get going."

Mackenzie catches the time on my phone screen. "Right," she says, shaking her head.

"Off to meet Khakis?" I ask.

Can't help myself, the same way I couldn't help myself from sending all those voice notes last night. I'd never do anything to get in the way of her happiness, but I've got no problem making myself miserable about it.

But Mackenzie is too focused on collecting her tote bag to notice. "Trying to catch Serena before she heads for LA," she says. "But I'll see you tonight."

I had Ben all morning, so I haven't given the pool much thought. "You're sure you're okay for that?" I ask now.

"So long as we don't end up all over the internet again," Mackenzie says.

I can't help but smirk at the memory. After that particular antic, it's no mystery why Twyla and Isla pushed for the pool as a "haunt" to revisit. Early in our joint touring days I snuck both our bands into it after we played Madison Square Garden, the same way I did with my old buddies plenty of times when I was a kid.

Turns out we triggered some new silent alarm. No arrests were made, but people sure did have a field day with the paparazzi pics of us trying not to laugh our asses off from the embarrassment of being dripping wet, half-naked, and barefoot on the curb.

But Twyla and Isla got clearance from the school this time. Even if they didn't, I'm not half as worried about becoming the meme of the week again as I am about Mackenzie, now that I know she can't swim.

"I meant with being in the water," I say.

Mackenzie shakes her head. "Oh, I'm not going past the shallow end."

"Sure you are," I say easily. "I taught Ben how to swim. I'll get you freestyling in no time."

Mackenzie lets out a laugh. "Pass."

"Aw, come on. You don't want my six-year-old lapping you at Hannah's lake party."

She pauses with her hand on the door. "Oh, you think you're scoring an invite to that?"

"I think you're scoring me one." I lean back on the couch, looking her up and down. "You're going to need your swim instructor to keep an eye on you, after all."

Mackenzie raises her eyebrows as she slides out the door. "But who's going to keep an eye on *you*?"

Not a damn soul, apparently. I'm already in so deep with Mackenzie Waters that I couldn't swim out if I tried.

PART THREE

"Sweet Spot"

chapter twelve

MACKENZIE

For all the times I've accused Sam of being too cocky for his own good, it's clearly rubbing off on me. Because for some reason I thought that this whole "hang out with Sam half-naked in an empty pool at midnight" thing was going to have no effect on me whatsoever.

Enter Sam, who is yanking his shirt over his head the second the security guard closes the door behind us. His lean, sharp form filled out satisfyingly over the past two years, enough that I can't resist the temptation to make a new map of him as he walks to the edge of the pool deck.

A map that ends at his entirely smug face. "Enjoying the view?" he asks.

Turns out becoming Sam's friend hasn't done anything to stop that impulse to get under his skin. If I can't do it by one-upping him anymore, I'll settle for the next best thing—riling him.

"We didn't make any rules against that," I say.

It works. Sam's brows lift in surprise, and this time when I look,

I *look*. From the ripple of muscle in his thighs to the toned plane of his chest to the satisfyingly stunned grin forming on his face.

"Please. I'm blushing," says Sam.

I roll my eyes. "You're too shameless for that."

He holds his hands up. "You got me," he says. "But you've looked long enough. Don't you think it's only fair if I get a turn?"

A tingle runs up my spine. A harmless tingle. Just because Sam isn't an option doesn't mean that I can't have some fun.

In fact, I'm entitled to it. I spent so long crying over bad boys who didn't love me back that I never got to enjoy the thrill of having their attention in the first place. So that's all that I'm doing, as I settle my fingers on the top front button of my sundress—getting my due.

"Well, then," I say. "If we're keeping things *fair*."

I undo the dress button by button, slowly exposing the bikini underneath—a retro-style red halter top with a matching cheeky bottom. It's more revealing than any suit I've worn before, and it's clear from the way Sam's throat bobs as he looks me up and down that it hasn't escaped his notice. A few long, gratifying moments pass before he collects himself enough to speak.

"Well, damn, Sparkles," he manages.

I walk slowly to the edge of the pool, soaking up every moment his eyes stay glued to me. "It's Hannah's," I say coolly. The instant she found out the photos we took tonight would end up in the album art, she had it messengered to my apartment.

Sam only shakes his head, his eyes caught on the tie strings of the bottom before meeting mine. "It's lethal, is what it is."

My cheeks are burning now, but so are his.

"Someone better warn your buddy Grayson."

If I were a better person, maybe I wouldn't smirk at the jealous edge in the words. Sam doesn't see it anyway, pitching himself backward and falling into the pool with a loud, graceless *splash*.

I take the moment to pull in a breath and collect myself. Damn. Something about being in a high school has turned me into a teenager all over again—all hot-blooded and flustered over nothing more than a few remarks.

Sam pops out of the water and shakes his hair out like a wet dog. "C'mon," he says, gesturing outward. "It's time for your swim lesson."

That's all it takes for the little thrill in me to sink. "I don't need you to teach me how to swim," I say, staying put.

"Oh, this isn't for you. It's for me," says Sam. He drifts closer to the edge of the pool, eyes skimming my bare legs before meeting mine again. "If I keep thinking about how you can't swim, it's going to distract from my artistic process."

I set my tote bag on the pool deck, pulling out my notebook and my phone. "I can't write from the pool anyway."

"Good thing we're not writing yet," he says. Then he tilts his endearingly floppy-haired, wet head at me and says lowly, "We've got the place for two hours. Give me ten minutes."

This seems to be a theme with Sam—negotiating for my time. Maybe it should worry me that the more time we've spent together, the more I'm willing to give.

But I'm not going to overthink it. I've spent the last two years in my head, overanalyzing every mistake I made in my relationships. Overanalyzing the nonexistent one I had with Sam. A man is offering to teach me to swim. It's only logical to take him up on it.

"Ten minutes," I say. I ease myself down on the deck, sliding in as far as my knees. "*No* minutes. Jesus, that's cold."

Sam lets out a laugh as he comes closer to me. "I didn't take you for a wimp."

"I didn't take you for a masochist," I say, shivering.

He raises his eyebrows. "Then you haven't been paying attention," he says wryly. "Speaking of, I'm going to have to break that little 'no touching' rule while I'm teaching you."

As if we haven't been finding little ways to break it right and left these past few weeks. "You better," I say. "If I drown on your watch, Twyla and Isla will be pissed."

Not a moment later his wide hands are settled firmly just above my hips. I let out a startled gasp, sure he's about to yank me into the water, but he's just watching me with a grin.

"It's easier to jump in all at once," he says.

My eyes flit to his face, the planes of it gleaming with pool water against the soft yellow light. I put my hands on top of his shoulders, tilting my chin in permission, and he pulls me into the icy water in one quick swoop.

I let out a yelp of shock, clinging to him as the cold plunges through me. It's instinctive, is all. Find the heat and stay in it. The firm, muscular, ridiculously well-toned heat.

But then it's not just the cold that's got me frozen, but the fear. I didn't think it would hit this hard or this fast. But it's been so long since I even hung out near a pool that being fully immersed has my heart jackhammering in my chest, my limbs stiff as boards.

Sam doesn't let go, arms still firm around me the way they were on the boat the other day. "You're good?" he asks, close to my ear.

Damn it. The only thing sexier than Sam teasing me is Sam *not* teasing me. I didn't think it was possible to be this embarrassingly afraid and turned on at the same time.

I nod, only untangling myself when my feet touch the bottom. The water comes up to just below my chest. I take a breath. When I meet Sam's eyes, they're soft and determined.

"We'll start easy and try treading water," he says. "Basically just holding yourself afloat."

This is, in theory, a simple task. But after a few seconds of me not moving, Sam puts a hand on my elbow.

"I've got you," he says patiently. "Just lift your feet up from the bottom first."

I do, and for a few seconds I stay afloat. But then Sam starts to ease his hand away and I start kicking madly like I've never used my own legs before. I let out a self-conscious laugh and plant myself to the bottom again.

"Well, shit," I say, embarrassed.

Sam doesn't miss a beat.

"Instead of kicking up and down, try fanning your legs out to the sides. Like this," he says, lowering himself down to show me. "Same with your arms. Gentler strokes. It takes a lot less work to stay floating than you think."

His voice is so calm, his eyes so steady on me. He's a good teacher. Or at least he would be, if I weren't so tempted to focus on him rather than the task at hand.

I attempt to mimic him. It's not good, but it's an improvement. But a few seconds later I panic and my feet are right back where they started.

"Better," says Sam. "Go again."

There's no trace of Sam's usual cockiness. Damn. I must look *really* pathetic.

"You make it look so easy," I say.

"My mom put me in lessons pretty early on," he says, his attention still on my feet. "Why didn't your parents?"

He takes me by the elbow again, prompting me to lift my feet.

"They weren't like your mom," I say, experimentally shifting my arms in the water.

Sam smiles to himself. "Nobody's like my mom," he says.

Anna Blaze really is something else. Whenever she could swing it, she was in the front row of our concerts, yelling every Candy Shard and Thunder Hearts lyric alike and jumping up and down in T-shirts she insisted on buying full price from the merch table. She doesn't even drink, but that never stopped her from partying us all under the damn table after every show.

"She loves you." I blink hard, my eyes stinging in the chlorine. "I mean—not that my parents don't. They just weren't all that involved in my life."

All this floating has me distracted. I didn't mean to say that. But Sam nods without breaking focus and says, "You never talked about them much."

I never talked to Sam much, period. But he's not wrong. Hannah would gush about her parents in interviews, and Serena and I were both all too happy to let her take the lead on that. Neither of us had all that much to say.

It's one of the reasons we were close early on, despite all of Serena's type A tendencies. When you grow up the way we did—with parents whose love you couldn't necessarily count on—you recognize it in other people fast. Like you're quiet allies on a battlefield, stuck in a war you never meant to fight.

"I think they liked the idea of having a kid," I say. "They both have really demanding jobs. My mom's in corporate law; my dad's a surgeon. They didn't have much time for me growing up, and when they did, it was like—they didn't really know what to do with me. Most of the time I felt like I bored them."

Oh, my god. There must be something in the chlorine scrambling my brain. I haven't talked so frankly about them in my entire life. After I left New Jersey to try to make it big in the city, I never wanted to look back.

Sam's voice is as quiet as the lapping waves of the pool. "That couldn't have been easy."

My throat feels tight.

"It wasn't that bad," I say, trying to keep my tone light. "Mostly I just tried to impress them. And then when that didn't work, I tried to shock them. And when they didn't work, well—I just said 'fuck it' and started a band."

I'm about to say something else to deflect, but Sam doesn't let me. "Are you still in touch with them?"

"We aren't on bad terms," I say quickly. "We see each other on holidays."

Sam is still watching me, like he's waiting for the rest. There isn't anything else to say, until quietly, unintentionally, I'm saying it.

"But it's funny. No matter what I do I feel like there's this disconnect," I hear myself saying. "Like they don't want to understand what we do, so they're not excited about it."

It's why I try to avoid them if I can. I sit down with them and just like that, I'm that little kid spinning her wheels again—trying to be *interesting* enough. Good enough. Worthy of their attention, of their love.

It took me a long time to accept that I wasn't going to get it. It took me longer to understand that when I went looking for it somewhere else, it was in all the wrong places.

We're both quiet for a long spell, me trying to stay floating, Sam keeping an eye on me.

"Well," says Sam finally. "You're the least boring person I ever met. And fuck anyone who made you think otherwise."

I let out a breathy laugh, my attention split between the conversation and the lapping water. But Sam doesn't laugh, his jaw ticking. He's upset. Enough that it almost startles me.

He softens when he speaks again. "And from where I'm standing, you made a much better family than the one you got."

It hits with unexpected weight. Thunder Hearts is its own family, tighter than any I ever thought I'd have. But now even the one we made is fractured.

I bite the inside of my cheek, casting my eyes down. Our legs ripple under the water, hypnotic and otherworldly in the half-light.

"I haven't seen your mom since we started writing," I say carefully.

"Oh, you will soon enough," he says. "She's our favorite taste tester."

It's a relief to know she's all right. I've been worried about her ever since I saw Sam's face fall earlier today. Worried about Sam, too.

"So that text earlier—it wasn't from her."

I'm worried it's crossing a line to bring it up, but when I look over at him, he seems relieved.

"No. It was from—" He clears his throat. "Well, it was from my dad."

My feet scramble to hit the bottom of the pool, only to realize that Sam has pulled us farther into the deep end. Before I start to panic, Sam has me by the hips again, holding me in place.

"You were doing just fine," he says.

"Your *dad*?" I manage. "I thought you didn't know who he was."

Sam pushes us back to the shallow end. "Well," he says, "turns out he knew who I was. He actually got in touch with my mom after the whole situation with Ben blew up."

He is remarkably calm about it. But he would be, if it's been two years. I blink, trying to keep up without letting my shock get in the way.

"Did he say what he wants?" I ask as he lets me go.

Sam shakes his head. "Just to meet up, but other than that, no."

Sam was right. I can float on my own now. I tentatively drift closer to him, head bobbing with effort.

"Will you?" I ask.

When his eyes meet mine, I know he's remembering it, too—the only other time we broached the subject. That night we stayed up writing "Play You by Heart" and he made some crack about how if getting famous wouldn't make his dad get in touch, nothing would.

When he confessed it might have been the reason he wanted to get famous in the first place.

"I haven't decided," he says. "Would you?"

If it were someone else, I might hedge. But he asks it so deliberately that I know he wants me to tell the truth.

"I think I might be suspicious about the timing," I tell him. "If he wanted something."

There's no doubt this already occurred to Sam. But I can't help but feel protective of him, especially in these past few weeks when he's been quietly protective of me.

"He's, uh—well-off," says Sam. "So I'm not worried about that, at least."

"But you're worried," I say.

He runs a hand through his wet hair. "I think if I met him—I don't know," he says. "I told myself a lot of stories when I was a kid. Reasons why he left, or if he was good or bad. If he'd even like me, when he got to know me."

He meets my eye, and there's an ache in his face I recognize. The ache of wondering why someone who is supposed to love you unconditionally just—doesn't.

Over the years I've written myself in circles, trying to make sense of it. But it's enough for a moment just to share it with Sam. Maybe the truth is there are no words that can make us understand that ache. Maybe all we can do for now is understand each other, and wait until someday when we can understand the rest.

I look away, remembering there isn't a *someday* for the two of us.

There's the few weeks it will take to write this album, record it, and perform the showcase. Then as far as I know, we're done.

"He would," I say sincerely. "It's impossible not to like you."

Sam starts to make a face. I reach out and squeeze his arm, fast and hard.

"I'm not just saying that," I say. "Believe me. I tried."

Sam lets out a surprised laugh. It echoes through the empty pool deck, warm and bright.

"You're right," he says. "If worse comes to worst, I could always win him over with my—'bad-boy charm,' as you call it."

He's the one deflecting now, but I let him. I've already come to terms with the situation with my own parents, but this is raw. I don't want to tap too hard on an open nerve.

"As witnessed by these hallowed halls?" I ask. I turn my head back toward the main campus, nearly dipping below the surface when I lose my rhythm.

Sam's hand is on my elbow again, a silent *I've got you.*

"I'll let you in on a little secret about high school Sam," he says, the mischief back in his voice. "But only if you tell me what it is you told my kid earlier."

My mouth drops in surprise. "He didn't tell you?"

"No," says Sam, indignant. "But he's been listening to Candy Shard all day. I'm worried he's been bodysnatched."

I hum as if I couldn't possibly know what brought that on. "So what you're saying is you want a secret for a secret."

Sam nods, then leans in so close that his warm breath raises goose bumps against my cold skin. "I was a big dweeb in high school," he stage-whispers.

I hold his eyes, stage-whispering right back, "That's not a secret. Ninety-five percent of hot adults were."

Sam makes a point of looking me up and down again, eyes

gleaming when he settles on my face. "Jesus, Sparkles. Then you must have been the biggest dweeb of all."

I tilt my chin at him, trying and failing to bite down a smile. "That's classified."

Sam looks way too delighted. "Were you a horse girl? A gamer girl? A fangirl?"

One of the above, but I'll jump off the diving board before I confess. "Maybe I'll tell you one day."

"You will," says Sam confidently. "But don't think I forgot you owe me a secret in the meantime."

"Oh, former big dweeb," I say, reaching out to pat him on the cheek. "I didn't technically agree to anything."

His brow furrows, indignant. "Yes, you— Oh. Damn," he says, replaying the conversation. "You're gonna pay for that, then."

He dips into the water, poised to splash me, but I plant my feet on his thighs and push myself back. I end up half launching myself on my back, paddling with the grace of a drowning bug, laughing only because I know Sam will put his hand on the small of my back to keep me afloat.

"Look at you," he says. "That was practically backstroke."

I lean into his touch to right myself, my toes skimming the bottom of the pool. "That was flailing," I correct him.

"That was progress," he insists. He puts his hands on my shoulders to brace me from the bobs of the water, his eyes catching on the base of my neck and lingering. "Wait. How have I not noticed that before?"

I touch the hollow between my collarbones, feeling the just barely raised skin prickling in the cold. Serves me right. I've been putting off this conversation so long that the universe decided to start it for me.

"I had surgery." It feels strange to say it out loud. The few people who know I told before it happened, so I haven't had to talk about it since. "There was a growth in my thyroid, so they took it out."

Sam blinks. His hands stay on my shoulders, holding me in place. "Like—a tumor?" he says.

The word has so much gravity when he says it. I look away from him, keeping my voice light and the words fast.

"We thought it was at first. The biopsy came back 'inconclusive.' So they took it out pretty fast, just in case," I explain. "But it turns out I just have a thyroid condition. Hashimoto's. It just sort of—slows you down, is all. Probably wouldn't have noticed it for a while if it weren't for good old Joyce."

His eyes are still on my throat, unreadable. "Joyce?" he repeats.

"I named the growth," I joke. "Weirdly, they didn't let me keep it."

His thumb is on the hollow of my throat, grazing over the thin scar so lightly that I can feel the tingle up my neck.

"And you're . . . okay now?" he asks.

A little too okay in this precise moment, with my body this close to Sam's and the soft lap of the water only nudging us closer.

"Yeah," I say. "It's easy to manage."

I blink hard, because that's a lie. Most of the time the medication makes the symptoms go away, but they can't undo the damage. And now that Sam knows about the surgery, I can't keep hiding what it did.

"That's why my singing voice changed," I say. "The growth—it was pressed against my vocal cords. The surgeon tried to avoid them the best he could, but it's just one of those things."

Sam's grip on me tightens.

"Shit. I thought—I thought you just had nodes, or you were out of practice. How did I not know?"

I've never heard his voice so shaky before. The surprise and guilt of it pulls the breath out of my lungs. I spent so long convincing myself Sam didn't care that it's almost painful, feeling how much he does.

"Well, you also had a surprise growth," I remind him gently. "A three-foot-tall one with an anti-dessert agenda."

And also because—Sam really did disappear. There was no invitation to come meet Ben. No follow-up texts or Christmas cards. If there was a time I was supposed to tell him, it never came.

"Were you scared?" Sam asks quietly.

"Shitless," I say with a laugh. Not because it's funny, but because it's the first time I've admitted it out loud. "But it wasn't cancer, in the end. It was just some weird genetic thing that happens all the time. So it felt like I had no right to be scared."

Sam's thumb goes still just above my collarbone. "Sure you did. I can't even imagine what was going through your head."

At the time, I couldn't, either. It felt surreal. Like it was happening to someone else. Even going online made it feel more like a dream—most of the other people dealing with it were older than I was, usually by decades.

But once the surgery was over and I'd had time to adjust to the new reality, I felt strangely grounded. Something radical had changed my life forever, and I had to change, too.

It didn't happen fast. I went to therapy. I spent a lot of time with myself. For the first time in my life, I stayed still.

"It made me reflect on some things," I say. "Like—the people I was worrying about. I spent a lot of time chasing after people who didn't deserve it. That energy should have just stayed with the people that were already there."

Only then do Sam's eyes fall to the water. I am desperate to know if he's wondering the same thing I am—where the two of us fall between those two categories.

I always assumed Sam would be one of the people who weren't worth it. Sam, who seemed to hate my lyrics before we even met. Sam, who called me Sparkles and avoided me offstage, only to torture me on it. Sam, who was always an arm's length away, but impossibly out of my reach.

Sam, who is freezing his ass off right now to teach me how to float, and asking questions none of those other men would have asked.

His eyes meet mine again. "Now I'm wondering what else you're hiding."

He is so sincere that I feel more naked now than I did shedding my sundress. It isn't a scary feeling, but maybe it should be. I don't know what to do with it—the sensation of feeling seen and feeling safe at the same time.

But I've put my trust in too many things that have fallen through—Sam included. I can't risk it. This will stay fun, and I won't put any more weight on it than that.

"Are you now?" I challenge him, lifting myself on the tips of my toes. "You realize you're talking to the Sweet Spot champion."

Sam's brows lift, surprised by the shift in tone. But then his lips curl to match my smirk, his hands dipping under the water to graze just above my hip bone. "That's the last place you had one."

"For all you know, I've got one on me right now."

Sam unexpectedly grips me by both arms and lifts me out of the water, making me squeak with surprise.

"Do you?" he asks.

I wriggle in his grasp even though I'm enjoying it a little too much—the firmness of his hands on me, the absurd ease it takes for him to lift me. "Wouldn't you like to know?"

He releases me, shielding himself as I splash him. He stays close, though. So close that I can see the shifting light reflect against each fleck of color in his eyes. So close that I can track the drops of water streaming down his face and catching on his nose, his lips.

"Maybe I would," he says quietly.

We're both very still for a moment. We have a script, me and Sam. And we've been off book these past few weeks as we've gotten to know each other, shifting from rivals to friends. But we're shifting again, and this time there's nothing gradual about it.

"I gotta be honest," he says. "The things I'm thinking right now—I think they'd make your boyfriend want to punch my lights out."

Shit. There's a brief flash of guilt—not because I'm doing anything that would upset Grayson, who was never anything more than a guy I went out with twice. But because at some point in the last half hour, I forgot Grayson even existed.

"I broke things off with him," I tell Sam.

"You did?" Sam asks. "Why?"

"We get along just fine, but there was no—" *Lock, click*, I almost say. "No spark," I say instead.

I brace myself, knowing what's next. The few times Sam deigned to acknowledge me on tour, it was to make fun of my exes. This time it'll be khaki jokes, Corporate Ken jokes, the works.

Or worse—maybe Sam won't care at all anymore. He'll be just like all the men who came before him, who didn't care about me half as much as the thrill of the chase.

But Sam's lip curls, so unabashed that I'm blushing.

"So what does a *spark* feel like?" His hands are on my hips again, and only then do I realize he was holding back. His fingers press deeper this time as he pulls me in, like he's relishing every inch of it.

"You tell me," I say, sliding my hands over his forearms.

Sam's teeth graze his lower lip. "I think I'd rather show you," he says, voice low. "We've never done anything to find out."

I lean in close. "Oh, but we did."

I don't mean to say it, but I don't regret it. We've danced around that kiss for too damn long.

Sam knows it, too. "We did," he echoes, without pulling back.

Our last joint performance was a full two years ago, at the Sunray Awards. It was a breezy, beautiful August night for it. Candy Shard had released "Kiss & Desist" earlier in the year, and the running bit the whole night was that Sam would kiss anyone who won an award. He kissed one starlet on the forehead like a '90s sitcom dad, cheekily pecked the front man of another band on the lips, full on made out with every member of a seasoned rock band to such raucous applause that it's a miracle it didn't devolve into a full-scale audience orgy.

It was all typical Sam antics until there was a twist at the end of the show we didn't see coming: "Play You by Heart" won Single of the Summer by fan vote. I was pushed onto the stage, dripping sweat in the sequined hot-pink crop top and skirt I'd performed in earlier. Sam was in a similar state, flushed and exhausted from all the running around for the cameras, but beaming at me with a conspiratorial *What the fuck?*

For the first time ever, I wanted to launch myself at him with a hug. I was so *proud*. But we had our roles to play. Sam held the mic over me to thank our team, using the top of my head as an armrest. I wrestled it away from him, darting across the stage in a game of keepaway as I handed the mic to other performers, making them score his kissing skills like a sporting event.

"Before they kick us off this stage, I'd like to thank all of you for voting for us and proving me wrong. I used to think Sam Blaze was good for nothing." I turned to level him with a smirk, putting a hand on my hip. "But now I know he's good for *one* thing."

Sam slid his hand around my waist, drawing me in as I straightened my back as if to challenge him, even as I let myself be moved.

"Be fair," he said, aiming a cheeky kiss at the audience. "I think I've more than proven tonight that it's *two* things."

"Hearsay," I said back.

"That's right, Sparkles," said Sam, turning to me with an unrepentant hunger. "You haven't had your turn yet."

The next few beats were familiar ones. Sam pulling me in tighter. Me reaching my arms up around his back, pressing my fingers into the planes of his shoulders to the point of bruising. His expression cheated out to the camera, a clear *You think I can't handle this?* And mine a clear *I'd like to see you try.*

By then we were both so spent that we were practically drunk with exhaustion. I couldn't even tell whose heartbeat was whose with our chests pressed against each other, with the roar of the crowd. He lifted a hand and cupped it under my jaw, tilting my head toward his, driving the crowd wild with the slow deliberation of it. I let my eyelids flutter shut and breathed in deep.

Burnt sunshine, I remember thinking. Like I wanted to taste the edges of him, sink my teeth into the center.

His nose grazed mine, his breath warm and sweet. Distantly I tried to remember the last time we'd done this—last week? The week before? I wasn't sure whose turn it was to pull away at the last second. The moment Sam's lips brushed against mine, I realized that neither did he.

The crowd was united in a disbelieving scream. *They're going to kill us for this*, I thought. Twyla, Isla, the label, our bandmates. A kiss would be like a series finale. It would wreck the whole rivalry. We were supposed to do anything, *anything* but this.

But it felt so inevitable that there was no stopping it. Like we'd leaned so far over the edge of something that we had no choice but to fall, and hold on to each other for dear life.

There was an abrupt *slam* of a curtain falling just in front of us.

Our eyes shot open into each other's in shock, and then mutual understanding. We couldn't stop ourselves, so somebody else had. Which meant we had one second, maybe two, before whoever it was caught us.

We took it.

He seized the back of my neck and I hooked my arms around his back, coming together with such force that it was every bit as much a collision as a kiss. The desire didn't swell in me, but pushed up with violence, angry to have been dismissed for so long. I had all kinds of designs—to jump and wrap my legs around him, to tug on the back of his hair, to pull back and hold him there and make him look at me so he'd know, he'd *know*, that after this he was *mine*.

"*Mack!*"

It was over before it could even start. Serena yanked me back by the arm, someone yanked Sam by the back of his jacket, and we were bodily pulled off the stage. Laughing, I remember. Sam was laughing, and then so was I, and then—

And then the next morning, he was gone.

I'm about to look away from him, but then Sam lets out a soft laugh of recognition. Like he saw the film reel of it reflected in my eyes.

"Do you remember what you said to me on the phone?" Sam asks.

He's still holding me, but there's something guarded in his tone. I can't have that. I already spent two years second-guessing that conversation, and I'm sure as hell not going to let myself get hung up on it again.

I tilt my chin at him. "Before or after you said you wouldn't be dating anymore?" I ask right back.

He said it offhand, without prompting. As if he worried it

might be the only reason I was calling. I'd be lying if I said it wasn't one of them, but mostly I just wanted to know he was okay.

It hurt like hell to hear, but it was good of him to say it. I never had to wonder where we stood. Unlike right now, with Sam so close that he's nudging his knee into my thigh under the water.

"After," he says, not denying it. "You said not to worry about the kiss. That it didn't count, because it was only five seconds."

I have no trouble believing him. It sounds exactly like something I'd say to protect myself. I nudge my own knee into him and dip low into the water so I'm at his chest, staring up at him.

"Well, yeah," I say easily. "That's basic kissing math."

Sam lowers himself to meet my eyeline. "Hmm. They didn't cover that in my classes," he says, voice low against the ripples of the water. "You're going to have to explain."

I swallow hard, my eyes flitting to his lips and back to his eyes. "The transitive properties of the five-second rule apply to physical acts. If I kissed you right now, for instance, and it was only five seconds—it wouldn't count."

Sam nods thoughtfully. He's pulling me closer to the shallow end of the pool. I let him, feeling the tension build with every ripple of the water against our skin.

"Oh. So in a sense, we've barely broken the no touching rule this entire time." His tone is innocent, but his eyes are anything but. "Since there's a five-second grace period."

Funny. The pool doesn't feel remotely cold anymore.

"See?" I say, the word half in whisper. "You're a quick study."

"Look at us, swapping lessons." We're in shallow enough water now that Sam can take a knee. He wastes no time putting me on the other one, flashing a wicked grin as my legs straddle him and he lifts his thigh *just* so. "Might help, though, if this one came with a demonstration."

I'm letting out a keen noise of agreement before I even know what it's for. The anticipation is already curling low in my belly, that same hunger rising up in me—not sharp and raw like the last time we kissed, but slow and brimming.

We're pressed together now, bare stomach to stomach. "I take it you're volunteering, then," I say.

He keeps one hand on my hip and uses the other to brush the wet curtain of hair off the side of my face, his eyes blazing and tender and entirely sure.

"I am," he tells me. "So show me how it's done."

His hand slides under my jaw and holds it there, hovering so deliciously in the *almost* that I can't help but savor it. Knowing that this moment isn't a performance for other people's sake, but one that's finally just for us.

Still, I can't shake it. Through the haze of want and *demand* and the honey smoke smell of him, I feel the faint tug of reality. The quick bite of fear that's spent years living like an animal curled under my ribs, afraid of getting too close—of giving anyone the power to hurt me again.

Of giving *him* the power to hurt me again.

"We have to work together," I breathe. "Rules still apply."

I brace myself for him to pull away, but he only nods. I see it in his eyes, then—the steadiness. The certainty. This will be a fleeting thing, maybe, but not a painful one. Like writing this album. Short and sweet and finished.

"Lucky thing I'm good at keeping time," he says, and then gently tips my head, and kisses me.

His lips are unexpectedly gentle, the kiss slow and savoring. There's a *tap* of his finger on my hip, right where I hid the last Sweet Spot. A quiet *one*. His fingers dig satisfyingly in the heavy, wet hair at the nape of my neck. *Two.* His tight muscles ripple under my palms as they slide down his back. *Three.* The hot coil in my stomach is burning all over my body—*four*—so demanding that by the time he's pushed me up against the edge of the pool deck it's consuming me, until—

Five.

Sam gently pulls away. I'm dizzy and dumbstruck, leaning against the wall as the water bobs around us, as his face comes into focus again.

"See?" he says, flushed and breathless. "Even bad boys can follow the rules."

I know I'm in trouble, then. Because I can't even remember the rules anymore. All I can think is how sweet it feels to break them.

chapter thirteen
SAM

If there is a drug more potent than Mackenzie Waters, I hope to god I never find out.

It was bad enough just to wonder about her all those years. How her thick hair would feel tangled in my hands, or how she'd taste with her lips crushed against mine. But the man I was back then was no good for her, with all her big declarations about love, so I told myself a lie—that I was making something of nothing. I only wanted Mackenzie because I couldn't have her.

All it took was one damn piece of her to know that all I'm ever going to want is more.

And if Mackenzie really is a drug, I'm hooked. It's been three days since we stumbled soaked and smug out of that pool with half of a new song and a handful of sloppily taken photos. We've seen each other twice since then, and we've barely got any music to show for it.

Not that I'm complaining. I've had to use more than enough

self-control around Mackenzie in this lifetime. If someone's responsible for getting us back on track, it shouldn't be me.

"I'm not worried," said Mackenzie as she slid her hand under my shirt in the back office of Sugar Harmony yesterday afternoon, my guitar and her notepad forgotten. "This is for our—what'd you call it? 'Artistic process.'" She splayed her palm over my heart, tapping *one, two, three, four. . . .* "We're learning about *keeping time.*"

It's the title we decided on for the next song. She slid her hand away on *five*, with a wicked grin. I caught it with my own hand and set it back on my chest.

"What are you doing?" she said, still grinning.

I raised my eyebrows, then lifted her wrist to my lips. "Keeping it."

Mackenzie was quiet, then let out a soft laugh. "Well, the reports of your charm were not exaggerated, huh?"

She kissed me before I could answer, but the words stayed with me the rest of the day and into this one. The rueful way she said them. Like I was exactly what she thought I'd be, when she never thought much of me in the first place.

Like this wasn't any different from what came before it, when it feels like my whole damn world got turned upside down.

I'm nowhere near used to that world as I take the elevator up to her apartment. Sweaty palms. Racing heart. It's like standing in line for a roller coaster, not knowing if that seat belt will work before the drop.

But the drop has to come. I've been a lot of things in this life, but what I'll never be is a coward. If there's a chance Mackenzie feels the same way I do, this time I'm not going to screw it up and let her go.

Hell of a weight to have on my shoulders as I knock on her

apartment door for the first time, but something stops me before I can. A song I've never heard before. The words are muffled, but the melody is slow and yearning. It takes a moment to realize it isn't a recording, but Mackenzie herself.

It's been a whirlwind since Mackenzie told me the truth about her voice. But somehow, I haven't heard her sing once.

Her voice carries as she moves closer to the door. It's Mackenzie, but with a new depth. Softer vibrato. A slight rasp in place of the usual bite. If her old voice commanded you to pay attention, this one is grounded enough to assume you already are.

The voice sounds oddly familiar—enough that I'm trying to place it. But of course it's familiar. It's still Mackenzie.

The door opens abruptly across the hall.

"Oh, shit," says Mackenzie's neighbor, nearly dropping her briefcase. "You're Sam Blaze."

I tip my head. "For better or worse," I confirm.

Mackenzie's door swings open so fast that the neighbor and I both flinch. Neither of us looks half as stunned as Mackenzie, whose hair is in a bun that adds a good half a foot of height to her small frame.

"How did you get up here?" she asks.

Not the hello I was hoping for, which involved a lot more of our hands on each other.

"The security guard let me in," I explain, crowding her in the door.

She blinks. She must have lost track of time, or she wouldn't be in a tight little sports bra and sweatpants. "Without ID?" she says, even as she leans in closer to meet me.

"He's Sam Blaze," her neighbor calls with a shrug.

Mackenzie is uneasy. "Were you just standing out here like some kind of ghoul?" she asks.

The elevator door shuts behind the neighbor. We finally close the distance, me pressing my palms into the small of her back, drawing her in as she snakes her arms around my neck.

"I heard you singing, if that's what you're asking," I tell her.

I feel the breath stop in her chest. "You did?"

I lift my hands so they're cupping her cheeks. She watches me, her blue eyes wary and sharp.

"Beautiful," I murmur.

Her eyes water. She blinks fast. "Shut up," she says, but leans into my touch.

"I should," I say. "I want to hear more of it."

She shakes her head against my hands, then draws me in for the kiss I've been waiting for since she opened the door. She's on her tiptoes to meet me, so instead of ducking my head I grab her ass and lift her to my level. She laughs into my mouth and hooks her arms around me, deepening the kiss.

I pull her tight against me, easing her back down as I touch the bare, hot skin of her back. She digs her fingers into my hair and tugs me down to meet her without breaking the kiss. My mind is in too many damn places at once—on the seams of that little sports bra I want to pull off her, on the sweet smell of her hair I want to bury myself in.

Letting her go only proves my little theory. A few seconds without Mackenzie's touch and I'm already in withdrawal.

"So what were you singing?" I ask, following her down the light blue entry hall to an open living room. "Something original?"

She's flushed as she turns to look at me. "Just finishing something up," she says, pulling on an old Thunder Hearts T-shirt that was resting on a chair. "A little ditty I call 'Nobody Knocks These Days.'"

I cross my arms, looking her up and down. "Well, don't get dressed on my account."

She tilts her chin up at me as she passes on the way to grab a guitar. "And here I was thinking you liked a challenge," she says.

Too much for my own damn good.

She goes looking for her guitar capo and I take in the space—a lot of light walls and inviting furniture with pops of color. Like a cozier version of all that neon Thunder Hearts glitz.

"So this is where you've been hiding all this time," I remark.

I take a few steps to see how far it goes back. The wide hallway is decorated with a long twisting music staff where she's hung sweaters and hats. One of the doors is ajar to a recording space with deep magenta walls covered in old Thunder Hearts posters. I'm wandering toward it when Mackenzie diverts me with a kiss in the doorway.

"I wasn't hiding," she says, shutting the door and leading me out to the living room.

I weave my fingers through hers and tug lightly, so she falls with her back against my chest. "Said the woman impossible to find," I say into her ear.

She looks up at me, eyes wicked. "Were you keeping tabs on me?" she asks.

No point in lying now. "Course I was."

Her eyes narrow up at me. "Keeping an eye on the competition?"

"Something like that," I say, my voice low in my throat.

Mackenzie's gaze softens on mine and lingers. I skim a hand on her waist. Now is the moment. The words won't be pretty like hers, but they'll be honest—I wasn't the man she needed then, but I am now, if she'll have me.

But before I can speak, Mackenzie looks away, pulling in a sharp breath. "Well—it's no Dad Side in here, but I like it," she says, pointing herself back to the living room.

I clear my throat. After we write, then. That's when I'll tell her.

In the meantime, I follow her down the hall. A week or two ago I never imagined the words "Dad Side" would ever leave her lips. Now she's been there long enough for Ben to rope her into helping brainstorm this week's creation and make her a friendship bracelet in Thunder Hearts colors like mine.

"It feels very you," I say, falling back on her plush couch.

Mackenzie sets her guitar next to me, then settles herself on my other side. "Does that mean you're going to call it Sparkles and make it want to fling you into the sun?"

I shift until her thigh is pressed into mine. "It means I like it. A lot."

She hums to herself and then against my lips. Damn it. The only thing I love more than writing with Mackenzie is touching Mackenzie, and it's impossible to do both at once.

After a whole lot longer than those five seconds we held ourselves to, she pulls away.

"Be honest," I say, hoisting the guitar into my lap. "How many Thunder Hearts ragers have I missed here?"

Her eyes are rueful. "As much as I'd love to give you FOMO, the answer is a resounding none."

"Right. I forgot you famously don't have any friends," I say, lightly thumbing her guitar's strings to tune it.

But Mackenzie's staring out the window, where there's a private deck with a sweeping view of downtown. She blinks and says, "It feels wrong to do much when it's still weird with Serena."

From the looks of things, they've been at odds since the band broke up, but it's gotten worse. Mackenzie took a call from Hannah during our last writing session. Mackenzie didn't want to get into it, but it didn't take much to figure that Serena had blown them off and they're worried about her.

"She can't be mad at you about us still," I say.

"Oh, she can be and she is," says Mackenzie.

My eyes drift to the thin scar at the hollow of her throat. It's still hard to wrap my head around it—that something so massive happened to her and I never knew. But I made damn well sure of that by pushing her away.

Still, I never meant to push her far enough to miss something as big as *this*.

"Did you not team up with her because of your voice?" I ask.

Mackenzie shakes her head.

"Some of it was—I just wasn't ready. She understood, but she kept pushing it anyway." Mackenzie's lips twist to the side. "She didn't get it, though. Even if we made new songs, people would come see us for the old ones. The big, loud crowd pleasers. And I can't really do *loud* anymore."

"Isn't 'loud' most of your discography?" I ask.

Mackenzie's smile is grim. "Yeah," she says. "The whole thing is a bitch."

My throat's gone tight. Maybe there's nothing I could have done when all this happened, but I can't shake it—not just the guilt, but the fear. If anything truly terrible happened to her, I might be the last to know. Letting Mackenzie go was one of the biggest mistakes of my life. It's nothing compared to the idea of losing her entirely.

My voice is rough when I break the silence. "No more crazy shit like this happening without you telling me, got it?"

"That an order?" she asks, her lips quirking.

"Maybe," I say. "But you're breaking so many rules these days, I think you've got authority issues."

"Pot, kettle," says Mackenzie, suddenly twisting her body to straddle me on the couch. I shift to attention, the blue of her eyes like magnets compelling me.

"Never did meet a rule I didn't want to break." I settle my

thumb on her lower lip, my hand holding her chin in place. "But let's not break this one. I don't ever want something like that to happen to you without me knowing. Not ever again."

Her throat bobs, her eyes not leaving mine. "Same to you."

The words feel more powerful than any lyric we'll ever write together. It's more than a rivalry or a partnership or even a romance. It's a promise. And no matter how this thing ends, it's one I intend to keep.

Mackenzie's half whispering when she says, "Are we just going to write the song like this?"

"Looks like it," I say.

Her smirk deepens, like I just issued a challenge. "You're sure it wouldn't be too distracting?"

"Trust me," I tell her. "You've been distracting me for years."

Her teeth graze my thumb.

"Years, huh?" she says. "Careful there. A girl might start thinking you actually cared."

She starts to tilt back, but I don't let go, nudging her chin closer to me.

"Mackenzie," I say hoarsely. "You can't possibly think I didn't."

Her eyes widen, her jaw slackening in my hand. I hold her stunned gaze, and there's no question that it's written all over my face—every damn word I'm about to say.

And she looks terrified.

"No love songs." She clears her throat, pulling her face out of my grasp. "That memo you sent last night—you changed one of the words to 'love.' We should change it back."

I stay as still as I can, even as my heart starts to sink. "I wasn't clear if we made that a rule."

"An understanding," she says carefully. "We're having fun."

There it is—the line drawn in the sand. I step to the edge of it.

"I think we both know this could be a hell of a lot more than *fun*," I say, my voice low.

Mackenzie eases herself off me. "We're friends," she says. "I think that's more than enough, all things considered."

No. God, no. It's laughable to think it ever could be.

"Friends who have fun," I say.

She leans in as if to kiss me, but she settles her palm on my forehead, weaving her fingers in my hair, and firmly pushes my head against the back of the couch. I feel her keeping time with her pinky, but the seconds are uneven, just like our breaths.

Not keeping time anymore, but keeping me in my place.

Before the ache can settle, she dips low on the last count, kissing me hard and fast.

"All right," she says. "No more *fun* until we finish the song."

I swallow hard. I knew what I was risking from the moment I walked into Lightning Strike the other week. If this hurts now, I've got nobody to blame but myself.

But that hurt is too big to let myself feel even a piece of it right now. Not when we've got a job to do and I owe it to her to get it done right.

Once her back is against the couch again I brush her hair off her neck, exposing the faint scar. "I want to hear you sing," I say. "I want to write to it."

She doesn't answer, but she doesn't pull away. I skim the scar with my knuckles as I pull away.

"Please," I add.

There's a quiet stutter in her breath. But when she turns to me, it's with resolve. "Well," she says, "since you asked nicely."

In some ways the writing is more intense than the touching. The adrenaline of building off each other, the hypnotic sound of Mackenzie's new voice in my ears. Once I've got her singing again the song comes together so fast that finishing it feels like getting yanked out of a dream.

We get a rough recording of the full draft. Even then I can tell Mackenzie's not using the full range of her voice yet, like she's afraid to let me hear it.

But this is progress. And I've got to get out of here before I crack deep enough for Mackenzie to see.

"I'm gonna tool with the tempo," I warn her as I set her guitar on its stand. "Like you did in that one song on the first album."

Mackenzie sets her notebook down and settles herself upside down on the couch, stretching out like a cat and letting her legs rest on my shoulder. "Oh, you mean your least favorite album in the world?"

I seize one of her calves and skim my hand down it, reaching her knee and then her thigh. "Only thing I hate about it is whichever assholes you dated inspired it."

Mackenzie laughs. "Yeah, well, you hated all the guys I was with," she says.

"Of course I did," I say. "You deserved better."

She slides her legs off the couch, skimming my neck and collarbone with her shin on the way down before sitting upright.

"What do you think I deserved?" she asks.

When I meet her eye, I see the same damn thing she must have seen in mine. The same damn unspoken, electric thing that keeps bringing us back together again and again.

The thing that tells me I'm not alone in this.

"All of it. Every damn thing you want," I tell her. "You better promise me you won't settle for anything less."

Her eyes well up so fast that understanding hits me like a bolt of lightning. Mackenzie's had plenty of men come and go, hooking her on all the things she thought she needed to hear. The last thing she needs is more words.

She needs time. Time enough to prove that the words aren't just words, but have weight behind them.

And even if time isn't enough, I'm not stupid enough to let her disappear again. Maybe it'll be torture every day of my life, wanting more of her than I can have. But if I've got a shot—if I'm not wrong, and god help me, I *know* I'm not wrong—then I'll give her however long she needs.

For us, that is. When it comes to hiding from the rest of it, I'm not giving her another second.

"I'm sending your vocals over to the label as is," I tell her, flashing the recording on my phone screen. "It's about time you let people hear it."

Mackenzie startles, shaking her head. "I want to hear it back," she says, reaching to grab the phone for me.

I hold it over my head. "I'm your archnemesis, remember? If I love it, everyone else is gonna go nuts."

"Sounds like something a nemesis would say to trick me into embarrassing myself," Mackenzie points out.

"Since when do you care what people think?" I ask.

Mackenzie winces. "I just—it's complicated." Her eyes cut to the closed door of the studio. "I thought I'd be more ready by now."

I put the voice memo in a drafted message to Twyla and Isla, then hand it to Mackenzie. "Just think of it like we did in the old days," I say. "Remind everyone how much better you are than me. Then you'll forget to be afraid."

She lets out a choked laugh. "Life hack. Try to best Sam Blaze."

"Either way, clock's ticking," I say. "You can't avoid it forever."

She blinks hard, bracing herself. Then she taps the "send" button. The Messages app pops back up, and right at the top is another message from Caspar's unlisted number, checking in.

"That so?" she asks.

The question is gentle, but pointed. She's caught me opening this text thread at least a dozen times these past few days. I can't help it. I keep thinking one of these times I'm going to open it and know what to do.

"I might go to Boston," I hear myself say.

She straightens up on the couch. "Yeah?"

"I don't know," I add quickly. "Maybe when we're done with all this."

We're quiet for a moment, Mackenzie intently searching my face.

"Would it feel less like a big deal if we just . . . went?" she asks.

After years of anticipating the wild things Mackenzie would say to get a rise out of me onstage, I'm pretty damn hard to shock. But nothing could prepare me to hear her ask that.

"Right now?"

Mackenzie nods. "Ben's visiting his grandmas this weekend, right?" She tilts her head toward the door. "It's not that bad of a drive. We could just go tomorrow. Day trip."

My throat is so tight it takes me a moment to speak. "You're offering to come with me."

"I mean—we were looking for another haunt, right?" She says it like this is the breeziest thing we've said all day. "Well, we were always on the road. A road trip was inevitable."

I'm no fool. I know she's making that up on the spot the same way she spins lyrics. But I'm too grateful to her to call it out, even to tease.

She rests a hand on my leg. "But only if you want the company," she says.

It's not that I want the company. I need it. I couldn't even admit it to myself, but now that Mackenzie is offering, the relief feels like a damn tidal wave.

I put my hand on top of hers and squeeze.

"Yeah," I say sincerely. "I do."

She weaves her fingers through mine and puts her head on my shoulder. Five seconds pass, and then another, and then another. I don't worry about losing the time half as much as I worry about making it count.

chapter fourteen
MACKENZIE

Weirdly, if you Google "things to pack for an impromptu road trip to your not-boyfriend, not-ex-boyfriend's estranged father in Boston," the results are less than helpful. Which is why I'm only just zipping my duffel by the time there's a knock at my door.

"Just a sec!" I call, but then the door opens. It's Hannah, chic as ever in a pair of black trouser shorts and a pale cream mock neck tank.

I glance down at my light wash jeans and crew neck. "Shoot. Did we have plans?"

"No, I just wanted to drop these off," she says, dangling the new Hannah Says–branded kitchen pans in various shades of pink. "Definitely wouldn't be mad if they happened to make it into an Instagram story."

I lift them up to admire them. "Bold of you to think I can cook."

"Bold of *you* to be hooking up with Sam Blaze."

I nearly drop the pans on my feet. "Did someone see us?"

It would be my own damn fault if someone did. As committed as we've been to keeping our *fun* under wraps, it's easier said than done. My hands drift to Sam instinctively now that I've come dangerously close to forgetting to keep them to myself when we're not alone.

But Hannah's eyes widen, incredulous. "I was bluffing, but damn."

I let out a breath of relief. I've got my artistic integrity to worry about, but that's nothing compared to what Sam's got on the line. A huge part of our working together is to make sure the media focus stays off Ben. If the press thought we were sneaking around, it could start a field day.

"Well, I can only assume from the moony eyes you had opening the door that he's on his way over."

My cheeks burn. "We're taking a road trip for the album. And we're not—it isn't serious."

Hannah turns abruptly, putting both of her tastefully bejeweled hands on my cheeks and holding me there. I brace myself for her to ask why things didn't work out with Grayson, but her eyes are surprisingly stern.

"That man broke your heart, Mack. I don't know the details, but that seventh song made it sound like it messed you up *big* time."

I can't deny it, especially now that Serena's brought it up. Still, we've been so focused on trying to lock Serena down that I was hoping Hannah would let that slide.

"Well—it worked," I say. "Writing the song, I mean. I'm over him."

Over him and on every side of him and just short of under him. If anyone finds my last shred of self-control somewhere out on the streets of New York I hope they let me know.

Or maybe I don't.

"Then why aren't you posting it?" she asks.

A fair question. Posting the last song was meant to give me closure, to end the story of what might have been. Only now I'm looking back and wondering if maybe I had the story wrong this entire time.

This could be a hell of a lot more than fun. The words are playing on repeat like their own song, one I can't get out of my head.

The scary thing is that Sam means them. Or at least he thinks he does. It's what could make him more lethal than any of the guys who came before him, if I let him in. The other guys knew they were playing me, but Sam—he doesn't even know how fast he'll lose interest, once the rush is over.

I've seen firsthand how much he loves the thrill of a chase. He's never even dated anyone long enough to be in a relationship. I'm ridiculous if I think that whatever we've got going on right now is going to magic him into wanting one.

So I'll have my fun. Take a page out of Sam's old playbook, and not let my feelings get tangled in it. Whatever Sam thinks he's feeling will pass before we go and wreck the perfectly good friendship we have now.

Hannah pulls her hands off my face. "Sam aside, you've got half of Tick Tune in a frenzy," she reminds me.

I wince. I had to hide the notifications from the app so Sam wouldn't see them flooding in, all of them asking Seven why the last song is overdue.

"Well, it's finished," I tell her. "I'm posting it. Ending the whole saga."

Hannah crosses her arms. "I'll believe that when I see it."

"Then behold," I say, pulling my phone out of my pocket. In the app there's a draft of a clip teasing the final song, and then the actual recording of it. The one I was working yesterday morning, when I lost track of time and Sam overheard through the door.

I finished it after he left. It's less about what might have been now, and more about what could be. Less about Sam, even, and more about me.

It's not like Seven's other songs. It's still guarded, but hopeful. No matter what my feelings are for Sam or any other man, I have learned from all the hurt that led to Seven. I'll never be so reckless with my heart again.

Hannah raises an eyebrow at me. I meet her eye, then tap "publish" on the teaser.

While it loads, I wait for that quick burst of relief. My heartbreak has been a pressure valve building for years, and every one of these songs has been letting a bit of the air back out, letting me breathe. But when the video posts all I feel is a flutter under my ribs. Like maybe it took something this time I didn't mean to give.

I pull in a breath, tapping the other draft and scheduling it to go up in a few days.

"There," I say. "Done."

But Hannah's looking at her own phone now, her expression pinched. I get the text a moment later—it's from Isla:

> Hey girlies! Thought I'd let you know before the news breaks that Serena has decided to go a different direction with her management. Love you all to pieces. Catching a flight now but around to chat this weekend!

I blink at the message. "Serena . . . fired Isla?" I manage. "Why on earth would she do that?"

Hannah knows as much as I do, which is nothing at all. Serena was so cagey at Hannah's apartment yesterday that we barely got two words out of her. At one point she fully pulled out her laptop and started typing in Hannah's office.

The screen was tilted when I walked in with her wine, enough for me to see that she was working out of a Google doc. Rocket's name was on it, along with other acts who had opened for her. She slammed the laptop shut before I could see more, and told me to worry about my own act when I asked.

"She still hasn't rescheduled those tour dates, either," says Hannah worriedly.

Hannah tried to bring that up yesterday, too. Serena curtly told her that she was looking at dates in the fall, and not to worry about it. But her eyebrow was twitching in that way it only does when she hasn't slept, and her usually immaculate nails were bitten to shreds. Whenever either of us tried to press, she changed the subject fast enough to give us whiplash.

I pinch the bridge of my nose. "We're her best friends. If she's not telling *us* what's going on, who is she telling?"

The answer, I know, is a resounding *nobody*. Serena was the boss when she had us as bandmates, but without us she's gone full lone wolf.

Hannah slides her phone back into her pocket. "I think you've got to get her alone, Mack."

I shake my head. "She's so angry with me right now," I say. "She'll stonewall me if you're not there."

"Maybe," says Hannah thoughtfully. "But I think—the few times Serena ever let herself crack, it was with you."

The guilt hasn't gone anywhere, but it sinks deeper. It took a long, long time for Serena to confide in us about anything—and even then, it was rare. But I was the only one she'd talk to about her parents not coming to our shows, or her younger siblings hitting her up for money. I was the only one she'd let watch her practice moves she hadn't nailed yet, trying to get them just right before rehearsal.

And I was the one who took that trust and threw it in her face.

"I hurt her," I say. "A lot."

Hannah surprises me by letting out a terse breath. "You said something shitty. You're human and you apologized. Whatever grudge she's holding now about the duo, she's using it to hide."

My eyes sting. "Even if she is, I think she really is just—done with me."

Now that I've let the hurt rise to the surface, it's startling how deep it goes. I'm worried about Serena. But I also *miss* her. She's hurting herself by pushing me away, but she's hurting me, too. There's so much I've wanted to tell her—about Seven, about my voice, about all the little, boring things we used to tell each other because we could. Now I can't even get her to tell me what's *wrong*.

Hannah puts a hand on my arm. "You two have always been close. That doesn't just go away."

Hannah's eyes drift to the wall and linger. It's the first-ever Thunder Hearts poster—neon-clad and laughing in a confetti blizzard, Serena dead center with her arms hooked around us, pulling us in. Her head's turned to one side, though. Looking at me.

"You're the one who's going to get through to her," says Hannah.

I blink back tears before they can fall. Hannah's right. I just don't know how. It took time to earn Serena's trust, and now she won't even give me that.

And the more of her time I try to ask for, the more it hurts when she shuts me out.

"Yeah. Well," I say, my throat tight. "I'll try her again when I get back from Boston."

As if summoned, Sam knocks on the door. Hannah gives me a

quick squeeze before letting me go. I'm fully collected by the time Hannah opens the door.

"Hey," says Sam, surprised to see Hannah, but not missing a beat. He scoops her into a quick hug and raises his eyebrows at me over her shoulder, eyes glinting with mischief. "Hot off the press—Seven is finally posting that last song."

I go still in the hallway. Sam has made plenty of offhand comments about Seven the past few weeks, but I didn't think he was following her *that* closely.

"Oh, is she?" says Hannah innocently as Sam lets her go. "I take it you're a fan."

"Yeah, but our girl here hates her," he says, winking at me.

Our girl. My face flushes, the kind of heat that starts in my cheeks and works its way down. It's not nearly as bad as when he said *Mackenzie* yesterday, but it's pretty damn close.

"I don't—not—"

Damn. If there's a way to defend yourself for not liking your other self, I sure as hell don't know how.

Hannah, on the other hand, is entirely too pleased by this turn of events. "Really, Mackenzie?" she asks. "I thought you had better taste than that."

I resist the urge to glare at her. "Who says I hate Seven?" I ask Sam.

"Anytime Rocket turns Seven on at the bakery, you make this face."

Sam flares his nostrils and frowns so comically that Hannah lets out a sharp laugh. The worst part is, I feel myself making the same face right now.

Part of it is just the weird out-of-body guilt of hearing these songs I wrote in front of the man I'm writing the next one about.

But then there is Rocket. Sweet, ridiculous, talented Rocket, who has been sliding into Seven's DMs to chat for weeks. I've never answered a DM as Seven and never plan to, so if he's trying to collab like he has with other Tick Tune artists, he doesn't know he's wasting his time.

Sam closes the gap between us. Kissing him is so instinctive that I tilt my head in anticipation, only to get pulled into his arms. Right—Hannah's here.

But his arms wrap tighter than usual and hold me there an extra beat. Some tender part of my chest cinches. He's nervous.

Everything comes into sharp focus then. For now, at least, I know exactly where I'm needed.

"We'll take my car," I say. "I'm driving."

"Damn. You're gonna regret trusting me with an aux cord for five hours on the road."

Hannah kisses my cheek on her way out the door. "The way Mackenzie drives that clunker, she could be Seven."

chapter fifteen
MACKENZIE

Turns out after navigating all these old and new feelings for Sam, navigating traffic out of New York City is a breeze. Before I know it, we're at a rest stop halfway between New York and Boston, pumping gas into my old Jeep. I should probably have gotten rid of it long after I bought it as a teenager, but it's easy to go incognito when today's car looks like tomorrow's scrap metal.

"I almost forgot." Sam sliding into the passenger seat in a pair of worn-out jeans that hug all the right places is a sight on its own. Then he has the audacity to hand me a loaded pastry bag. "Ben's Creation this week."

I split the croissant open. Inside is a glob of chocolate, pretzels, and peanut butter that would put Willy Wonka to shame. I press a hand to my chest and turn to Sam.

"Did your dessert-hating son make me a Take 5 croissant?"

It's the first time I've gotten a full Sam grin for the whole drive.

"Sure did," he says. "Trying not to take that personally when the kid turned his nose up at my birthday cake last month."

I take a bite that's nothing short of heavenly. Lizzie and Kara don't know how to miss.

"Mmm," I say, licking my lips. "Tastes like betrayal."

Sam checks the windows, then leans in to kiss the chocolate off the corner of my mouth. "Huh," he says. "Dunno. Gonna have to check again to make sure."

I'm expecting him to go for the croissant, but instead he kisses me, slow and deep, his tongue skimming the chocolate off mine. I let out a laugh of protest and he doubles down, his teeth grazing my lower lip.

"Hungry?" I ask as he pulls away.

His grin settles into a smirk. "Starved."

But by the time we're merging back into the freeway, Sam's jaw is set again. He checks his phone the way he has the entire drive, opening his messages app over and over like he's waiting for the whole thing to fall through. I'm weighing whether to bring it up when something makes him let out a low whistle.

"Shit," he says. "Did you see the news about Tick Tune?"

My stomach lurches, but I keep my voice steady. "What news?"

Sam goes quiet as he scrolls. My eyes stay on the road, but my fingers stiffen on the wheel.

"Looks like they're selling to some sketchy new streaming company. If artists don't claim their songs or fully delete their accounts, they'll have all the rights to anything they've ever posted. Even songs they already pulled."

It's shady as hell, and we both know it. But Sam doesn't even sound surprised. Just resigned. We've been in the industry long enough to see people jump rope with morality when it comes to artists and their rights.

But I assumed Tick Tune was separate from that. Nobody was making any money. Rights were never supposed to be involved. It was the people *outside* of Tick Tune I thought to worry about, like the label that screwed over Rocket.

"Most of the artists are anonymous, though," I say weakly.

Sam nods, still reading. "That's why people are pissed. Guess if you want to claim your work you have to identify yourself. Otherwise, they just own the rights to your stuff forever."

My heart sinks. Not for myself, but the other artists on Tick Tune. People have plenty of different reasons to use an app where their music is fleeting. To get things off their chest, like I have. To practice somewhere they won't feel judged. To try to get a modest following, so they can leverage it into a deal if they decide to come forward.

If they delete their work, they lose all their stats—all the comments and streams and followers. And even if they find some way to keep a record of them, some of the artists on the rise will lose their momentum. They can't all possibly jump ship to a label at once.

But if they don't delete it, someone else gets to steal it. And no matter how uniquely weird my position is here, it's no mystery what most artists would choose.

"So people are just taking their stuff down," I say quietly.

"They're trying," says Sam, blowing out a disbelieving breath. "According to Serena, the app has conveniently started glitching."

I blink. "According to my Serena?"

Sam closes out of the browser and sets his phone on the console. "She's the one posting about it. She's pissed."

This tracks a little too well. Serena may be allergic to letting anyone help her, but even when Thunder Hearts only had an inch of clout, Serena was using it to look out for other artists. Rocket is only the latest example—there's no saying how deep a lawyer must have gone into that contract that screwed him over to find a way to let him be one of her opening acts.

But that doesn't prepare me for what Sam says next.

"She's calling out Tick Tune and Seven."

For a moment all I can hear is the traffic and the beat of my own heart between my ears. When I speak, my voice is remarkably calm. "What's Seven got to do with it?"

Sam just shrugs as he leans back. "Seven announced the last song today, right when the sale was announced. And the song is set to drop the day the change takes effect," he says, with a faint disappointment.

Jesus. I couldn't have timed that out worse if I tried.

"And you think she's going to go public right then, and capitalize off it," I realize.

"Makes sense. I mean, what else would she do?"

My actual options are clear, because there are only two. I can immediately delete the account. Let the seventh song stay buried, and stay out of this before it starts.

Or I could release the seventh song now. Let it play for a few days, get the closure everyone is expecting before the change takes effect, and delete it then.

But it doesn't feel right. Pulling a stunt like that would only pull attention from the artists this will actually affect. Whatever is happening here is a whole lot bigger than me.

"I couldn't say."

There's no reason to worry Seven will get traced back to me, but my heart is still jackhammering. I want to pull the car over and yank out my phone. I want to read every word of what Serena's written to *Seven* when she can barely look me in the eye.

"Well, we better brace ourselves. Seven's about to be our biggest competition."

I bite the inside of my cheek, trying not to smile. "What makes you say that?"

"She's the only alternative writer on your level right now. Hell, her lyrics sound like she took a Mackenzie Waters master class," he says.

A manic, bubbling laugh escapes me. Jesus. Good thing I never want to spin this singing thing into an acting career.

"That last one especially. I don't know if you heard it, but it was brutal."

That's the one I wrote for the last man I dated when we were on tour. I don't think of him much now; writing the song really did cure me of it. But of all of them, he lasted the longest. Nearly a year. I thought he was it for me.

Not because we had anything special. Just because he didn't leave. He was ambivalent most of the time. Bored of me, even. After the tumult of all the other guys I was with, it felt like a relief.

But it wasn't love. It was the first time I broke something off. It hurt worse than the others in some way, because I had nobody to blame for the wasted time but myself.

"I heard it," I acknowledge.

Sam's head turns to look out the window, so his voice sounds far away. "That lyric where she cuts off after 'almost.' The pause after it. It's uncanny how you know exactly what she means."

"The lock without the click," I say, without thinking.

Sam turns to me in surprise. "Yeah."

His eyes stay on me. I swallow hard. "Well. At least we'll have a head start on her," I say lightly.

"But she's got the market cornered on heartbreak."

"Says the original heartbreaker," I tease.

Sam is quiet for a long moment, his gaze shifting from me to the front window. I don't think anything of it. We've had a lot of long pauses on this drive. I can't even imagine the kinds of things going through his head right now—I've just tried to give him the space to talk if he wants.

Enough miles pass that when he straightens up and looks over at me, I think he will.

"I got around, but I didn't—break hearts," he says quietly. "I was always clear I could only do casual. Everyone I was with wanted that, too."

"Okay," I say, too stunned to say anything else.

There's nothing defensive in his tone. If anything, he sounds unsettled.

"I just—need you to know that," he says. "If I thought someone might get hurt, I didn't get involved."

I bite the inside of my cheek again.

"Is that why you steered clear of me?" I'm teasing, but I'm not. "You were worried I was gonna fall for you?"

Because if that was his little plan, it didn't work. He stayed away from me, and he hurt me anyway.

My throat tightens. *No, he didn't*, says the little voice in my head. The one that's been interrupting me for weeks. The one that made it so hard to write Seven's last song.

Sam was no saint, but he never meant to hurt me the way I got hurt. That part I did all on my own.

"Nah," says Sam. "I was just afraid you'd kick my ass. You hated everything about me."

"Not everything," I protest.

Sam lets out an unexpected laugh. "Well, shit. That's a relief."

I don't mean to say anything else, but we're so separate from the rest of the world that it's almost too easy to be honest.

"It was just—all that partying and the women and rolling up to rehearsals hungover. You did whatever you wanted and everyone thought you were so *cool* doing it," I say. "It drove me up the wall. It was like you didn't even try."

And I'd spent my whole life trying. Trying to get my parents' attention. Trying to get boyfriends to stay. Trying to prove Thunder Hearts deserved the hype we got right off the bat, when it made us easy targets for people like Sam to brush off in the first place.

Trying to earn my place, when Sam took the one he had for granted.

"I'll let you in on a secret," says Sam. "I was trying *really* hard to look like I wasn't."

I glance over at him. Our eyes only meet for a split second, but I see it anyway—that flash of recognition. Maybe I didn't hate Sam because he wasn't trying. Maybe I hated Sam because I could tell he was, and he was a hell of a lot better at it than me.

"But staying away—it didn't mean I didn't care," says Sam, his eyes still on me. "I did. I do."

Now I'm the one who's quiet. Turning the words in my head over and over, holding them up to inspection. Looking for the holes in them, for the tiny tears. For the evidence that he doesn't really mean it and he's just saying the same things the other six did before they turned into Seven.

"I did, too," I say softly.

Sam goes very still.

"I *do*," I add.

But I can't say anything more than that. No matter how I feel about Sam, I can't give that much of myself away yet. With every song I've posted as Seven, I've started trusting myself more and more, but I'll never get to post that last one about Sam now.

I need to close the old book with him before I open a new one. I don't know how long that will take, but this much I do know—Sam could very well lose interest in this whole thing before I get there. And that might hurt more than anything that's come before.

It's uncanny, the way Sam seems to read my mind.

"Good," he says, stretching back like a cat. "Because you're never getting rid of me now."

"Oh yeah?" I ask wryly.

"Afraid so," he says. "You can't go writing songs like that with me and ever expect me to settle for anything less."

I smile. I don't have anything to say to that. I'm proud of what we've written so far—my words feel sharper and brighter with his melodies pulling them along.

"So," he says slyly. "Are we gonna write another one or what?"

I planned on us making up for the time later. But if he needs the distraction right now, well—so do I. Anything to block out the whir of the Tick Tune news and Serena's posts and the songs I'm going to have to pull, and the one that will never see the light of day.

"Right now?" I ask, just to make sure.

Sam grabs his phone. "No time like the present."

I check the clock on the dashboard. "We might run out of road before we finish," I warn.

"Ah, Mackenzie, I'm not worried," says Sam, with a slow grin. "You're always taking me for a ride."

chapter sixteen
SAM

My mom doesn't know I'm here. It's a hell of a thought to have at my age, but I can't shake it from the moment we park the car. It feels like when I was a kid and my mom would let me race to the next crosswalk the way we do now with Ben. She's so short that sometimes it was hard to spot her when I turned around and I'd think, *I went too far.*

Only this time when I turn, Mackenzie's there, matching pace on the sidewalk next to me. Eyes steady and waiting. Her lips cut into a conspiratorial kind of smirk that calms my nerves.

Or at least it does until we turn the corner on a sunny, crowded Boston street and nearly barrel into the last person I'm expecting to see.

"Rocket?" Mackenzie exclaims.

Rocket blinks at the two of us in our sunglasses and baseball caps. "Holy shit! What are you two doing here?"

"Working on the album," Mackenzie says without missing a

beat. I stand dumbfounded as she pulls Rocket in for a hug. "What are *you* doing here?"

Rocket's eyes track down the street and then back to us. I pat him on the back and he flinches. He's jumpy. Or maybe it's me.

"Visiting my folks," says Rocket. "Plus, an open mic down the street tonight. You should totally come."

"We'll be out of here by then, but knock 'em dead," says Mackenzie.

Rocket nods, then disappears down the street so fast that we might have hallucinated him. Mackenzie looks just as bewildered as I am, blinking at the spot where Rocket just disappeared.

"Well," I say, "it's official. This might be the weirdest day of my life."

"No kidding," says Mackenzie.

She puts the address to the bar in her phone and leads the way. My eyes graze past the little storefronts as I follow Mackenzie through the brick buildings of Newbury Street like a beacon in a storm. I want to tell her how grateful I am, but the words are stuck in my throat.

Mackenzie knocks her shoulder into mine. "You good?"

Only then do I realize we've come to a gradual stop.

"I'm something," I murmur.

I'm half expecting her to offer to call it off. To pack up the car and head out like this whole trip was a blip. But she doesn't have to offer—we both already know she'd do it, no questions asked.

"I'll be down the block," she says instead, then pulls me into a firm, grounding hug. She lingers, saying the next words right into my ear. "Just remember. He's *lucky* to get to know you. You're a good man."

I let myself into the bar in a daze. It's old but dignified, the kind of place that has been here a lot longer than I have. According to

Caspar, who retired in Boston a few years back, this is the one place in the city he can trust to be "discreet."

"I'm here for a reservation under 'C.'"

The hostess's expression stays entirely serene. "Of course," she says. "Right this way."

I'm led past the dark, wooden interiors of the bar to a small back room. There are a few high-top tables and only a bit of sun illuminating the dark wood from high windows, and the place smells like old tobacco smoke and leather.

"I'll lead him back when he arrives," says the hostess.

I settle on a stool. A minute passes, and then another. I keep my eye on the door, trying to calm the embarrassing pounding in my heart. I've had too much experience with making first impressions to get worked up about one now.

But this isn't just my dad's first impression of me. It's his first impression of three decades of me. Everything I've made out of my life, without him in it.

The hostess comes back after a few minutes and tells me he's been held up. I pull my phone out. No messages. Why tell the hostess and not just text?

Mackenzie's kept me calm all day, but now the nerves I've been ignoring are crawling under my skin. A half hour passes. Then an hour. The hostess asks for the fourth time if I want anything to drink while I wait. God only knows how much time passes before the door opens and I turn, exasperated, only to see the man himself.

Caspar Quentin is every bit as much "larger than life" in person as he is on a stage. There's the pirate-like swagger as he walks into the room. The distinctively scruffy hair, now gone a pepper gray. The metallic studs in his ears and cuffs around his wrist, the ripped denim jacket, the steel-toed boots.

The broad, rubber band smile against his piercing eyes that I realize, in that instant, are the exact shade of hazel as mine.

"Sorry about the wait, kiddo. Had a group of fans recognize me out front and it was pandemonium." He jerks his thumb back at the hostess. "Glad Bella here could run interference."

Bella nods, happy and flushed. "The usual?" she asks.

"Yeah. One for me and one for the rug rat," he says to me, with a quick, mischievous wink.

I bite down my unease, knowing how many times I've made that same wink myself.

Caspar walks over to me, grabbing the back of the stool next to me with one hand and easing onto it like it's a rodeo horse. He lets out a satisfied sigh, then puts a hand on my shoulder, giving me a long look as if to drink me in.

It feels oddly like a performance. Like he rehearsed this in his head the same way he must rehearse spoken bits between songs onstage.

"Sam," he declares.

I raise my brows, swallowing down the sudden urge to laugh at him. "Caspar," I say back.

Bella is already back with two beers. He waves without even looking in her direction, then says to me, "But why am I apologizing? You know all about the pitfalls of fame, so I hear. Apple didn't fall far from the tree!"

I take a sip of my beer, trying to stave off the flat disappointment. It's only been a minute. But I have an uneasy feeling that it will only go downhill from here.

"Guess not," I manage.

He ribs me so hard that I slosh beer on the table. "Didn't you ever wonder where you got it from?"

He takes a long swig of his drink, watching me out of the corner of his eye.

"My mom sings," I remind him coolly.

He smiles with fewer teeth when he sets the glass back down. "So she does," he says, and then straightens up. "How is that gem of a gal?"

"She's great," I say. *No thanks to you*, some petty part of me wants to add.

But that isn't entirely true. After my mom told me about Caspar, she explained that he sent checks when I was growing up. She used a portion of the money to send me to a nice school in Manhattan and to pay for my music classes, but other than that she put every cent of it away for me, determined to raise me on her own terms.

I made plenty of money with music right out of high school, so she didn't mention it until I knew about Caspar. I tried to make her take the money when I found out. She compromised, and put it in Ben's name. As far as I know, Caspar's never asked.

"Good to hear it, good to hear it," says Caspar.

We both go quiet, sipping our beers and not looking at each other. I have my second childish thought of the day: *I just want to go home.*

Caspar claps his hands together, the sound echoing like a gunshot through the empty room. "So—what do you want to know about me?"

A few minutes ago, everything. But already most of my thoughts are on the door.

"Because I was thinking—we wrap up this quick drink here, go hang with some of my buddies at a spot downtown. You'll love 'em."

He starts listing off names of a few other rock stars—all men around his age, most I've already met myself—watching for my reaction. My disappointment gives way to a faint revulsion.

I'll be the first to admit I've got a cocky streak. But I hope to god I've never sounded like this much of an ass, and that I never will.

"What I want to know is . . ."

I force myself to look at him. At my same eyes. At my same unaffected posture. The resemblance is so uncanny that I wonder how I never noticed, with all the times I've seen him on-screen.

"Why now?" I ask. "I mean, what made you finally get in touch?"

Caspar turns his gaze from me to his beer, but not fast enough for me to miss it—the quick shift in his eyes. A window to something sharp and deep that shuts as fast as it opens.

"Well," he says gruffly, and then shrugs. When he finally does turn to me, it's with a self-assured smile that doesn't reach the edges of his lips.

"I'm not—sick or bankrupt or some shit like that," he says. "I've just reached a point where I'm wondering what the point of it all is, you know? This fame stuff. It is what it is. But I want something else. Something more."

He's looking at me expectantly, like he's waiting for me to put him at ease. But I've got nothing. I wasn't supposed to be the one who did that here. He's the—parent, for lack of a better word.

"You know what I mean," he says, shrugging again. "It's a weird, lonely road we chose. You lose a lot of so-called friends along the way."

He raises his mostly empty glass to "cheers" me. I don't touch my own.

"I've kept all the people I love close," I say.

There's a cutting edge in Caspar's eye then. "Not always, I hear."

The tension finally snaps, fast and brutal. Still, I keep my voice even.

"What's that supposed to mean?" I ask.

Caspar leans back as if to assess me.

"That we're not so different, you and me," he says. "With a son you didn't mean to have. That you couldn't be around for."

It's uncalled for, but it still does exactly what he meant for it to do. It hits me in the weakest spot. I came here thinking Caspar wanted to meet me at his level, but he's been trying to knock me down a peg since before he walked into the bar.

I have no idea why, but it doesn't matter. It doesn't change the truth. I thought we might be able to relate to each other. Now the idea that I might be like him makes me feel sick.

"I couldn't because I didn't know. You could," I say, my jaw tight. "You chose not to stick around."

Caspar levels me with a look of smug disbelief. "You're telling me you really had no idea that kid was yours?"

The fury that rises up in me is so white-hot that it scares me—not just because of how fast it hits, but how fast it gives way to something worse. Something like anguish.

I meant what I said to Mackenzie in the car. I may have been reckless in my heyday, but I did my damn best to make sure nobody got hurt.

But didn't someone, in the end?

Ben spent the first four years of his life without a dad—and then when he got one, he got *me*. A lifelong liability. No matter how much I love him, no matter how much I'm able to provide, he'll always have a dad whose reputation follows him wherever he goes.

You're a good man. Mackenzie's words still have just enough weight to ground me. I won't give Caspar the fight he's looking for. I've got enough of a fight in myself.

"Believe what you want," I say. "But I love Ben. I wouldn't trade a damn second with him for the world. So no. We're not the same."

Caspar opens his mouth to protest, but I stand from my stool.

"Thank you for meeting with me. It was—thank you," I say, as sincerely as I can.

Only then does Caspar's facade start to crumble. His hand shakes against his glass, his eyes watering. He doesn't look like a legend anymore, but a cautionary tale.

To his credit, he follows me to the curb. We clap each other on the shoulder. We say empty things about staying in touch. I stumble across the street, not sure where else to put myself except far from him.

And then Mackenzie is pulling me into a quiet alley and I'm sinking into her arms. She doesn't say a word. There is nothing but the even in and out of her breath against my chest, nothing but her cool hands braced comfortingly on my back. Nothing but the words still echoing between my ears—*I've kept all the people I love close*—and the sudden understanding that Mackenzie is one of them. Someone I love and lost once, and could still so easily lose.

chapter seventeen
MACKENZIE

We are definitely not going to make it back to New York tonight. Even after a few miles of Sam's aimless wandering through Boston, he is so vacant that I've barely gotten a few words out of him. Not even words like, *Hey, by the way—my secret dad is Caspar Quentin, one of the most famous rock stars in history.*

Or at least I assume it was, given the guilty look Caspar cast Sam before he slid into a black car and drove out of sight.

Not that it matters who he is. Whoever put Sam in a state like this deserves to rot.

We alternately walk and sit on benches by the river. Nobody's expecting us to be here, so with my hair tucked into my cap and our sunglasses, we're left alone. At some point we pass some shop owners closing up for the night and Sam startles at the sound of their keys.

"Shit," he says. "It's so late."

"I booked us an Airbnb earlier," I tell him.

He shakes his head. "If you're tired, I can drive—"

"There's a big storm coming," I say. "I don't think my clunker is built for it."

Sam runs a hand through his hair. "Sorry. Fuck."

I take his wrist and squeeze it lightly. "New rule. No apologizing," I say. "At least not until we get some food."

We do the most Boston thing possible then, and stop in a Dunkin' for decaf coffee and donuts and settle on a park bench in Boston Common as the sun starts to set. Sam explains between bites what his mom only recently explained to him: that once upon a time she was working as a barista to put herself through school, in a spot right next to Caspar's bachelor pad. He'd ask her out every morning and every morning she'd laugh and say no. Then one night they ran into each other at a club. He was leaving the next morning for a tour, so they danced. They went back to his place together. By the time his mom realized she was pregnant, she was four months along and Caspar was skyrocketing to fame.

Caspar didn't want to be involved. Anna wasn't surprised. She said that if he ever wanted to get in touch with her about Sam, he could. But Caspar never did. At least, until now.

"So what happened this afternoon?" I ask carefully. "You were in there a long time."

Sam leans forward on the bench, recapping a conversation that quite frankly makes me want to break Caspar's nose.

"He's—every cliché you can imagine," he says at the end. "It was like talking to a cardboard cutout of a man."

The last thing I want to do is defend Caspar. But I can tell that despite everything, Sam doesn't want to believe it. He wants to hold on to the idea of what his dad was supposed to be. It's a feeling I can understand, even if I've never felt it like this.

"Maybe he was just nervous," I say.

Sam lets out a bitter laugh. "I was nervous to meet *him*."

We're quiet again, and it's getting dark. I'm about to pull up the address of the Airbnb when Sam says suddenly, "Let's go to Rocket's open mic."

On the list of possible words that might come out of Sam's mouth right now, I can't say that was near the top. "You're sure?"

"Yeah," says Sam. "If we're stuck here, we might as well get some of Boston in while we're at it."

I cast my eye at a touristy vendor stall on the corner. "In that case," I say.

A few minutes later, we've swapped our incognito disguises for ones that are just as effective, if not far more ridiculous. I pick out a pair of Red Sox sunglasses and a hat that says WICKED PISSAH for Sam, and he picks a Sam Adams trucker hat with an oversized T-shirt of a most certainly unlicensed Baby Yoda drinking out of a Dunkin' cup for me.

"Well, shit," says Sam, reaching up to tuck a loose curl back into my hat. "They're not going to let us back over the river."

"Damn. I'll never get to try Ben's pizza muffins now."

We shoot Rocket a text. Just as he drops us the address to the open mic, a few raindrops start to fall, before abruptly turning into a sheet of water so thick we can hardly see past our noses. Sam grabs my hand and *tugs*, and the two of us take off, cackling and yelping as the rain pelts us for the entire five blocks to the cafe.

We're breathless when we tumble through the door, a mess of wet limbs and dripping clothes.

"You made it!"

Rocket hops off the stair step that makes up the "stage" in the cozy little cafe. He hugs us so hard and so gratefully that I know not to turn and look to see if his parents are here. In fact, by the time he presents us coffee and cookies and sits us down at a table right by the stage, bashfully and excitedly introducing us to his friends, I'm starting to feel like *we're* his parents.

Rocket sticks a clipboard under our noses with enough gusto to make us flinch. "Can I sign you guys up for a slot?" he asks. "Doesn't have to be anything fancy. Everyone here's pretty chill."

Sam looks at me with his eyebrows raised gamely.

"Sam does some impressive Taylor Swift covers if you get enough of this into him," I say, poking at the coffee.

Sam isn't letting me off that easy. "Let's do 'Run Out of Road,'" he says.

I blink. "The song we wrote two seconds ago?"

Sam puts his hand on the back of my shoulders, rattling me like a boxing coach. "C'mon, Mackenzie. We got this."

Damn. He needs to stop saying my name. If he had any idea what kind of hold it has on me, he'd be too damn smug for his own good.

Still, I hold firm. "It's not ready yet."

I'm not ready yet.

It's not even that I'm nervous about my new voice. I'm worried that I'll open my mouth, sing one note, and someone will recognize it as Seven.

I've been careful. Sam thinks I'm holding back, but it's more strategic than that. I keep my voice in a particular register when I'm rehearsing with Sam, and practice the songs in it, too. Only Hannah has heard, but she has a discerning ear. She doesn't think they sound enough alike for anyone to make the connection.

But I haven't had a chance to practice the new song in it yet, so Seven might leak through. And the last thing I need is to have my alter ego revealed just before I pull it off the app forever. As soon as the glitch gets fixed, I'm logging into my account and deleting the whole thing.

"All right," says Sam, giving my shoulders another squeeze. "But it's on you when I bastardize 'Shake It Off' in front of these innocent people."

We spend the next hour entertained by a sweet-faced, pixie-cutted cellist, a stammering comedian who makes us all howl, a few singers with guitars, and, of course, Rocket, who does a stripped-down version of a wacky synth song we hadn't heard yet. We're at a pause between performances when Sam's phone lights up.

"My mom," he says. "I should probably update her."

I nod, making room for him to head to the back of the cafe to take the call. The tiny cellist is struggling with her instrument and several tote bags, causing a near collision with Rocket as he tries to slide past her to the bathroom, so I help her pull out her stuff and take it out to the front where she can wait for a car. By the time she's squared away, Sam is off the phone with a grim smile.

"Let's head out," I say.

He nods and I send Rocket a quick text so we don't have to wait. This time when we walk out into the rain, we don't make a run for it. There's something welcoming in the warmth of it, in the way it has emptied out the streets.

The Airbnb is close enough to walk. We let ourselves in with the hidden key, turning on the lights to reveal a small living and kitchen area and a hall that leads to a bathroom and two bedrooms, one of which is the master suite, the other a child's bedroom complete with cloud-painted walls and a genuine race car bed.

"Dibs," we both say at the same time.

I turn to him in mock affront. "I drove here," I remind him. "I get the race car bed."

He steps backward into the room, making a show of how at ease he is in it. "My estranged dad turned out to be an egomaniac. *I* get the race car bed."

I step so I'm inches away from his face. I haven't kissed him in hours. It feels like a debt that needs collecting, a deadline overdue.

"Nice try," I say. "But that doesn't mean—"

The argument swiftly ends then with Sam's hand on the back of my neck, pulling me in for a kiss. It's sweet and simmering, with a distinct kind of ache. I can still feel the weight of this day in his touch.

I ease us both to the edge of the little race car bed, kissing him lightly before asking, "What did your mom say?"

Sam blows out a breath. "She said he's always an ass the first time you meet him."

"Will you see him again?"

Sam pulls the baseball cap off my head, letting my damp hair fall onto my shoulders. He runs a hand through it, considering.

"This probably makes me an ass, too," says Sam. "But I like my life the way it is. I don't need him in it."

I shake my head. "You don't owe him anything. Especially not after the way he treated you."

Sam is so quiet that I worry he doesn't believe me. Then he turns to me, uncharacteristically careful.

"Is that how you feel about your parents?" he asks.

I blink. "Oh," I say. "I mean—I don't think about it that much anymore, to be honest. God, that probably makes me sound like an ass, too."

"Nah." Sam settles his hand on top of mine, weaving his fingers through it. "But it doesn't make it suck any less."

The rain patters against the glass windowpanes, lulling and gentle.

"I, uh—I went to therapy, during that break," I tell him. "Maybe

I'm not happy about the way my parents are, but I'm at peace with it. They just weren't built that way. It's got nothing to do with me." I squeeze his hand. "I hope you know that about Caspar, too."

Sam nods, staring down at our laps. "You really don't think about it much?"

I'm still for a moment, considering.

"I do," I say. "But mostly to explain other parts of my life. When guys came on strong and made all these promises, I just—wanted to believe them so badly that I ignored all the red flags. They felt safe, in the beginning, and when things started to go bad I just . . ." I swallow hard. "It was my parents all over again. Trying to earn their love. Keep it. Like I was playing the same story over and over, thinking I could change the ending and fix all the other ones, too."

Sam doesn't say anything. He just keeps his hand on mine and leans in, tucking me into him like a port in the storm still picking up outside.

I close my eyes in relief, but keep them shut because I'm afraid it's happening all over again. That Sam will become one more ending I can't fix.

"Sorry," I say quietly. "That was a lot."

More than a lot, even. I've never said that much out loud to anyone. Not even Hannah.

But Sam shakes his head against my temple. "You know you can tell me anything."

When I pull in another breath, the words are at the tip of my tongue: *I'm Seven.*

Maybe there's no harm in telling Sam now. I trust him not to tell anybody. I trust him not to judge me for the way I held on to the past, writing those songs in the first place.

I may even trust him with the scariest thing of all. I trust him to stay.

"I know," I tell him.

Sam kisses my temple. "Good," he says.

But Seven is mine, and tomorrow, she'll be buried. I used her to close a book so I could start a new one, and I think—I hope—it might be starting right now. With the last person I thought it would be, in the least likely way.

I pull back to look at him. There's no mischief, no posturing, in the familiar planes of his face. When he's stripped of everything that makes him Sam Blaze, he's just Sam. *My* Sam.

Maybe it's an absurd thought. But the more time we spend together, the harder it gets to push it away.

I shiver. Sam pulls me in closer. "I saw some robes hanging in the bathroom," he says.

"And I spotted a cheap bottle of wine at the door," I tell him. "I don't know about you, but I could use a damn drink."

Sam's lips curl. "Lead the way."

PART FOUR

"Keeping Time"

chapter eighteen
SAM

Mackenzie's drying hair is fanned out across the couch like a halo, her body fully stretched against mine on the couch with her bare feet on the coffee table. I take a sip from the open bottle of Pinot Noir and pass it back to her, watching the rain from the window cast shadows on her face. It's been one of the wildest days of my life, but the end is simple as ever—I still want as much of her as she's willing to give.

"Mackenzie," I say lowly.

Her face immediately flushes. I do my best not to smirk. The only thing I like more than saying her name is watching her hear it.

"I need a favor."

She raises an eyebrow. "Convenient of you to ask when we're half a bottle deep," she says, taking another sip herself.

"It's about damn time I hear you sing." She opens her mouth to protest. I don't let her. "I mean *sing*. You've been holding back."

She doesn't deny it. Just stares at the rim of the wine bottle, lips twisting.

She knocks her head against my shoulder. "Okay. We'll practice 'Run Out of Road.'"

"Nice try. I want pure, undiluted Mackenzie," I tell her. "Sing something you already know."

"I don't really have a repertoire these days," she says wryly.

It's been weighing on me ever since she told me about her voice. She said it so easily, but the grief in her eyes was so plain. Years and years of writing a history of herself, and now she can't even touch it.

"'When I Was Green,'" I suggest.

Mackenzie blinks at me. "I've never even performed that live."

It's a bonus track on Thunder Hearts' second album. Mackenzie is the only one singing on it. It's unlike any of her others—not a love song, but a quiet, personal one about the time it takes to come into your own.

"It's slower than the others," I say. "It would be easy to scale back."

"Yeah, I know. But how do *you* know?" she says.

Now it's my face getting hot. I swipe the bottle from her, pulling myself up to my feet.

"I told you I don't do anything halfway," I tell her. "Especially not scoping out the competition."

Mackenzie lets out a stunned laugh. I pull out the old guitar we found in the closet earlier. I tune it, then play a few chords until I get the pattern right. When I look up, Mackenzie's eyes are incredulous.

I clear my throat. "I'll try lowering the key. Stop me if it isn't working."

Mackenzie watches my fingers on the strings like she's in a trance, but at the last second, she pulls in a sharp breath and sings. In the first verse her voice is still soft. Uncertain. But as we reach the chorus, she finally meets my eye and sings not just from her throat, but her whole body.

Her voice is rich and soft and—familiar, somehow. I can antici-pate how she'll use it, when she has to change it from the original.

But as soon as I have the thought, she stops.

"Hey," I protest.

"That's enough of that," she says lightly, reaching for the wine bottle again.

I pluck it from the table before she can. "You can have the whole damn bottle, if you admit your voice is a knockout."

"It's raspy now," she says.

"It's got depth. Like a fine wine," I say, holding the bottle above my head.

She rolls her eyes. I wait for them to meet mine again; then I lean down to level with her.

"It matches the song better," I tell her. "It was meant to be sung that way."

Mackenzie sighs. I take a performative sip of wine, waiting for her to admit I'm right. But her lips settle into a small smile.

"I'll tell you something funny," she says. "I wrote that song because of you."

That's the last thing I'm expecting her to say. "How?"

"In that interview with Noted Scene—you called us 'green,'" she says. "I got stuck on it. What it means to be *green*. What I'd have to become, so I wouldn't be. The song just fell out of me."

I know better than to think it *fell* out of anything. Mackenzie's always had a way of polishing scraps into something that shines.

"Damn," I say. "So you're saying I should mouth off more often."

"You and that mouth of yours have done plenty."

It's about to do a whole lot more tonight, judging from the way Mackenzie's leaning in right now. Her robe is loose enough that I can see her bare shoulder and the top of her pale breasts.

"What if I told you I wrote a few lines because of you, too?" I ask, using the knot on the tie to her robe to pull her closer.

Her blue eyes are like sparks against the dim light. "Oh yeah?" she asks.

"'Kiss and Desist.' That line about wanting to taste the edge of your smirk," I say.

That same smirk is deepening now. Enough that I can see the faint dimple on her left cheek. When she leans in, I can smell the sweetness of the wine on her breath, feel the tickle of her hair on my shoulder.

"'Nice to Un-meet You,'" she says, listing a song off Thunder Hearts' third album. *Fallen-angel face with a devil tongue.*

I skim my tongue over my teeth. "Bold claim," I counter. "You hadn't tried it yet."

She presses a thumb over my lip then, using it to hold me in place. "But was I wrong?"

Her other hand settles on my thigh, slowly moving it higher.

"'Forget Me Not,'" I say as evenly as I can. *I'd never cross a line, but I'd do anything to cross your mind.*

She looks me up and down. "I can think of some lines we can cross right now," she says idly.

"Like this one?" I press my lips to her shoulder. "Or maybe this one," I add, pressing another to her collarbone.

I ease back to see the flush on her cheeks, the heat in her eyes. Already I feel her burning through every other touch I've had on my skin, like she's branded me for good.

"And most certainly this one," I say.

I don't just taste the edge of her smirk then, but every inch of the broadest, most shameless grin that has ever crossed her lips.

chapter nineteen
MACKENZIE

No matter how hard I tried not to feel anything for Sam, I could never fully shake the dream I had about him the night we met. We were at the trailer where he introduced himself, with that smug lean and cocky grin. Before I knew it, we were tearing off each other's clothes, so fast and heated it bordered on punishing.

But then I met his eyes. They were so tender. So warm and steady on mine.

I'd never seen anyone look at me like that in real life. It made me realize it was a dream so fast that I jerked awake.

But whatever is happening between us now is no dream. Sam meets my lips for another slow, searching kiss, sliding his arms beneath my knees and around my back. He lifts me from the couch so easily that I let out a little gasp, feeling as weightless as I did in the pool.

This time when his eyes meet mine, it's with a current so electric that I know I'm not waking up from this. And if I waited all these years to let myself feel it, I'm damn well going to take my sweet time.

"Oh, you think you get me that easily?" I keep my arms hooked around his neck, but ease my feet onto the floor. "Years of driving me up the wall and you can just *have* me without settling the score?"

His hands wrap around the small of my back, migrating down. "I wouldn't dream of it," he says lowly. "Remind me of my crimes?"

I tilt my chin up at him. "There are enough that it might just take all night."

He leans in slowly, kissing me just above my ear. "As long as you're the one deciding the punishment."

"Well," I say sweetly. "In that case."

I take a step back and plant my hands on his chest, pushing him on the couch so he's laid out on his back. I take my time straddling him, dipping low and sucking just hard enough under his jaw to leave a mark. He tastes sweet, like salt and rainwater, but the groan I feel rise up in his throat is anything but.

"That," I say, "is for the time you wore one of my ex's ugly sneaker brands onstage for a month."

He snickers, then plants his hands firmly on my hips to settle me on top of him. He lifts his hips and I let out a gasp at how achingly hard he already is underneath me.

Then he skims down the robe, hoisting me up a slow kiss that ends with him dragging his teeth along my lower lip.

"That's for the time you set off that glitter cannon in the middle of our set."

I push my hand on his chest again, dragging my fingernails down his torso as I deliberately roll my hips over the hard length of him between our underwear.

"Fuck, Mackenzie," he says.

I've never loved the sound of my name more than when it's coming out of Sam's mouth.

"We'll see," I tease. "But first, that's for acting like a total jerk to any guys I brought around."

One moment I'm on top of him, and the next I'm in the air again, his arms firmly hooked under my shoulders and knees. He takes me down the hall and all but tosses me on the bed.

"In that case," he says, his eyes dark, "that was for making me watch you date jerks."

I tighten the robe around myself, smirking as I sit up. He saunters over, grabs me by my ankles, and tugs me to the edge of the bed, stepping between my legs. He reaches for the tie to the robe. I shift up in silent permission, and then I'm letting the loose fabric slide off my shoulders, and he's staring at every inch of me as I stare back.

"Well?" he asks. "Any last misdeeds to punish me for?"

I nod. "Just—trying to remember which ones."

"Maybe we can stir up some memories."

Doubtful. Any thoughts I have are entirely consumed by the sight of Sam sinking to his knees, by the warmth of his mouth on my inner thigh. I reach for a fistful of his hair, and he kisses upward, sucking so lightly that tremors roll up my whole body.

The tips of his fingers graze my underwear. He looks at me with mock innocence as he slowly slides it off.

"Anything yet?" he asks.

"Don't worry," I say, trying to keep my breath even. "I'm sure it'll come to me."

He teases a single finger at my entrance. I'm so wet that I don't feel the first finger he slides into me until he hooks it upward and I let out a sharp pant.

"Sooner than later, I'd say," he tells me.

"Please," I say, in a voice I've never heard before—quaking, but with a bite.

"Patience," says Sam, sliding his finger back out. "I have a few things to get back at you for, too."

He dips his head between my legs, sliding his tongue with torturous slowness before sucking lightly on my clit. I spread wide as he pulls back, kissing my inner thighs again almost like he's mapping them—*here* and *here* and *there*. I brace myself on my elbows, letting my head fall back.

"I must have done something really—*bad*," I say, hitching on the last word. Sam's tongue is only at my entrance for a few seconds before sinking in deeper. My hips buck in surprise and he grips my thighs like anchors as I tug on the back of his hair, already so startlingly close to coming that I am dizzy with the shock of it—the way it's swelling in me, so overpowering that I already know I'll have no choice but to give in to it soon.

"Fuck," I say. "This—you—I'm gonna—"

He twists his tongue just so, pressing his thumb to my clit, and I see *stars*. The pleasure slams into me so unexpectedly that I cry out just as the first strike of lightning hits, the immediate, booming thunder drowning out the tail end of it.

Once I catch my breath, the only words I can summon are, "What the *fuck* was that?"

Sam is still on his knees. "Revenge," he says huskily.

I sit up and reach for his robe, which is inexplicably still on him. "Well, that's not fair," I say, breathless. "I still haven't gotten any."

As he rises to his feet, I slide the tie off his robe, drinking in more of Sam than I've ever seen. The lean ease of his body. The full woven tapestry of his tattoos across his arms and legs, the ink fresh and old, telling stories I know and stories I have yet to hear. The sharp cut of muscle that dips into his low-slung boxers, the tempting tuft of dark hair just above the seam.

I press my palm over his boxers, the length of him so warm and hard that I shudder in anticipation. Or maybe the shudder is Sam's; his lips are parted, his breath uneven, as I gently, firmly stroke upward.

Just like that I forget all plans to make him wait for it, to make him beg. I'm too eager to dip below the seam of his boxers, to hold him firm and pulsing in the palm of my hand.

"Of fucking *course*," I say as I pull his boxers off him. "Of course this is as infuriatingly perfect as the rest of you."

I'm expecting a cocky response, but from the look of him he might have lost the power of speech. Good. I want to undo him every bit as much as he just undid me. Maybe we aren't rivals anymore, but this is a competition I am determined to win.

I might just be losing track of the rules, though, because Sam's hands find mine, weaving through my fingers. He uses them to lift my arms over my head, putting my naked body on full display for him.

"Mackenzie," he says in a low voice. "If you're going to punish me, then—the worst thing I can possibly imagine—" He's closer to the edge of the bed now, his fingers squeezing mine possessively, his eyes burning with intent. "Is doing whatever I have to do to see that look on your face again."

For all my years spinning lyrics, I have no words left. There is just the pulsing, immediate *need* to have as much of him as I can possibly take, and nothing else.

He releases me, only to pull his fingers through my hair and slowly push me back onto the mattress. Another strike of lightning crackles outside, illuminating him like the very fallen angel I've always imagined him to be: sharp-edged and beautiful and impossible to look away from.

When he lowers himself the weight of him is so satisfying that I wrap my arms around his back, pulling him in even tighter. The crush of his ribs against mine steals my breath, but I keep him there, listening to the unsteady beats of our hearts. When he looks down at me it's with the kind of awe that makes me scared to blink and miss one split second of watching what this is doing to him.

"Whatever I do next," he says, "is payback for knowing my *tell*, when I've spent years trying to read your mind."

I'm dizzy with want, a dam on the verge of collapse. But something else spills out of me then. The secret I've been keeping from him. The one that's been stuck in my throat for so long that it's impossible to keep for another minute.

"I was a big Candy Shard fan before we met."

Oh, *fuck*. That's not the secret I thought I'd tell him. Somehow, it's worse.

Sam doesn't move, his voice wry when he says, "You were?"

My cheeks are searing. "I had posters. I knew all the words to your songs. I just—" I let out a breathy laugh. "I never told anyone. But you thought I hated you when we met. But the truth is, I didn't."

I crush my eyes shut. Jesus. I'm no stranger to self-sabotage, but this might take the cake. Every inch of me is burning for him, and if I lose this now, I've got nobody to blame but myself.

It's just—we spent so long pretending. Using the rivalry as our only excuse to get close. In a way, we're even doing it now.

I can't pretend with him anymore. I want the real damn thing or nothing at all. Even if it means giving him this piece of myself I swore I never would.

"Mackenzie."

Sam runs his fingers through my hair, pushing back the loose curls.

"Mackenzie," he says again. "You know what I thought the first time I saw you?"

I finally meet his gaze, and there it is. That look in his eyes that I dreamed about. It feels so much like love that I don't know what to do with it except brace myself.

Except this time, I don't wake up.

"That's a lot of glitter?" I say weakly.

He shakes his head. "I thought—that woman's either gonna change my life, or end life as I know it."

I let out another laugh. Sam's eyes stay steady and resolved on mine.

"Damn if I wasn't right about both," he says. "I admired you. I was scared of you. Hell, sometimes I still am."

Those eyes are still on mine and I want—god, I want too much. I want to be loved by him so badly, but I know if I let him, it will be terminal. I could come back from the others. I don't think I could ever come back from him.

But if I don't take this chance, I'll never know.

"I don't want to be scared anymore," I breathe.

His expression cracks long enough for me to see something I recognize. That quiet line between hope and fear. I've been straddling it for so long, and never once thought he was on it with me.

Maybe this means as much to him as it does to me. Maybe, for the first time, I'm not falling alone.

He buries his face in my neck. "You've got nothing to be scared of," he tells me, pressing the words into my skin like a promise.

I don't trust promises, but I trust Sam. I always have. Our rivalry wouldn't have lasted a second if it hadn't been there—that quiet understanding. That inherent faith.

It isn't quiet anymore. I lift my hips, searching for him, *needing* him. All of him. Like something was sealed that day we first met and it's high time we get to collect.

"Have you got a—" he starts, and when I shake my head, he says, "Hold on," and comes back from the bathroom with a condom. He approaches the edge of the bed, his eyes near starved, but I lift my bare foot up to catch him by the chest.

I'm not afraid of this. But now I'm something else entirely.

"Sit," I command, shifting my gaze to the top of the bed.

He raises his eyebrows, but does as he's told. I wait until he's settled on the pillows, raking my eyes up and down his body, the lightning briefly illuminating the sheen of sweat on his skin. I ease myself on top of him, hovering just above his lap.

"Don't move," I say, lowering myself. Just the tip of him against my entrance is enough to make my breath hitch in my throat, but I stay in command. Slowly, slowly, watching the high flush in his cheeks and the rise of his chest as he tries with impossible effort to stay still.

I slide farther down, opening myself up to him, feeling every slow, pulsing inch of him fill me. That look is in his eyes again, but this time I let it wash over me. Let it anchor me.

I wrap my hand around the back of his neck, lifting up one pinky off the top of his spine. *Tap.* He's still watching me, not catching on yet. *Tap.* He blinks slightly. Stirs. *Tap.*

"You wouldn't," he pants. "Mackenzie. Don't make me beg."

"Then you better tell me what you want," I say, pressing the fourth tap into him with more pressure than any of the others.

The rivalry may have just ended. But the games have just begun.

"Please," he says, his hands on either side of my face, then burying themselves into the thick tangle of my curls. "You have no idea how good you feel. Please, Mackenzie, please—"

I settle the last *tap* just as I slide the last few inches, taking him all the way inside me. We both gasp at the suddenness of the plunge. I rock on top of him, the sensation so consuming that I dig my palms into his chest to anchor myself. He's got me by the ribs, steadying our rhythm, every thrust so satisfying that I have to bury my face in his neck to muffle my own noise.

"No," he says. "I want to hear you."

I'm stunned there's anything to hear at all. Nobody has ever made me sound like this. I've done this before, I've done *all* of this before, but never imagined how much more of me there was to feel.

Our foreheads meet and we're scorching against each other, sweat pooling from my hairline, mingling with his. Another bolt of lightning streaks light, and I see it in his face, too—the shock and the reverence. The impossibility and the inevitability. The way we never could have imagined this moment, but it was never going to lead anywhere but this.

He pushes my damp hair off my shoulders and kisses me. "Beautiful," he murmurs.

He tightens his grip on my ribs, slowly sliding out of me. I let out a choked noise at the temporary loss of him, putty in his hands as he eases me onto my back on the mattress. When he settles himself above me this time it isn't with urgency, but intensity. We must be in the eye of the storm; everything is quiet but our rasping breaths and my heart thrumming all over my body.

There are no quips and comebacks. Not one word left to hide behind. He never once takes his eyes off mine as he slides back into me and we set a new pace, one that starts deliciously slow before it builds—a quiet verse building up to a thundering chorus—a swell that starts low and pitches higher, and higher still, until it starts to peak.

"Sam, Sam, Sam," I gasp, louder than I've ever been, his name chased by words I've never said to anyone before: *I love you, I love you, I love you.*

It's the sweetest, most terrifying, most divine thought I have ever had. It brings a crest of pleasure so intense that all I can manage is a whimper, like my body can't fully fathom it.

His voice is rough in my ear, so ragged that I know he's close to coming himself. "I've got you," he says. "Always."

For the second time that night, I'm entirely unprepared for the crash of my own orgasm. My body trembles through the crest and aftershocks, Sam clutching me against him as he follows just behind with a deep moan. He buries his face into my hair as he pushes in and out of me, giving me the strangest out-of-body sense that maybe we are in some new infinity—that we'll never *stop* feeling this—that we've reached a peak impossible to climb down from.

Then there's the comforting weight of him on top of me, and his lips between my brows again, on the tip of my nose. Then there's the few minutes we lie there, trying to catch our breath, sneaking glances at each other and smiling like we've got some new secret between us that nobody in the world will ever understand. Then there's Sam sitting up and hoisting me by the elbows, leading us to the bathroom where we wash each other in the shower, slow and gentle in the warm spray.

The rain is still pattering on the window outside when we ease back into bed. I press my forehead into his collarbone and he wraps his arms around me, pulling me in as I breathe in that burnt-honey smell of him.

For the first time, I'm not tempted to lie awake and wonder. I have nothing I need to say, and nothing I need to hear. I feel it already, in the steady beat of his heart against my open palm. In the way his knuckles stroke the top of my spine, a gentle up and down, lulling like a tide.

My eyes slide shut, but my lips are still moving. I let myself mouth the words one time—the lyrics I chased these past few weeks, but could never catch until now: *I love you.*

They wash over us so sweetly that I'm still smiling as they carry me to sleep.

chapter twenty
SAM

When I wake, Mackenzie is still in my arms, her chest rising and falling against mine. The sun is streaming in through the window, glowing against Mackenzie's wild curls, brightening the curve of her pale hip.

I wanted to tell her when she first offered to come to Boston. I wanted to tell her as she was running her fingers through my hair in the shower, staring up at me. I wanted to tell her the day we met, and I want to wake her up to tell her right now.

I love you.

I've known it for a long time, but now I know that nothing I do in this life could ever make me stop.

She stirs. I stay very still. I know what last night meant to me. I know what *she* means to me. But if she still thinks we're having "fun"—well, I don't have any idea what that'll do to me now.

She blinks the sleep out of her eyes. When they meet mine, they're steady and unsurprised. There's a smile curling on her lips. It's still blooming when she tilts her head up to kiss me.

The relief is dizzying. I pull her in tighter, savoring every soft, warm inch of her pressed against me, breathing in that flowery Mackenzie scent. She's still smiling when we pull apart. I take her chin, tracing her lips with my thumb.

"Something funny?" I ask, hoarse from sleep.

She nods into my palm, grazing her teeth over my thumb.

"I thought I wasn't a morning person," she says, hooking a leg over my hip. "Turns out I am if I wake up like this."

Damn if I don't know the feeling. Turns out I'm an *everything* person if it means I've got all of Mackenzie Waters in my arms.

We're slower and sweeter about it this time. She is surprisingly shy in the light of day, but not for long. I was proud of myself last night for finally getting Mackenzie to sing, but I'm a whole lot more satisfied with the sounds I'm getting out of her now.

The sun is casting shorter shadows through the window as I lie back on the mattress, Mackenzie's head on my chest, my hands in her hair. The city is coming to life. Cars on the road. Lawn mowers whirring to life. My phone buzzing with a text, letting me know that Lizzie and Kara will be an hour late getting back with Ben tonight.

I press a kiss to Mackenzie's temple. "You stay here," I say. "I'll grab breakfast."

"I'll come with you," she offers.

I shake my head. "I want you right here when I get back," I say. "Don't move an inch, you hear me?"

The August air is balmy and heavy from the storm as I walk out of the Airbnb, but for once my head is clear. The thing is, I've spent most of my life waiting for the other shoe to drop. When Candy Shard finally made it big, and I was so scared I'd fuck it up for us. When Lizzie told me about Ben, and I was so scared that I'd fuck everything up for *him*.

When Mackenzie crashed back into my life, and I realized I'd fucked everything up for myself.

But my feet are firmly planted now. I'll drive us home after breakfast. I'll tell Mackenzie how I feel. I'll close the book on Caspar.

We'll finish the album, do the showcase, and then—I don't know. For once, I'm not worried about not knowing. I saw enough of the future in Mackenzie's eyes last night. Maybe I don't have the words for it like she does, but I know she's in this as deep as I am.

But just as soon as I have the thought, the words come. Fast and easy, like a song—one I've lived with for so long that it feels less like I'm writing something and more like I'm remembering it. A song that started the day I met Mackenzie, and has been stuck in my head ever since.

I stop on a bench, recording what I can before the foot traffic starts to pick up. I point myself back to Rocket's cafe and pass the bar where I met Caspar on the way. It's shuttered from last night. I glance in the window, catching my reflection.

Messy hair, hands in my pockets, public face set on the verge of a smirk. I do it without thinking now. I know how easy it is to be caught by a random camera lens. But for the first time I don't just resent it because it feels like a lie—I resent it because it reminds me of *him*.

I stand up straighter. Drop the face. Ease my hands out of my pockets.

And turn to a flash directly in my eyes.

"How do you respond to the accusations that you're a nepo baby?"

These days when someone puts a camera in my face, it's usually a fan. But this is a damn pap. The worst kind, too—the kind that gets under your skin to get you to react. When I first found out about Ben, they'd wait outside Sugar Harmony like snakes.

"Do you have other half-siblings, or are you the only secret love child?"

Jesus. There isn't one pap, but two.

"Why did you lie about being Caspar Quentin's son?"

The panic doesn't even have time to set in. I know the drill by now: Find a restaurant. Find a cafe. But when I turn and start walking, there's nowhere to go—it's too early for anything on this block to be open, and as I walk down the street the paps are shouting at me loudly enough to wake the damn dead.

"What does Ben think about all this?"

My ears are ringing, but my next thought is clear as a bell: *There goes the other shoe.*

PART FIVE

"Running Out of Road"

chapter twenty-one
MACKENZIE

We're quiet for most of the ride home, aside from Sam making and taking calls as I drive. At one point he even gets a call from Caspar. "I'm sorry," he says over the speaker. "I really don't know how it got out."

I think I do. And I so, so desperately want to be wrong.

I drop Sam off around the corner from his place. There are already paparazzi in front of Sugar Harmony. He just barely shook them off in Boston before coming back to get me at the Airbnb— the last thing we need is a picture of us together in the car to add fuel to the fire.

When I stop the car Sam hugs me so tightly that it reminds me of the way I needed to hold on to him when I was learning to swim. He thanks me hoarsely. Then he cuts in through a back entrance that takes him up to the apartment to find Ben and Lizzie.

I peer into the window of Sugar Harmony as I drive past, where Kara and a few customers are braving the camera storm at the front.

Rocket's table is empty, but I already knew it would be.

I head straight for the Hudson. There are benches on the bike path where Rocket often makes a small spectacle feeding the pigeons. But he's all on his own today, slumped on a bench and staring at New Jersey like he's waiting for it to slam into him and put him out of his misery.

He flinches when he sees me standing there, his eyes bloodshot.

"Rocket," I start.

It's a good thing I didn't bother preparing a speech, because I don't need one. Rocket folds like a card table, lanky limbs caving, face crumbling.

"Fuck. I'm sorry," he says. "I didn't think—shit."

I sit next to him, strangely calm. "Did you follow us to Boston?"

Rocket turns to me, looking more like a little kid than an up-and-coming anything. "I wasn't—Serena wanted to—"

"*Serena?*"

Rocket nods miserably, settling his hands on his face. "It's ridiculous, I know," he says, pressing the tips of his fingers into his scalp. "But I heard her on the phone with Hannah. She thought—she thought maybe you were Seven. That you were going up to Boston to record new versions of the tracks before you went public."

The heat is blistering on this bench in the August sun, but the hair on my arms rises. One of our favorite producers just relocated and opened a studio up there. It tracks that Serena might think I'd record with her.

The rest I can't even begin to explain.

"And you what? Wanted to expose Seven?" I ask, keeping my voice even.

Rocket just shakes his head. "No. I wanted to know because—the guys behind the company buying Tick Tune? They're the same ones who fucked me over on my contract. So I guess I just thought—if you were Seven—I dunno. Maybe you could do something about it."

I've been so wrapped up in what's happening with Sam that the Tick Tune drama seemed beyond me. But it isn't, really. Not if people like Rocket think that Seven has enough power to do anything about this.

It feels wrong not to tell him the truth, but it won't help him. Or rather—Seven can't help him. But maybe I can.

"I'm sorry," I start, but Rocket isn't done.

"And also, I guess—because Serena's been so fixated on Seven," he says. "I figured if we found out it was you that she wouldn't try to find the actual Seven to replace me on the tour."

Of all the things Rocket has said in the last minute, this is the wildest. "She would never replace you," I tell him.

Rocket looks near tears. "Oh. I don't know about that." He's shaking so hard that I couldn't stay angry with him if I tried. "The tour's been delayed again, and I already quit my freelance gigs, so I'm just—zip, zilch, out of money. And fully evicted. And I don't actually have any family in Boston or anywhere, really, so I—when I heard Sam talking on the phone about Caspar back at the cafe, I just . . ."

He hangs his head. It takes me another moment to process.

"Hit up the press for money," I finish for him.

Rocket doesn't look up. "He and Caspar had already been spotted together outside the bar. It was all over social media, so I guess I just thought—if it was going to get out eventually—" He shakes his head again, his face tinged gray. "I'd take it back if I could. I was just—it was enough money to get a motel room for the night. So I could figure out what to do when I got back here."

Jesus Christ, this kid. He gave away a six-figure secret so he could spend a single night lying on a moldy bed and drinking stale coffee.

"You could have come to us for help," I tell him. "Or Serena."

Rocket nods with his entire body, sniffling wetly. "I know. I know."

"So why didn't you?"

When he finally answers me, his voice is impossibly small. "I just thought I'd—handle it on my own."

Before he even looks at me, those words tug against a heartstring that's been sore ever since I can remember. I put a hand on his arm, knowing precisely what he needs to hear—the same words I needed to hear, after years of feeling alone in my own parents' home. The ones I was lucky to hear variations of from so many people in my life. Hannah. Sam.

Serena.

"That's too damn bad," I say. "Because you're not on your own."

Rocket shakes his head, freeing a loose tear that rolls down his cheek. "Sam's never gonna forgive me."

I squeeze his arm. "He will," I say. "He'll need some time, but he will."

Rocket stares mutely at his hands, and then back at me. I pull in another breath, grounding myself. Decisions need to be made, and right now I'm the one who has to make them. It's not a feeling I'm used to—when it came to the big decisions back in our Thunder Hearts days, Serena was always the one in control.

Ever since the band broke up, I haven't had to make any decisions, either. I hid behind Seven while things happened around me. I was a passenger in my own life.

But it's different now. It has been ever since Sam came back into the picture. Like he shone a light on everything—not just the parts of me that were scared to love again, but all the things I've been avoiding, too.

Now I've got no choice but to face it all head-on. If my whole mess with Seven caused this, then it's time for me to step up to the plate and fix it, one step at a time.

"Hannah has apartments all over the city she rents out," I tell Rocket. "We'll get you into one for now, while we figure something out."

Rocket just keeps shaking his head. "Don't," he says. "Seriously. I mean, shit. I was trying to blow your spot up, too."

I put a hand on his back. "We'll hash it all out later," I say. "But first, let's get out of here before someone tells the press you're my secret nephew."

His eyes brim again, a few more tears spilling over. "Thanks, Mackenzie," he finally says.

But the next steps can wait for a little while—for however long it takes after I wrap my arms around him and let him cry.

chapter twenty-two
MACKENZIE

Serena's apartment isn't a cozy loft in the East Village like mine or a retro chic Upper West Side penthouse like Hannah's, but a quiet, understated high rise on the Upper East. Her voice is clipped on the other end when the doorman calls to let her know I'm downstairs, but she lets me up.

She answers the door in a bathrobe; her face is bare and her bob tucked into curling rods. For a split second I straddle two realities—the old one where I saw her like this every night, and this new one where any version of Serena feels like a stranger.

Serena's eyes search my face, her own unreadable.

"I knew it," she says.

She turns back into the apartment before I can answer, but leaves the door open for me. I can count on one hand the number of times I've been here. From the looks of the empty walls and the barely touched furniture, so can Serena. But no matter where Serena goes, this much I know: she always has an emergency bottle of rosé.

I wordlessly pull the open bottle out of the fridge. When I turn, Serena is already washing the dust off two wineglasses.

She sets them on the kitchen counter and turns to look at me. She doesn't seem angry. She doesn't seem anything, really, except tired.

"You're not going to ask how I know?" she asks.

My hands are steady pouring the wine. I'm not anything, either, I realize. Only—tired.

"Just who else does," I say.

Her jaw ticks. "Nobody. I only figured it out because Hannah left a text thread with you open on her iPad. She'd screenshotted the comment section of a Seven song, and you responded with a bunch of melting emojis."

That was the afternoon we all met up at Hannah's apartment. Serena finished a meeting she had downtown early and beat me there. I chalked up the tension to the Mack & Sam news, but she must have been working it out about Seven right then and there.

I hand her one of the wineglasses. There's a split second where we both hover, holding the stems. We'd usually "cheers" something silly. *To not biting it onstage*, we'd say after performing in a rainstorm. *To prescription strength deodorant and fashion tape*, we'd say after an awards show.

Now there isn't anything to celebrate between us, no matter how ridiculous or small.

"I haven't said anything to anyone," Serena adds.

I take a sip of wine. "Rocket heard you asking Hannah about it."

She blinks, the surprise cracking her exterior. "And he asked you about it?"

"No. He followed me up to Boston to see for himself," I tell her. "He's got his own reasons for trying to unmask Seven, I guess."

After a strained, quiet moment, Serena asks, "Did he figure it out?"

I shake my head. "No. But he was the one who figured out about Sam's dad. He's in a tough spot right now. He's the one who sold the story."

Serena spends a long moment staring into her wineglass. She may not care about Sam, but she must care what it's doing to Ben. She lets out a low, "Shit."

"Yeah."

She swallows hard. "Where's Rocket now?"

I nod. "He's okay," I say. "He's just got a bad habit of not telling people when he's in over his head."

Serena lets out a terse breath. I turn before I have to see the rest of her stiffen up, walking myself out of the kitchen and into the living area. There are framed photos resting on the floor by the couch, as if she meant to hang them up. A quick glance and you'd think Serena's life started when Thunder Hearts did. There are no photos of her parents or her siblings, or anything that came before the band.

Not anything that came after, either.

"Why didn't you just ask me about Seven?" I say. "Then he wouldn't have followed us in the first place."

"Is that why you're here?" Serena asks sharply. "You want me to apologize about Rocket?"

It was only a matter of time before I set her off, but one glance back at her and I'm worried I've done a whole lot more than that.

"No, I just—"

"And what kind of question is that, anyway? Why didn't you just *tell* me?" Serena stalks out of the kitchen, towering over me as she gestures out the window, toward the West Side. "Hannah knows. Hannah's known a long damn time, apparently. Do you have any idea how stupid I felt on the phone with her, while she basically had to *lie* about it, telling me to—"

She cuts herself off so abruptly she almost tips over.

"Telling you to ask me yourself," I finish for her.

And here we are again: Two immovable objects. Or just two stubborn idiots. Serena pulls in a breath and stops herself, because she must realize the same thing I do—if we keep playing this "you should have" game, we'll go in circles until we drive each other mad.

I set my wineglass down on the bare coffee table, straightening up to look her in the eye. "I wanted to tell you," I say. "About that and—a lot of other things. But you've been so angry with me. I wanted to fix that first."

Serena can't hold my gaze. Instead, she takes a few steps toward the wide window, her eyes trained on the sunset-stained buildings downtown.

"I wasn't angry with you," says Serena.

My voice is wry. "Sure. You just publicly declared war on Seven, knowing full well it was me."

"I said I *wasn't* angry with you. But I'm pissed at whatever the hell you're doing with Tick Tune," she says. "I mean, Jesus, Mackenzie. You saw what those assholes did to Rocket. There are dozens of other kids just like him they've already screwed over, and now they're doing it to *thousands*, and you're—what? Going to prove the label wrong for not backing your solo career? Cash out as Seven and screw over Sam for breaking your heart?"

It feels like my heart is breaking right now. She must see it streaked across my face, because she takes a step back like it ricocheted.

"You can't possibly think that of me," I say.

But she knew it would hurt me to say it. The same way we were standing in my apartment two years ago and I knew exactly what to say to hurt her.

Exactly what to say to push her away, *fast*.

Serena's eyes sweep to the floor. "I don't know what to think," she says tightly. "You lied to me."

The apartment is so bare that I feel small, standing in the center of it on my own. Smaller than I ever did when I was on massive stages, with Serena and Hannah at my side.

"Well, you're wrong," I tell her. "I'm deleting Seven's account before any of this goes down."

"You can't," Serena says bitterly. "The app's still down. I've got Hannah's lawyer exploring options to stop them going through with the sale before artists have a chance to log back on. But who knows how much time it'll buy us."

Us. Serena has always gone to bat for underdogs. But she doesn't call people out on social media, or get lawyers involved. Whatever is going on here, it's personal.

I cross the distance to join her at the window. "Why do you care about this Tick Tune thing so much?"

She still won't look at me. Her throat bobs, her fingers tight against the wineglass. "I'm the one who pushed Rocket to take that contract two years ago," she finally says. "I didn't read the fine print and he got screwed over because he trusted me. So much that some of his friends did it after he did, too. I've been trying to fix it for them, and I just—can't." Her face twists into a hard scowl that doesn't stop her eyes from watering. "But I can damn well stop it from happening again."

The spreadsheet on her computer. The one of her opening acts—the ones who notoriously do almost all covers, and occasionally new songs. Everyone assumed it was a strategy to pump up the crowd. But really, it was the only loophole in that terrible contract that let them perform live without breaching it.

Rocket isn't the only one Serena's been looking out for. She's been trying to keep an entire sinking ship of new artists afloat.

Enough that she must have fired Isla, knowing full well that it wouldn't be fair to expect anyone else to try to steer it. Serena would rather drown trying to do it alone.

That's what scares me. Serena was built to handle this kind of thing. If she's falling apart now, there is more she hasn't said.

"There's something else going on, though," I say gently. "Not with that. But with you."

With one sharp shake of her head, Serena's back in her shell. Cool and indifferent. "You keep saying that," she says. "There's not some—big secret. I'm not like you. I don't lie."

My eyes sting. The thing is, I've already done this. Over and over and over again. So many people have pushed me away through the years, and I've just short of pulled myself apart trying to make them stay.

Of all the lessons I've learned over the years, the most brutal is knowing when it's time to let go.

"I'm trying here, Serena. I really am. But I can't do it alone."

My voice cracks. Serena's eyes flit up to meet mine, and for a moment I see her. One of my best friends. Someone who has seen me at my ugliest lows and my sparkliest best. Someone who speaks a secret language of inside jokes and millisecond-long glances that would be lost on anyone else. Someone I let myself think of as a *forever* person, despite all the people who came and went too soon.

My phone buzzes in my pocket. By the time I pull it out and see Isla's name on the screen, the glimpse of the old Serena is gone. She looks emptied of herself, jutting her chin toward the door with a silent *Go on.*

I do. It hurts like hell. But it's the tip of the iceberg compared to the hurt to come—a different kind of forever. One that might not have Serena in it.

"Don't delete anything yet," says Serena.

I stop halfway to the door, turning to look back. "Why not?"

"You can come forward before the sale goes through. You're Seven. You have more power in this than I do."

It's no easy thing for her to admit. She wouldn't unless she really needed my help.

But for the first time, I don't know if the help she wants is the kind I can give.

"I need to think about it," I say. "We're finishing the album soon. The label has a showcase for Mack & Sam scheduled for next week. So if anything happens, I'd have to tell Sam about Seven first. Anything I decide to do with this will affect him now, too."

I'm so preoccupied with thinking of how I'd break it to Sam that I startle at the sound of Serena's sharp laugh.

"Sam doesn't know?"

My voice is grim, my feet firmly planted. "Serena, I never wanted anyone to know."

The last of the laugh drains out of her as she meets my eyes. She softens, then. For the first time since I arrived, I feel like we're on the same side of a line, and not trying to cross one.

"Your voice is beautiful," she says. "I just wish you had told me about Seven. Maybe I . . ."

She trails off, but I hear it. *Maybe I could have helped.* That's always what Serena did best. But somehow, we've gotten so tangled in trying to help each other that all we've done is hurt.

My throat is almost too thick to speak.

"The way my heart got broken over and over—the way we *all* struggled back then—it was so public, and we were never, ever allowed to crack," I manage. "But it hurt. All the pretending only made it worse. Seven was my way of finally processing it all, without feeling like I was letting anyone down."

Even now, Seven feels like a strange dream. There was no way of knowing how people would respond to my new voice. I spent so long building this tough, shiny exterior in Thunder Hearts that I thought it was all anyone would want from me. The way I saw it, singing on Tick Tune was like singing into a void.

But then the void started singing my lyrics back, and everything got complicated.

Serena is the one who crosses the distance now, setting a cold hand on my arm. It's the barest touch, but that's all it takes for my eyes to fill with tears. I shift closer, setting my own hand on top of hers. I wonder if she feels it, too: that of all the heartbreaks we've endured in our lives, none would come close to losing this.

"The only way we got through all that was because we never had to pretend with each other," I tell her. "Hannah and I are your best friends. But we still have no idea what's happening with you, or why you keep delaying the tour."

Serena keeps her hand on my arm, but doesn't speak for a long time. The sun is sinking low into the skyline, streaking deep pinks and blues across the clouds, dimming the apartment light.

When she pulls her hand away, she gives mine a light squeeze first.

"The app is still down," she says, her voice barely above a whisper. "Don't make any decisions yet. But think about it."

I nod, blinking the tears back. It's not much progress. But it's enough to hope.

"I will."

I shove on a bucket hat and walk along the East River, but my mind is no clearer by the time I get home. The only thing I know is this: I am a grenade. At least, as far as Sam is concerned.

If it weren't for me, we never would have gone to Boston. Rocket never would have followed us up there and found out about Caspar. Sam wouldn't be in his worst nightmare, the one we teamed up together to prevent: putting Ben in the spotlight again.

And Sam wouldn't have sunk all this time and effort into an album that might get screwed over the instant the world finds out I'm Seven.

I open our text thread, but I don't type anything. It isn't fair to tell him right now, when he's got so much on his plate. And besides— maybe it won't matter. Maybe this whole thing will resolve itself on its own, before anybody has to know the truth.

Or maybe everything in my life is about to explode and take Sam down with it.

Jesus. All this time, I've stayed away from Sam to protect my-self. Now after everything we've been through, the truth is clear as day—I should have stayed away to protect him from me.

chapter twenty-three
SAM

Caspar Quentin is making pancakes in my kitchen.

"Morning, kid," says Caspar, lifting up the "#1 (Surprise!) Dad" mug Ben got me for my birthday. "Your girls let me in through the back."

Lizzie and Kara must have just gotten back from New Jersey, then. We packed up Ben to hang out with his grandmas for the day so he can take a step outside without getting shouted at by a bunch of assholes with cameras parked in front of our building.

I wait for the shock to register. But after all the messed-up things that have happened in the last three days since the news broke, I can take a famous rock star breaking into my apartment in stride.

"Hi," I manage.

He flips a pancake with a smiley face spatula. The whole scene is so domestic that I feel like I was dropped onto the set of a sitcom. It only gets weirder when he hands me a stack of mildly charred pancakes in a large, flat salad bowl.

"Couldn't find the plates."

"Thanks," I say warily. "But, uh—what the hell are you doing here?"

He takes a seat on one of the tall stools by the kitchen bar, gesturing for me to do the same. Leave it to Caspar Quentin to walk in somewhere uninvited with the ease of someone who owns the place.

"Figured it's the least I could do after fucking up your life," he says.

My jaw ticks. If this is some performance of guilt to win me over, it's a bad move on his part. I wouldn't tolerate it on a good day. But he's got me on a day when I'm so worried about my own kid that I haven't slept more than two consecutive hours since god knows when.

Ben, at least, has taken the whole thing in stride. Poor kid already found out he had a dad he didn't know about. By the time the three of us sat him down to tell him about Caspar, all he did was blink in mild surprise.

"I have *another* granddad?" he asked us. "But that's so many."

It was the first I'd laughed since the shit show began. We've kept him distracted with soccer practices and the mushroom Funfetti cupcakes he insisted on making this week, so I don't think he has any idea about the chaos going on outside our door. But it's only a matter of time. And if it's not this, it's something else down the road.

Turns out it doesn't matter how careful I am. Caspar was right. I'll be just like him, in the end—the kind of dad whose kid will always deserve better than what he got.

Caspar clears his throat. He's waiting for an answer.

"This wasn't your fault," I mutter.

His shoulders slump. I turn, irritated, thinking this is another part of his act. But there's no bravado anymore. He seems older than he did only a few days ago, stripped down in a plain black

T-shirt and faded jeans, his signature hair and the studs in his ears obscured under a worn-out baseball cap.

"Yeah, well," he says, his voice gruff. "A whole lot else was."

Maybe another man would be more understanding, but I am not that man. Everything I've got belongs to the people I love right now, not to this man who knows the staff of some bar in Boston better than he knows his damn son.

"I don't need any apologies from you," I say plainly. "I don't need anything from you. And if you need something from me, well— tough."

I expect him to leave then. Hell, I want him to. I can't stand seeing the guilt on his face. Can't stand the way it looks like a reflection of mine.

But Caspar doesn't go. He doesn't look at me, either. Just stares ahead and then back down at his plate and says, "You asked why I got in touch, back in Boston. And I bullshitted you."

"That's one way of putting it," I say.

His lips thin ruefully. "I said a lot of stuff to your mom she said I should just say to you. It's not pretty. But it's the truth." He hazards a glance at me. "I wasn't going to be a good dad. I know that sounds like a shit excuse. But I'm just saying it to explain. That's the kind of thing you do all the way, and I think I would have just fucked you up if I'd tried."

I don't bother arguing with him on that. It is a shit excuse. But I've seen enough to know that he's probably right.

I've lived enough to know he was probably right. Hell, that was the same reason I avoided relationships for so long. I knew it meant the kind of commitment that back then, I just couldn't give.

But avoiding a relationship with someone you choose is a whole lot different than avoiding one with your kid, who didn't get to choose a damn thing.

"I thought maybe when you were older," Caspar continues. "Then your crew hit the big time, and it just didn't feel right. You earned that on your own. Didn't want anyone thinking any different, and I—didn't want you to think I only cared because of what you were doing."

It's true what I told Mackenzie back in the day. When Candy Shard started getting traction, I thought maybe my dad would recognize my name. Look me up. Maybe even get in touch.

It never occurred to me that Candy Shard would give him one more reason to stay away.

"I wish you had said something," I tell him. "I was still a kid when that was happening. I was in over my head. It would have been nice to have someone to talk to about it—someone who understood."

Mackenzie may have judged me for all the partying back in the day, but she doesn't even know the worst of it. I was so fucked up in the beginning, thinking I might let the band down. I tried my fair share of things to turn off the noise. Nothing that turned into a habit, but plenty that could have ended in disaster.

Enough that I thought I was too much of a liability to get close to anyone. To get close to Mackenzie. Instead, I just sat there and watched her get her heart broken over and over, while she had no idea she was breaking mine.

Maybe Caspar wouldn't have been able to say anything that helped. But I guess we'll never know.

Caspar hangs his head. "Yeah," he says.

My throat is thick, but I swallow it down. "So what changed?"

This could very well be the last time we ever see each other. Might as well make sure it's all on the table.

"Ben," he finally says. He skims a hand under his baseball cap, squeezing the top of his hair. "Guess I just thought—maybe we had something in common, now. Give us an opening to talk."

I let out a terse breath. Caspar nods, like he knows he deserves it.

"But you were right. We don't have that in common." He's gone still now, finally looking me in the eye. "You're a good dad."

It doesn't mean much, coming from Caspar. But I know that can't be an easy thing for him to say. He's struggling to hold my gaze even now, as if the words are more of a judgment of his character than mine.

They are, in a way. Because being a dad to Ben is just one more thing I didn't get any blueprint for, thanks to him.

"Doesn't mean I don't get scared I'm fucking him up, too," I admit.

Caspar lets out a breathy laugh. "Guess I'm the last person who can give advice on that."

"Guess so."

A silence settles between us. I don't feel any obligation to fill it. It's a sad thought, but a relief—I don't need anything from him that I don't already have in spades. He's the one here with something to lose.

"I know it doesn't count for shit, but I thought about you all the damn time. Still do," says Caspar quietly. "I'd like a chance to get to know you."

I lean back on my stool. I don't know if I believe him, but he came all this way, and came as himself this time. I can give him the benefit of the doubt.

"What do you want to know?" I ask.

His cheeks get ruddy, his chin lowering. "Hell," he says self-consciously. "This sounds nuts, but it's like—I just got stage fright."

Maybe he was just nervous. I knew Mackenzie was right, but didn't know just how right until now.

I push my plate toward him. "We could start with how to make pancakes," I tell him. "I wouldn't feed these to the pigeons."

"Well, shit." He laughs. "All right. Show me how it's done."

We pull out ingredients. He asks questions. He listens. He brags about himself plenty, but there's something endearing in it. I get the sense he wants to impress me. If not with his ability to use a pan, then everything else.

Over the next hour we talk about the bakery and odd jobs we had as teenagers. We one-up each other over who's done more embarrassing shit onstage. We talk about how he met my mom, and how I met Lizzie. But mostly, we talk about Ben.

"Fucking wild," he marvels.

The fridge is so littered with photos and invitations that it takes me a moment to figure out which one he's looking at. It's a picture from Ben's last birthday, a big picnic in the park. Ben is standing on my feet and holding my hands, making me walk for him. Lizzie and Kara are on either side of us, laughing. All of our moms are huddled over the birthday cake on the picnic table, helping set up the candles, interrupted by blurs of little cousins running around with the balloon animals Divya and Rob attempted to make.

"Yeah," I say. "Ben's got plenty of fans, too."

I brace myself. Caspar might want to meet him, and I'm not sure if we'll ever be ready for that. But Caspar's still staring at the photograph, his eyes misty.

"I always thought—this kind of thing wasn't in the cards, for people like us," he says. "You know. The normal shit. The good shit."

He turns to me abruptly, and settles his hands on my shoulders. It's awkward, but heartfelt. Like he's so used to touching people out of obligation that he has no idea how to do it out of love.

"I know I've got no right to say it, but I'm proud of you. Not for the music shit. But for this," he says, tilting his head at the fridge. "Knowing what was important before it was too damn late."

He looks so lost when I meet his eyes, like he's hoping I'll help him find himself. Like I'm the only one who has the power to tell him he's wrong.

Like I'm the one who needs to take care of *him*.

I come to a quiet understanding, then. Caspar and I will never be like a father and a son. But if I let the idea of that go, maybe there's something else worth holding on to that we don't know the shape of yet.

This time when I say we'll stay in touch, I mean it. This time when he hugs me goodbye, it's gruff and stilted, but leaves a real warmth behind. This time when he leaves, I don't feel anything but an unexpected peace.

I spent my whole life terrified of becoming a man like my dad. I'll never be able to undo the years I didn't know about Ben, but for the first time I can forgive myself for it. It took seeing the regret of a man who lost too many chances with me to be grateful for the lifetime of chances I still have with Ben.

I won't take a single moment of that for granted. I'll never be perfect. But there will never be one damn day of that boy's life that he doesn't know how much I love him, or that he doubts that I will always, *always* be there.

chapter twenty-four
MACKENZIE

One glimpse of the door to the Hole is all it takes for me to feel sad, horny, and spooked all at the same time.

The ominously named broom closet remains perfectly preserved in the back of Lightning Strike, along with everything in it—two rickety folding chairs, a flickering lightbulb hanging from the ceiling, some dusty shelves holding bar glasses that are older than I am. The Hole was a catchall kind of place. You went in to either squabble or hook up with someone or cry. In a city where we'd get recognized on every corner, it was the perfect place to hide.

Which is why it's only fitting that Sam and I are meeting here after the circus of this week.

When I open the door, Sam is already waiting in the dim yellow light. He gathers me up so easily that it feels like coming home after a long trip. I breathe in that smoky sunshine smell of him, pressing my cheek into the soft cotton of his shirt.

"Are you okay?" I ask.

He kisses the top of my head. "Better now," he says. His voice is rough in that way it was when we were getting ping-ponged all over Europe at the height of a tour.

I lift my chin to get a better look at him, but he kisses me, slow and deep. I can't help but savor it. I've missed him more in these past two days than I did in the two years we weren't speaking. Now that I'm not hiding from the way I feel about him, it's all-encompassing. Like a seed inside me that's been waiting for years to fully bloom.

Sam's eyes are on mine as we pull apart, bruised with exhaustion. I reach for his jaw and he leans his head into my touch.

"Caspar went back home?" I ask.

Sam nods against my hand, then puts his own hand on top of it, grazing his lips across my knuckles. We've been talking on the phone and texting, mostly to check in on Ben or do our best to stay on the label's time frame. It's how I know Caspar dropped in this morning, and that he and Sam had something closer to the talk Sam had expected in Boston.

And how we know that the label wants our last song by the end of the weekend. Hence, the Hole. The place where we accidentally wrote our first song all those years ago will be the place we write the album's last.

"He's lucky you handled it well," I say.

Sam hums, letting my hand go. "Speaking of," he says, "seems like you and Serena are good."

Thunder Hearts made headlines of our own yesterday. Hannah and I took to social media to call out Tick Tune with Serena, and even revived the old Thunder Hearts accounts to do it there, too. And just in case that didn't give the posts enough momentum, a fan filmed the three of us walking on the street.

We were only meeting up with Rocket, who is putting his free-lancing skills to the test helping us generate a new website, and

Grayson, who's been so diligent about looking into class action options for artists affected by the sale that he's with Hannah nearly every time I call. But by the way fans lost it seeing the three of us side by side in our signature colors—me in pink, Serena in yellow, and Hannah in blue—you'd think we'd been photographed walking without helmets on the moon.

"Yeah," I say. "Things are better, at least."

Serena's still got her guard up. But the more we work together on this, the more glimpses of the old Serena I start to see. The one who lets me in. The one who lets me *help*.

The plan for now is that if Tick Tune doesn't fold, I'll upload one last "song" as Seven—one directing listeners to a website where anonymous artists can preserve their old Tick Tune stats and songs, while still keeping their identities private. Unlike Tick Tune, the stats will be public, so artists who *do* want to come forward have a much better shot of pitching themselves.

It's not foolproof. There's a good chance people will start digging about Seven, and it'll only be a matter of time before they trace it to me. But Grayson thinks we might kick up enough of a stir threatening legal action before then that it might not even come to that. The app is still "glitching." At this point they must be too scared of what artists will do if they push it live again.

"Seven's probably pissed," says Sam, smirking. "No way in hell she doesn't try and crush us now."

I swallow hard. Now that Sam's standing in front of me, so weary and relieved, I'm glad I haven't said anything to him about this mess. The last thing I want to do is give him another *what if* to worry about.

Sam must catch the flicker in my expression. I make sure it's gone by the time I meet his eye.

"Well then," I say. "I guess we're going to have to write a song good enough to kick her ass."

Sam eases his guitar off himself. I pull out my notepad, using my phone light to see better.

"Aw," I say, pressing my thumb to the doorframe. My handiwork is still on the wall in metallic silver ink: *crappy shard was here.* Sam's black Sharpie ink is crossed over it, writing *blunder hearts* below it instead.

"I'll chalk that up to one too many drinks," I say wryly.

Sam comes up behind me, chest grazing my shoulder. "I wasn't drunk that night," says Sam.

My ears burn. "Me neither," I say.

Not for lack of trying. I was attempting my third shot of Fireball at the old dive bar when Sam reached over my head, plucked it out of my hand, and took the shot himself. I pulled in a breath to tell him off, but Sam put a palm on my forehead like he was holding off an angry terrier.

"I don't get paid enough to watch you vomit glitter onstage," he said.

Hannah swiped whatever drink he just ordered from the bar and handed it to me. "She's got booze immunity for the night. She and Cal broke up."

Cal was the man who would become song number six. The one who didn't just make promises, but stuck around long enough for me to believe them. Who didn't even bother leaving when he let them fall apart, so I had to call it off myself.

It was hard to see much in the dim light of that bar, but impossible to miss the flicker of surprise in Sam's eyes. He cleared his throat.

"Tough break, Sparkles," he said.

I rolled my eyes, sipping his drink. "Oh, fuck off. You hated him."

"Says who?" said Sam.

That's when it hit me. Sam roasted my other exes like my love life was a damn barbecue, but in all the months I'd been dating Cal, he hadn't said a word. There was nothing wrong with Cal, really, except that he didn't care about me.

There was nothing wrong with him *except* for me.

I went straight to the Hole after that. I closed the door and waited for the tears to come. But there was just—nothing. Like I'd spent so long pretending everything was fine that I didn't know how to feel it anymore. All I felt was numb.

Then the door opened, and there was Sam.

"Jesus, you move fast," I said. "Make sure to lock the damn door this time."

But there was no pretty girl lingering behind Sam as I pushed my way out. Instead, Sam caught me by the wrist.

"Hannah said you went home, but I didn't see you leave."

I stared down at his hand, bewildered. "Congratulations," I said, shaking myself loose. "You won hide and seek."

But Sam didn't move. "You heading home?"

I didn't want to. Home wasn't *home* yet. I needed to strip the sheets. Needed to box up some records and ratty sweatpants and baseball caps. Needed to get rid of an extra toothbrush.

"No," I said. "I've got shit to do."

I walked back into the Hole and shut the door in Sam's face. Or at least, I tried. He stopped it with his foot.

"My drink's in there," he said, nodding at the untouched glass.

I held it out to him. "Here."

His eyes grazed the drink before settling back on me. "Could be poisoned, knowing you," he said. "You take a sip first."

I did. I meant to be a brat about it and drain the whole thing, but I didn't hate myself enough.

"*Fuck*, that's awful."

"Well, that's no way to drink perfectly good sewer water." He took it from me, his lanky, leather-clad form looming large as he eased himself onto one of the seats. "Stay put and I'll show you how it's done."

I crossed my arms. "If you think I need a pity hookup right now, you're out of luck. Go try the bar."

"Can't," said Sam, knocking back half the drink. "Everyone cleared out. So you might as well tell me what the *shit* is that you're doing."

I did the fastest thing I could to get rid of him—I lied.

"I'm writing a song."

Sam made a show of making himself comfortable. "Well, don't let me get in your way."

At that point I had no choice but to sit down, if I wanted to stake my claim on the space. "You're the competition."

Sam let out a laugh, leaning down to meet my eye. "We're rivals, Sparkles. But you're no competition."

"True," I said, without missing a beat. "You're not much of anything when I write you under the table."

His eyes flickered, a challenge in them. "You write shiny pop anthems."

I was unused to having Sam's full attention offstage. I didn't know if I liked it, but I couldn't help wanting to keep it. Having his eyes on me felt like catching a firefly in my hand.

"Oh, and your sad emo songs are the *height* of taste," I said right back.

Sam abruptly leaned in closer. "Say what you want, but you couldn't write one if you tried. You're all glitz and no grit."

"You're all punk and no damn fun," I countered.

Sam skimmed his tongue over his teeth, and said two words that changed the course of our lives forever. "Wanna bet?"

We wrote "Play You by Heart" in under an hour, but stayed in the Hole until the sun came up. We talked more in that night than we had since we first met. Me about my exes, Sam about his dad. Things we'd done and things we'd hope to do. Things I hadn't told anyone, because I'd just never thought to say them out loud.

At the time I chalked it up to the Hole. It was a space where nothing counted, so of course that talk didn't, either. Only now that I'm staring into the eyes of that same man after all this time do I know the truth: even then, I was falling for him. I loved him long before I could give the thought room to grow.

When I turn my head back to look at him, those same eyes glint with mischief. His fingers skim my waist, pulling me in so my back is against his chest.

"The rest of Candy Shard was convinced we hooked up that night," he says, close to my ear.

I lean my weight against him. "And what did you tell them?"

He presses his lips to my temple. That bare touch is enough to make my entire body hum in anticipation.

"That you'd never," he teases.

I turn slowly so we're pressed chest to chest, tilting my chin. He is so solid and warm in my arms that I can't help but breathe in deep, like touch isn't enough. I want every sensation of him. His voice in my ear. His smoky sweetness in my lungs. His fingers digging into the small of my back.

"'Never' is an awfully strong word," I say. "'Not yet' is better."

Sam takes a step that presses me between him and the door. "So you're telling me you never hooked up with anyone in the Hole," he says.

I shake my head. "Not once," I tell him.

His hand skims under the flimsy fabric of my dress, easing up my thigh. "Well, hell," he says. "You've been deprived."

I wrap my arms around his neck. "Not for much longer, I hope."

I gasp as he slides a finger into me, and then another. His eyes stay steady and smug on mine, savoring every second of what he's doing to me as I start to pant.

"The only rule you need to know about the Hole," he says hoarsely, "is that you have to be very, *very* quiet."

He hooks upward, hitting the *precise* spot that makes me whimper.

"Sam," I breathe out, half in praise, half in warning.

His tongue skims his lower lip, his eyes drinking me in.

"What did I just say?" he asks, hooking his fingers deeper, finding a rhythm.

Jesus Christ. I try to hold my breath, but it doesn't work—I let out a keening whine, bucking against his hand. A few more strokes and I am pressing my face into his shirt, trying to muffle myself. Damn impossible when he's using his teeth to graze my earlobe, using his lips.

"You know how I love breaking rules," he says, voice rough with desire. "I want to hear you come."

I shake my head, crushing my eyes shut and holding my breath again, but I can't resist it. Not the crest of pleasure that comes with every curl of his finger, not his voice crooning, "That's my girl," in my ear. It sends a possessive thrill through me—I am his, and he is *mine*.

After all these years, I am staking my claim. It's loud and shameless, a cry that would rattle the whole damn bar if it was open for the night.

When it's over I ease back against the door, boneless and satisfied.

I can taste Sam's self-satisfied smirk as he pulls me in by the back of the neck, his touch firm and his kiss rough.

I'm still panting, electrified, as I reach for his belt buckle. But Sam pulls back, shaking his head.

"Let me," I plead. I can feel how hard he is. I'm *aching* to feel more.

He presses another kiss to my lips, soft and fierce. "Patience," he says. "We've got deadlines, don't we?"

I snake my arms up his back, pressing my fingers into the hard planes of his shoulders. "You can't do *that* to me and not let me return the favor."

Sam laughs. I feel the warm rumble of it against my own chest.

"If you wanna repay the favor—let me break one more of your rules."

I raise my eyebrows at him. "You bad boys just don't know when to quit," I tease.

But Sam doesn't laugh. He lifts a hand to my face and holds me there, his thumb skimming my cheek. In all the time I've been alive, I've never been looked at like this before. Like I am not just wanted, but fully, wholly known.

When he speaks, his voice is softer than I've ever heard it.

"We said no love songs," he says. "But I think that's gonna be a problem for me, Mackenzie. Right now, it's the only kind I can write."

He swims in front of me, but I cling to him like an anchor. I swallow hard.

"What if—something got in the way of us?" I manage.

It takes a moment for Sam to answer. "Of Mack and Sam?" he asks.

I shake my head against his palm, my voice wobbly. "Of *us*," I say.

Because if this is the anchor, the world outside is a brewing storm.

Sam's nightmares about Ben coming to life. My looming secret that was never meant to be one. And the two ordinary truths that loom larger than anything else: Sam has never been in love enough to stay, and I have never been good at staying loved.

Sam lifts his other hand so he's cupping my face between them, so I have to meet his eyes.

"For all we know, this whole thing could crash and burn," he says. "But you listen to me right now. No matter what happens with this—with *anything*—it's not gonna change the way I feel about you. You have to know that. Tell me you do."

I let out a hiccupping breath. It's so much more than the relief of hearing it. It's years of wondering what it would be like to feel loved enough that I don't have to question it, and knowing now that it feels like *this*. Like sinking into the arms of someone who has seen every part of me and loves the whole.

I used to think I'd never trust words like that again. It turns out it's easy to, when the right person says them. It turns out everything is easier, when that person is Sam.

"I know," I say. "I feel the same."

We don't write a love song that afternoon, but make it, slow and sweet. We hold each other for a long time in the quiet that comes after. It strikes me that I've been spending my whole life trying to put love into words, but now I know what it sounds like—it's the beat of Sam's heart against mine. It's his warm breath of relief against my neck. It's the silence between two people who understand each other well enough not to need any words at all.

chapter twenty-five
SAM

I'm no stranger to embarrassment. When you're in a punk rock band it's part of the job description. I've burped mid-song. Stuck my foot in it during interviews. Even mooned half of Madison Square Garden trying to pull off baggy pants.

But my son figuring out how to open my Voice Notes app while I'm stuck in Lincoln Tunnel traffic might take the damn cake.

"That's you!" Ben pipes from the back.

It's all terrible lyric ideas that should never see the light of day, but like any parent, I know if I flinch, he'll only want to hear it more. Sure enough, he skips ahead—straight to the quick recording I made in the park after that night in Boston with Mackenzie, and then to the one where I tried it with a guitar at home.

I say something then that I haven't said in all my years of fatherhood. "Want me to turn on Thunder Hearts?"

"Noooo," Ben protests. "I wanna hear this."

Damn. That was the one and only card I had up my sleeve.

"It's not finished," I warn.

Ben turns it up. "I don't care."

And then Ben does something *he* hasn't done in all my years of fatherhood—he goes completely, utterly silent for a full three minutes. We're fully in New Jersey by the time the recording stops, and I can feel Ben's curious eyes on me in the passenger mirror.

"Is this one of the songs you're doing with Mackenzie?" he asks.

"Nah," I tell him. "Just something I'm playing with."

Ben's brow furrows like he wants to say something, but can't puzzle out how. "I think she'd like it," he decides.

"That's what I'm hoping," I say. "I wrote it based on one of her songs."

Ben's face lights up. "Like how Mackenzie said she wrote some of the first Thunder Hearts songs trying to be like you?"

I bite down a smile. "Did she say that?" I ask.

When I catch Ben's face again, it's red enough to rival a tomato. "That was supposed to be a secret," he says.

I try not to laugh, but the way he's wiggling like a criminal in his booster seat is making it hard. "*That's* the big secret she told you?"

His head bobs guiltily. "She said that's why I should listen to more Candy Shard," he says.

My throat goes tight. I've never minded if Ben doesn't like my music, or anything I like, for that matter. But knowing Mackenzie is the one responsible for Ben singing snippets of Candy Shard songs like a pocket-sized punk these past few weeks makes my chest warm.

"You can't tell her I told you," Ben adds quickly.

I wink at him in the mirror. "I won't," I promise.

Even if I weren't a dad of my word, Mackenzie and I don't have the time to spare. We're running up so close on the deadline for the last song that when I told Mackenzie I was dropping Ben off in New Jersey for his cousin's birthday party, she sent me a screenshot of the address to Hannah's lake party a few miles away. Turns out I *did* score that invite in the end.

It's anybody's guess how much writing I'll be able to do with Mackenzie in a swimsuit drinking one of those cherry-flavored drinks that turn her lips all red, but miracles happen every day.

We arrive at Kara's sister's place a half hour later, where cousins from all sides of Kara's and Lizzie's families are tearing through the backyard. I open the car door for Ben, who spills out with his backpack full of baked goods from Sugar Harmony and sunscreen and baseball cards.

"You'll let me listen to the song again when it's done?" he asks.

I ruffle his hair.

"You bet," I tell him. "Your moms are coming by in a few hours after they drop off that wedding cake, but I'll be home when you get back tonight. Love you."

"Love you, too, Dad."

I wave at the aunts as they collect him. I'm plugging in directions to Hannah's lake house when a bunch of Tick Tune notifications pop up on my screen. The app is back, and the name Seven is at the top under the list of artists who have new songs up.

Guess I was right about her working with the app, then. No doubt she goes public first thing tomorrow morning. Good luck to her, whoever she is—it's going to be rough launching a career when half of Tick Tune's artists have it out for her.

I hit "play" as I pull out of the driveway. Three minutes later, I'm a goddamn wreck.

"Jesus," I mutter. Maybe it's for the best that you can only listen to a song once a day. This new one is beautiful, but sad enough to make Mary Poppins drive into a ditch. The kind of sad that makes me wonder if it needs to get cleared by the FDA.

Maybe we won't know who Seven is until the sale goes through tomorrow, but this much I already know: Whoever she wrote the song "Last" about broke her heart so bad that it's about to break anyone who listens right along with it. It's devastating. It's transcendent. It makes me hope that after she finished it, she put a hit on the guy she wrote it about.

I pull up Ben's Thunder Hearts playlist to shake the despair out of the car. I'm still playing it on full blast with the windows down when I roll up to Hannah's lake house.

Mackenzie's sitting on the railing of the deck, wearing a bright pink bikini that glitters in the sunlight. She bounds up when she spots the car, her lips stained red from her drink and her hair blown out from the humidity. She looks sweet enough to take a bite out of and wild enough to let me.

I stop the car and she leans into the window, smelling like cherries and sunscreen. She lowers her sunglasses, her eyes sparking with delight when I almost lean in and kiss her. It's such a reflex already that it feels like highway robbery when I can't.

"Can't" might be an exaggeration. But we don't know everyone here. Better not to risk any rumors about us when we haven't been an *us* long enough to talk about it.

Although it's hard to remember anything we should talk about, the way that bikini top seems one light gust away from sliding off her shoulders.

"Nice tunes," she says. "But aren't they a little too *sparkly* for you?"

Nobody can see us from this angle, so I slide my finger under one of her glittering bikini straps. "Turns out I'm a big fan of sparkles."

She leans in closer, licking the flavor off her lips. "Good. Because if I get my way, they're about to be all over you."

I'm already too riled up for my own damn good by the time I

park the car. I jack up the volume on "Neon Love" right at the part where Mackenzie lets out a belt powerful enough to wake the dead. Sure enough, half the patio is looking over at us now.

Mackenzie clearly hasn't noticed, because her fingers are digging into the back of my shirt before she's fully pulled me in for a hug.

"You're lucky I can't make that sound anymore," she says, "or you might be hearing it right in your ear later."

"Well, damn. That's a challenge if I ever heard one." She feels like sunshine against my skin. I just barely resist the urge to lift her up from the ground and into a kiss. "But funny thing is—I do miss hearing you sing those songs."

Mackenzie stiffens. "Well," she says.

I ease back. "I've got something for you," I say.

She raises her brows. I give her ass a playful squeeze low enough so the patio gawkers can't see, then turn back to my car to grab the beaten-up folder in the front. It's the one I used to keep on the floor of the stage with our setlist in it during shows. She tilts her head as I hand it to her.

"Open it," I say.

She does. I watch as she pores over the old songs, suddenly self-conscious as her finger traces the notes I left by them. New chords and patterns. A few notes in the margins—*slower bridge?* and *try with piano.*

She looks at them so long and so silently that I'm damn near sweating when she looks up at me, her cheeks bright pink, her eyes sparkling.

"Did you—" she manages, before letting out a breathy laugh. "Sam, did you rearrange all my old songs so I could sing them again?"

"It's a work in progress," I admit. "I haven't heard enough of your voice yet to know if I did any good."

Mackenzie's eyes drift between me and the folder and back to me again, her lips parted, her expression unreadable.

"You don't have to try it if you don't—"

The rest of the words are cut off by Mackenzie leaning in and kissing me so deeply, so resolutely, that I kiss back on instinct. To hell with it. We know everyone here, and I spent too many years resisting her not to give in to every inch of her now.

When she pulls back, she digs her fingers into the back of my shoulders. "Thank you," she says.

She's so close to tears that I give her hips a little squeeze. "Well, you told me some of those lyrics were secretly about me," I say. "Be a downright shame if you weren't still singing them just because they weren't in your range."

She steps back from me, twisting a finger under the strap of her bikini. The way the light is hitting her every curve makes it look like the sun was just put there so she could shine in it.

"Well, then we better go find some place where we can test it," she says, eyes sparking with mischief. "I'm going to put this in my car and come find you so we can—*rehearse*."

It's a good thing everyone else is already tipsy, because I can't wipe the grin off my face to save my life. I drop off the baked goods Lizzie and Kara sent me with, stopping to talk to old friends from our touring days. I wander out to the pool, where there's a huge spread of food from one of Hannah's parents' restaurants that Grayson is helping restock while her sisters tease him for wearing neon-blue swim trunks from Hannah's line.

I don't spot Mackenzie, but I don't see Serena or Hannah, either. I decide to wait before I call so I don't interrupt anything, but as I head back into the house to find a bathroom, I hear them. They're in a room at the end of a hall, and Mackenzie sounds so panicked that I head toward the door on autopilot.

"But I deleted it," she insists. "How the hell did it go live?"

"Did you delete it?" Hannah asks carefully. "Or did you just unschedule it?"

Her voice is so cautious that I stop before I reach them. They don't want to be overheard. But I can't just leave when Mackenzie's next words sound like she just ran a marathon.

"I—I don't know," she says. "Why?"

Serena's the one who answers. "Tick Tune was down because they were preserving all the songs before people deleted them. When the app restarted, it didn't just restore them all. It pushed everyone's drafts live, too."

I'm at the edge of the door now, completely still as my head spins itself in circles trying to process.

"So your seventh song went live," says Hannah.

The rush in my head stops, snagging on those two words: *seventh song.*

"No. An early version of it went live," says Mackenzie miserably. "The video that had one of Hannah's pieces in the frame."

"But it's deleted now, right?" Hannah asks.

"Probably not fast enough," says Serena grimly.

"Fuck," says Mackenzie. *"Fuck."*

Serena is sympathetic, but firm. "Take a breath. We were going to have Seven go public as a last resort anyway," she says. "We'll just pretend this was intentional. I'll get Isla on the phone right now."

It feels like I'm underwater. I've heard the words. I know what they mean. I just can't make them real.

"Yeah." Mackenzie's voice is dazed. "But first I have to tell Sam."

It's the way she says my name that makes it snap into place. Mackenzie doesn't hate Seven. Mackenzie isn't worried about competing with Seven.

Mackenzie *is* Seven. She has been this whole time.

"Sam still doesn't know?" Serena asks.

"It's been so crazy," says Mackenzie. "I didn't want to tell unless there was something *to* tell."

There's a pause long enough that I think they'll head for the door. I step back, then think better of it. I have no idea how the hell to process all this, but this much I know: the rest of the world is not going to wait for me to figure it out. If Mackenzie thinks she's been exposed as Seven, there isn't a second to waste on deciding what to do next.

"Well, there probably is now," says Serena. "Are you going to get him?"

When Mackenzie speaks again, she's so quiet I can barely make it out.

"It's the song. I wrote it before Sam and I started working together. If he knows it's me, he'll figure out it's about him."

Next thing I know I'm headed for the closest door that gets me outside. I run both hands through my hair, leaning against the wall at the back of the house, breathing hard.

I did this. I'm the guy she should have put the hit on. I'm the guy who made her write "Last."

I spent years trying not to hurt her. I was goddamn *smug* about how many years I resisted temptation, about how I'd never be like the men who broke her heart. And it turns out I'm such a fuckup that I hurt her more than any of those assholes combined.

The worst part is that even after all this, Mackenzie couldn't bring herself to tell me. Not about the heartbreak. Not about the song.

And not about this entire side of herself she's been hiding behind the whole time.

My phone rings in my pocket. It's Lizzie. She's talking before I can say a word.

"It's Ben," she says. "How fast can you get back to the house?"

Everything else falls away in an instant. I yank my keys out of my pocket and run.

chapter twenty-six

MACKENZIE

There are no two words more perilously at odds with each other than "if" and "when." "If" can fill you up with false hope or false dread. "If" is an infinite number of ways a scenario can shake out, in or out of your favor.

"When" is a hammer drop. There's no undoing it once it lands.

Right now, I am stuck between the two. Nobody has tracked the deleted video back to me. But there are screenshots of it all over the internet. It's only a matter of time.

"I thought you were okay with this," says Serena.

It's just the two of us in the reading room now, a cozy space on the first floor of the lake house with wide windows and built-in window seats, bookshelves, and a pillowy blue couch. We sent Hannah back out to the party. She was reluctant to leave, but technically nothing's happened yet. There's still a chance nothing will happen at all.

But not a likely one. I sink onto the couch, pressing my palms to my face. "That song was never meant to go live."

"Last" is scathing. Unfair, even. I poured all of my hurt into it because there was no place else for it to go. Not just because I was too proud to admit that I'd fallen for him, but because I knew, deep down, I couldn't blame him for it. Sam was a lot of things back in the day—reckless and cocky and a pain in my ass—but he was honest with me from the very start.

"Are you two together?" Serena asks.

I give her a bare nod. "Yeah."

She clears her throat. "He's changed, then?" she asks.

I glance up warily, but there's no trace of judgment in her eyes. "We both have," I say.

She's quiet for a moment. "Well. He'll understand, then. He's an artist, too."

Some of the tightness in my chest finally eases up. She's right. It doesn't make the guilt disappear, but it helps with some of the fear.

I know Sam isn't looking for an easy out like so many others did, once they were bored of the chase. But I can't turn off that anxious voice in my head. The one that reminds me this would be the *perfect* out if he was.

Because not only is Sam going to figure out the song is about him, but the rest of the world will, too. I know all too well how it could play out. Poor Mackenzie Waters, America's perpetually tragic sweetheart—versus Sam Blaze, a former bad boy too easy to turn into a villain.

Serena sits next to me and does something she hasn't done in ages, and did rarely even back in the day. She wraps an arm around my shoulders and presses me to her. It's stilted and awkward. But it means more coming from her than the perfect hug from anyone else would.

"The rest of it will be fine," she says. "We planned for this possibility. Isla will be surprised, but she's trained to handle things like this."

I let myself take my first full breath in an hour. "Thanks."

She squeezes my shoulder. "I know I've been—" She stops short. "Distant," she says. "But I'll always have your back."

I close my eyes. I don't know if that's true. I know in my heart that Serena would do anything she could to protect me from the rest of the world. But there's not much in this world that would feel as hurtful or personal as the way Serena has pushed me out of her life.

"Serena," I say carefully. "Why are you delaying the tour?"

I feel her chest go still against mine. After a moment she says in a quiet voice, "Why are you so worried about it?"

"Because I love you," I say, without hesitating. "Because *I'll* always have your back."

She pulls her arm back, setting her hands in her lap and staring down at them. "I've been awful to you."

It's the last thing I'm expecting her to say. It's not an apology or an explanation, but it's a relief to hear it. To know the hurt wasn't just in my head.

I nudge my shoulder into hers. "We've both had our moments. But you and me—we're each other's family. The one we chose."

I don't have to go any deeper than that for her to know what I mean. My relationship with my parents might feel hollow sometimes, but hers is transactional. They were treating Serena like an ATM even before we made it big. The money she supports them with is drops in a bucket now, but I know that doesn't make it hurt any less, that their love comes with an agenda.

Still, I'm not expecting the way she starts to shake.

"I can do all this on my own. But I just—didn't think the pressure would be so different, when it wasn't all three of us." She lets out a breathy laugh. "So many people's careers depend on strangers *liking* me."

I try not to sound too surprised, but I can't help it. "People love you," I insist.

Serena shakes her head sharply. "You know how it goes. They love the idea of me. And that's fine. It's easy to be in control of an idea. I was so good at being in control of everything in Thunder Hearts that I thought it would be *easier* when I was just doing it alone."

She pulls in a shaky breath, her fingers curling and uncurling.

"It turns out it was you two who made things easy. Hannah kept everything so calm, and you were always a natural. You didn't need people to love an idea of you. They already loved *you*."

Serena's words from Hannah's launch flash back to me: *You got to be the fun, messy one that everyone loved.* I chalked it up to her trying to get a rise out of me. I didn't realize it went so deep, but maybe I should have. Serena has always been so particular about the way she's perceived.

"They just liked me because they thought I was a mess," I remind her wryly. "I didn't want people to see me that way. And I know deep down you don't, either."

Serena swallows hard. "The funny thing is, deep down I don't want anything. I don't care if people like me. But I know what happens if they don't. There's so much money on the line. So many people depending on me. Not just my family now, but the label, and the crew, and these *kids*—" Her eyes well up fast. "The ones who have been opening for me. Every single one of them took that shit contract. They're all tied up in it."

She puts a hand to her chest, as if she's anticipating the hives before they come. There's an ache in her face that I recognize. It's the same guilt I'm feeling right now.

But I knew what might happen if I lied about Seven. Serena was only doing what she does best: trying to help.

I know she doesn't want to hear it, but I say it anyway. "It wasn't your fault, what happened to Rocket and the others."

Serena is shaking her head before I can get the words out. "It was," she insists. "I thought I was right. I always do. And I bullied him into taking that deal, the same way I bullied you into trying to do that duet with me, because I just—always think I'm *right* about everything." Her eyes well up. "But all I did was hurt people."

Her voice cracks, and then the rest of her does. Silent tears stream down her face. She blinks, stunned at herself, but doesn't stop. Instead, she looks to me like she's lost, and doesn't know what to say next, or how to say it. Like she's looking for that wavelength we used to share, and can't find it anymore.

But I will. For so long I've been worried about saying something that might push Serena away. Instead, I tiptoed and let things slide, and it let this tension between us go on so long that it almost finished us. If I don't want it to happen again, I have to tell her the truth.

"You pushing for the duet didn't hurt me," I say. "The way you pushed me away did."

Serena closes her eyes. "I never meant to hurt you," she chokes out.

"I know," I say easily. "Because I know you. And I think you were doing it to hurt yourself."

She pulls in a shuddering breath, but it still takes her a few moments to collect herself enough to speak.

"I was angry about the way things were," she says. "Things that weren't your fault, but—things you didn't have to deal with anymore, so I felt angry at you, and then angry at myself for feeling that way. So I just—had to avoid you, because that wasn't fair to you, either." She presses her hands to her eyes, shaking her head into them. "I know that sounds crazy."

No, it doesn't. It sounds a hell of a lot like what I did to Sam. I thought I was alone in the way I felt for him, so I pulled back hard and fast before he could see how much it hurt. Before he could think *I* was crazy for feeling that deeply at all.

"You can just tell me stuff like that," I tell Serena. "After all the shit we've been through, we passed 'crazy' a long time ago."

Serena doesn't laugh. Instead, she holds my gaze, blinking back another round of tears, and says, "I'm so sorry."

I don't need her to say it. I felt it a long time ago. I felt it before she was willing to admit anything was wrong at all.

But I nod and tell her, "I'm sorry, too."

I should have checked in more. If anyone was going to see the hairline fractures before Serena cracked, it was me. But I was so wrapped up in my own feelings that I buried myself in them, one song at a time.

It clicks, then—the real crux of this tension. Serena has always avoided her pain by trying to fix everyone else's. I held on to my pain as if it could protect me from taking on any more of it. We were so at odds that it was only a matter of time before we hit a breaking point.

These past two years have been a seismic shift between us, but all the love is still there. We may spend our lives pushing up against each other, changing each other for the better, but we will always find our way back to this.

Serena puts her head on my shoulder, and I wrap my arms around her.

"They haven't rescheduled the tour dates yet," I remind her gently. "If you want to do it, you can. But if you aren't sure, this is the best time to call it off."

Serena's throat bobs. "If I stop, Rocket and the others won't have anywhere to perform. They won't get enough buzz to get new contracts after they get released."

"You know that's not true," I say. "There are plenty of other ways to help them that don't involve you being miserable."

Serena pulls back enough that I can see her face. "Like what?" she asks.

"I don't know yet," I say honestly. "But I do know we'll figure it out together. It's like you said—we'll always have each other's backs. You have to let us have yours, too."

Serena swipes a lone tear off her face. "Thanks," she says wetly.

We sit there and breathe, listening to the happy clamor of the party outside. No matter what happens with Tick Tune, I'm grateful that it brought us here—back to each other, where we belong. The three of us learned to love each other in the whirlwind of Thunder Hearts, but it's the aftermath of it where we'll get to see all the ways that love grows.

After a few minutes Serena straightens her spine, taking a breath.

"I'll call Isla," she says. "You should go find Sam before anything happens."

I let her go, the pit in my stomach already starting to drop. I have no idea how to tell him about Seven, but there's no time to think about it. He deserves to hear it from me before he hears it from anyone else.

I step outside, scanning the party for Sam. But it's not the same party I left an hour ago, when everyone was clamoring for seconds of the food and belting eighties hits with the karaoke mic. Now it's just eerily quiet, and every pair of eyes is staring at the door.

No. Staring at me.

It's Rocket who darts forward, grabbing me by the arm, eyes comically wide. "It's all over the internet. I swear I didn't say anything. I *swear*."

And just like that, the *if* becomes a *when*.

chapter twenty-seven
SAM

When the news about Seven breaks, I'm the last person in New York to hear it. I'm too relieved to have Ben in one piece in the back seat of the car to process anything else. He's going to have some ugly bruises on his left arm from his incident on the Slip 'N Slide in the backyard, but according to the doctors at the ER, nothing's broken.

Nothing other than every damn nerve in my body, but that comes with the territory.

Ben is in high spirits when we make it back to New Jersey, thanks to all the attention from three panicking parents, and the Happy Meal we got him on the way home. But my heart is still beating like a battering ram. I don't take my eyes off him for a damn second until he's gone to sleep, and even then, all three of us stand outside the door like we're keeping guard.

"Is it legal to Bubble Wrap a kid for eighteen years?" I ask.

We all let out quiet, exhausted laughs, but I'm not kidding. That call scared the shit out of me. I'll do anything it takes not to get one like it again.

Lizzie picks my phone up from the counter. "I sent Mackenzie a text to let her know Ben was okay on the way home, but you've got a lot of missed calls."

Shit. The rest of the world starts seeping in like a draft under the door. That gutting song. Mackenzie's secret. The shock and guilt I didn't even have time to process before Lizzie's call hit me like a brick.

I open Mackenzie's texts first: Did you leave? Call me when you get a chance, says the first one. The missed calls come after that. Then a second text: I'm so relieved Ben is okay. I can't even imagine. Don't worry about anything else, we're taking care of it.

She doesn't say anything about Seven, but a quick Google search tells me the rest of the world is:

**Seven Is Already Someone Famous—
And You Definitely Know Her Name**

**All The Embarrassingly Obvious
Connections Between Mackenzie Waters
And "Seven" We Missed**

Mackenzie! Waters! Is! Seven!!!!!

I'm about to call her, but there's a knock at the door on Dad Side. I cross over to open it fast, but it's not Mackenzie on the other end. It's Twyla in a bright green ensemble, sporting a grim expression and a bottle of scotch.

Her eyes narrow when they meet mine. "Did you know about Seven?" she asks.

"No," I say. "You didn't?"

She lets out a bark of a laugh, letting herself in. "Damn. Can't believe that kid pulled a fast one like that on me *and* my sister. Isla's a shark."

I'm too damn tired to think of a better way to ask. "So why are you here?"

Her answer is to prop the scotch on the counter, tapping the cap so I'll undo the plastic and she won't mess up her nails.

"Well," she says.

My hand stops over the bottle. "Mackenzie's not in trouble, is she?"

Twyla blinks at me. "No," she says slowly. "But you and I— we've got to come up with a game plan here."

I pop the cork off. "It's been a crazy day. Can it wait until tomorrow?"

Twyla is pulling out glasses as if I haven't spoken. "Have you been online?"

"No," I say, pinching the bridge of my nose. Too little, too late. My head's been pounding for hours. At this point the booze can't hurt.

"That last song," says Twyla slowly. "People think it's about you."

I lean against the counter, staring down at the amber in the glasses. *This is the last song I'll ever write about you*, the song starts, before listing all the other *lasts*. The last of her tears. The last of her love. The last of her faith.

The lyrics are subtle, but now that I know the truth, I can trace back every word. It isn't just a song. It's a timeline. A brutal history of the years I spent avoiding her, and the years she spent hiding from me.

All the wasted time I didn't just hurt myself, but hurt her more than I ever knew.

I knock back half my pour. "It is," I tell her.

Twyla takes a sip from her own glass, her eyes on me, waiting for an explanation. But I've got nothing to say. At least, nothing I want to say before talking to Mackenzie.

Eventually Twyla sets the glass back down, blowing out a breath. "No easy way to put this, so here goes," she says. "The label is thinking about putting a stop to Mack and Sam. They want Mackenzie to put all her effort into Seven, this time with them backing her."

I wait for the blow, but at this point there isn't much of me left to hit.

"Good," I hear myself saying. "She deserves that. Hell—we knew from the start I needed her more than she needed me."

Twyla shakes her head sternly. "Don't say that."

"It's the truth," I insist. "Seven is a legend. She should be proud. I know I am."

Twyla's brows lift. This isn't how she expected this conversation to go. It takes her a moment to recover, but I am eerily calm.

"You should be proud of the work you did, too," says Twyla. "The songs you wrote together—they're incredible."

They are, but it doesn't change the truth. If they have to choose between a sure bet they already have and a sure bet they don't, they'll pick the first every time. And Mackenzie isn't just a sure bet. She's a damn star.

Twyla leans into the table sharply, like she's trying to snap me back to attention.

"We'll make a new game plan. See if Mackenzie will be open to letting you use some of the songs you wrote together for your own solo career."

Ah. I see now. Twyla didn't just come here to warn me about Mack & Sam ending. She came here for damage control on my career.

"Nah," I say easily. "I can't go singing those without her."

Twyla blinks. I'm not used to surprising her. It would be funny, on any other day.

"You've got other songs you were working on. Pull those out for me. We'll regroup." She pauses. "After the stuff with Seven dies down."

It's her grimace that clues me in. I let out a sharp laugh. "Shit," I say. "People are out for my blood, huh?"

Twyla doesn't deny it, lifting her glass at me adamantly. "Ignore all that. It's all just internet garbage," she says. "This is just one of those weird chapters in your *very* long career."

But it's not my career I'm worried about. It's the people I love, and all the things I haven't been able to protect them from. I couldn't protect Lizzie from raising Ben without me those first few years. I couldn't protect Ben from my infamy, or even a damn toy in someone's backyard. I couldn't protect Mackenzie from all that heartbreak.

I couldn't protect her from *me*.

Mackenzie calls again after Twyla leaves, but I don't pick up. I already know what she's going to say—that she's determined to keep on with the duo, the label be damned. Her own success be damned.

But she knows there's no world where I let her do that.

I take my scotch and head back over to Mom Side, sitting outside Ben's door. A few hours ago, all this would have felt complicated beyond belief. But right now, everything is simple. My kid is safe. All the people I love are safe. As long as that's true, there's nothing else worth worrying about.

I fall asleep with my head against the door and my heart beating all over my body, terrified and grateful and certain of what I need to do next.

chapter twenty-eight
MACKENZIE

I try not to think about it now, but there was a time between being Mackenzie Waters and being Seven when I wasn't anything at all. Thunder Hearts was over. My voice wasn't my own. And suddenly everything was so—quiet. No color-coded weekly calendars from Serena in my inbox. No more of Hannah's raucous dinners with Thunder Hearts and Candy Shard on the road. No more belted songs, no more roaring crowds, no more *me*. Everything that had defined the beats of my life for years was gone.

Suddenly there was space for too much to crawl back in. The heartbreak. The shame. The losses I never got over, but thought I did because everything was *go, go, go* for so long that there wasn't time to feel anything. You can't see the pain at the bottom of yourself when you're standing at the top of the world.

I didn't realize how bad it was until I came unglued at Serena about the duo idea. After that I went to therapy. I went as far as I could into the ugly parts of myself, trying to pull them back out. But once I had ahold of them, I didn't know how to let them go.

So I turned to the only cure I could think of—I pulled out my guitar. I tried to sing. It wasn't my voice anymore, but it didn't need to be. All it needed to do was *release* me.

I posted to Tick Tune. "Seven," I called myself. A tally of the men who had let me down, and a countdown to when I could finally be free of them.

It worked too damn well. It's been a day since I was unmasked, and now Seven is making headlines all over the internet, and Sam hasn't returned a single damn one of my calls. I'm right back where I started—thrust right back to the top of the world, trying not to look down at the pain below.

On top of the literal world, even. I've been holed up in Serena's high-rise apartment all day. The paparazzi are planted on my sidewalk and all the talk from Isla and the label has been making my head spin, so this was the only place other than the damn Hole I could go to hide. These stolen moments I'm taking up on the roof are the first times I've been able to take a breath all day.

I don't turn when the door to the stairwell opens, expecting Serena. There's a storm coming. She'll want us to get inside before it hits. But then a few seconds pass, and the shift in the air is unmistakable.

It's Sam. Rueful and tired and way too far from me. I want to cross the distance to him, want to bury myself in his worn-out T-shirt and breathe in the burnt honey of him, but I can't. Not when he's staring at me like he's every bit as much at a loss as I am.

I swallow hard, drawing myself up. I will not be weak. I will not put any more of my mess on him. Especially not if he's here to do the one thing I fear most.

"I'm sorry," I tell him.

The words come out steady, but then everything else goes to shit. My eyes well up so fast that Sam is just a blur against the clouded skyline. My body is shaking so hard that I don't feel Sam pull me in until he has his arms around me, holding me to him like a port in a storm.

I shake my head. He can't be the one comforting me right now. But Sam settles a hand on the back of my neck, lightly digging his fingers into my hair to stop me.

"I'm sorry," I say again, "and I'm so glad Ben is all right."

Sam nods against the side of my head. "Scared the hell out of me. But he's already running around like nothing happened."

I have no trouble picturing that. If there's one thing Ben got from Sam, it's toeing that fine line between determined and reckless. My throat goes thick at the thought. Of all the awful things I've considered in the past day of Sam's silence, the idea of not being a part of Ben's life anymore is among the worst.

Sam's voice is a low rumble against my chest, hoarse in my ear. "Why didn't you tell me?"

There were so many times I rehearsed this conversation in my head, but now that it's here, I'm drawing a blank. I don't want to say another word. I want to stay right here in Sam's arms, as if it might be the last time I ever get to be held in them.

But he deserves answers. That's the least I can give.

"I didn't mean to tell anyone about Seven," I say.

Sam's fingers press comfortingly into the back of my neck, weaving into my hair. "I meant about the way you were hurting."

My eyes are still crushed shut against him. I'm afraid if I open them, the tears will spill out.

"That song was never supposed to go live," I say as evenly as I can. "I wrote it before we started working together. It's not how I feel about you."

"But it was how you felt," says Sam quietly.

My fists curl around the back of his shirt. "I couldn't. You knew it, too. You were right to stop anything from happening back then. You needed that time with Ben, and I needed that time to process."

He pulls back just enough to look at my face. I'm right about the tears. They stream down my face, chasing after each other so fast that I can barely see through them. He settles both hands on my cheeks, catching them in the crook of his thumb, staring at me so tenderly that for the first time, I wish he wouldn't. I don't deserve it.

"You snuck up on me," I say as evenly as I can manage. "I would have told you how I felt before the bands broke up. But it just— *happened*, after we wrote that first song together. It was all just bad timing."

The breath Sam pulls in is ragged, his words thick. "It didn't sneak up on me," he confesses. "From the first damn day I was—so in over my head, the way I felt about you. I was trying to do the right thing, staying away. I didn't think I could be what you needed. I didn't get there fast enough." He strokes his thumb on my cheek. "It wasn't bad timing. It was me."

This confession isn't what stuns me from my tears. It's the stark difference between this conversation and too many that I've had just like it. The conversation where something has gone wrong and someone needs to take the blame.

Only now nobody's trying to give it to each other. We're trying to take it on ourselves. The way two people do when they have something neither of them can bear to lose.

I tilt my chin into his touch. "All of that was in the past," I say. "It doesn't matter anymore."

Sam shakes his head sharply. "It *does* matter. *You* matter." He draws me in, touching his forehead to mine. "It kills me thinking I ever let you think anything different. If I'd had any idea, I wouldn't have—"

He stops himself short.

"What?" I prompt him. When he doesn't answer, a chill goes up my spine. "You wouldn't have done Mack and Sam?"

Sam keeps his hands framed on my face as he pulls back. "I'll never regret a moment of that," he says, eyes steady on mine. "But we both know it's got to end."

My blood runs cold. "Don't say that."

"Twyla told me the plan. I think it's a good one," he insists. "You're a once-in-a-lifetime talent, Mackenzie, and you deserve all the success with Seven coming your way."

Sam still hasn't let go, but I put my hands on top of his like I'm scared he might. I need him to hear this. I need him to understand.

"Seven is finished," I tell him. "Everything is deleted. I'm never going to talk about it publicly. I spent the whole day making that clear."

To everyone but Sam, it seems. "You haven't heard them out," he says lowly. "Twyla said the label could use you to advocate for the other Tick Tune artists. You might change your mind. Give it a few days, at least."

Serena and I have done enough digging today to know that's not true about the label, but it isn't worth getting into right now.

"I won't," I say.

Sam tilts my face as I try to look away. The love in his eyes isn't just plain, but burning. Like he's ready to light himself on fire with it.

"I want the whole damn world for you," he says, his voice hoarse. "You've already got it in the palm of your hand. Nobody's stopping you on my watch, least of all me."

I swallow hard. The words he said that night in Boston cut through my panic like a knife: *That woman's either gonna change my life, or end life as I know it.*

He's not the one stopping me. I'm the one stopping *him*.

I stumble back from his touch. His eyes widen, stunned and hurt. I reach out and grab his hands before he can lower them, intertwining our fingers, pulling them to my chest.

"You're not listening to me, Sam. I don't want to be Seven. I never did. From the moment I made her, it was to get *rid* of her," I say, squeezing hard. "I didn't want to live with all that heartbreak anymore, so I let it go. But I don't want to let *you* go."

Sam's eyes search my face, the hurt shifting to bewilderment.

"I'm not going anywhere. You know that, right?" he says. "This isn't me walking away from you. This is me telling you that whatever future we have, Mack and Sam isn't in it."

I shake my head, because this isn't happening. Not after all this. We didn't get past this whole rivalry, past two years of unbearable silence, past these weeks we've spent picking up every broken piece of that past to give up on the future we started building with them.

"We'll show them at the showcase," I tell him. My heart is pounding, the adrenaline a tidal wave in my blood. "I have a whole plan. Or at least an idea of one, but Serena's got Grayson looking at the—"

"I pulled out of the showcase," says Sam.

I drop his hands. The words feel like a collision, and I'm too stunned to figure out how hard I've been hit.

"You what?" I manage.

Sam's eyes search mine, sorry but resolute. "I thought you knew," he says. "They're billing it as a Seven show. The tickets are already on sale."

I knew about the tickets. Serena and I spent the morning negotiating a deal to let Tick Tune artists perform on either side of

Mack & Sam, to get them some exposure and raise awareness about what the app was doing. When they agreed and pushed the tickets live without Sam's name, I just assumed the worst from them. I never dreamed that Sam would give them the okay without telling me first.

The pounding in my heart is so loud now that I can barely hear myself over it.

"Come anyway," I insist. "If we're going to save Mack and Sam, I can't do it without you."

Sam says it so gently this time that I finally believe him. "There isn't a Mack and Sam to save," he says.

Whatever last stitch was keeping me in place comes undone. I pull in an awful, hiccupping breath. It isn't just tears this time, but the mortifying, full-body kind. The kind of tears that feel irrational because you can't fully explain them yet, except this time I can. I've lived this enough times to know how it ends.

Maybe Sam thinks he's just walking away from the music, but it could just be the first step before he walks away from us.

"Please don't do this." I hate myself for what I say next, but I can't help it. "Please don't go."

Here I am again, in a place I never thought I'd be: begging a man to stay. I am my own damn self-fulfilling prophecy. Maybe I didn't have a right to the heartbreak I felt about Sam when I wrote that song, but I will now.

No. This time is different. Sam isn't letting go. I'm the one who pushed him away—one lie, one lyric, one silly *rule* at a time.

This time I've got nobody to blame but myself.

But Sam's arms are around me again, his hands in my hair, his voice warm in my ear. "Hey. I'm not going anywhere. I promise."

I sink into him, but there's no relief. They're only words—so easy to say, so easy to forget. I built a fortress out of the promises people already broke. I let Sam into it, and now I'm terrified I've started a fire that will burn us both from the inside.

Sam draws me tighter into him. "But I'm going to clear out for a little while," he says. "Spend some time in New Jersey with my mom. I need to get out of the city, and you need space to do what you have to do. I would never forgive myself if I got in the way."

My skin feels numb, my thoughts coming to a slow, stunned stop. I believe him. I believe him. I know that I should.

But it feels too much like all the other times I believed, and it hurt twice as much to be let down.

Sam pulls back and presses his lips to mine, and then to my forehead, lingering there. He steps back and searches my face again, waiting for an answer that I can't give. It feels like I've been reading a book only to stumble on the last few pages and realize I've read it before and I already know how terribly it ends.

But I spent two years tearing those pages out of the book. I am not that woman anymore. And Sam is not that man.

I meet Sam's gaze.

"I know what's best for me. I'm not going to change my mind. I want what we have." I take a step toward him, but I don't reach for him. I need him to hear every word, and I need them to stick. "You said you didn't know you hurt me then, but that was on me. I didn't tell you how I felt. But I'm telling you now."

Now Sam's eyes are swimming and I am the one who is calm.

"I want to do this with you," I tell him. "I always will. So please. Be there."

Sam's throat bobs. I've never seen him this close to tears. He doesn't try to hide them, but instead reaches out his hand.

"Come down with me," he says. "It's going to rain."

I don't move. "Come to the showcase," I say quietly.

Sam looks down then, taking a moment to collect himself. It doesn't work. His eyes are almost spilling over when he looks up.

"Tell me you'll forgive me if I don't," he says.

I will. Of course I will. But I won't forgive myself.

Every moment of the past two days has been spent trying to undo this. Now that it's over, the shame I've been too busy to feel hits so hard that my body has to brace itself. My bones go stiff. My nails cut into my palms. My eyes cut to the dark, swollen clouds descending on us, but it still doesn't rain.

I can't bring myself to look back at him yet. He deserves an answer. But if I give one, it'll make the whole thing real.

Then Sam pulls in a breath that sounds like it's caught in his throat. When I turn back, his expression is wretched, like my silence was answer enough.

"Sam—"

"I can't lose you," he says, his voice so broken that it cracks something in my heart right with it. "Please. Mackenzie. You have to know I'm doing this because I lo—"

"Don't say that," I beg.

A tear streaks down his cheek. He lets out the rest of the breath in a shudder, lowering his head so I can't see his face.

I'm the storm. I fixed my own heart so I could hurt his.

I take a step toward him, softening my voice. "If we say those words to each other—it won't be here. It won't be like this."

Sam's throat bobs. "If," he repeats.

"When," I correct myself. "I hope—I hope a lot of things. But mostly I hope that you change your mind."

The storm never breaks. It looms above us like a threat as Sam clears his throat and gives me a tight nod. As his gaze lingers on mine and his mouth opens, but he doesn't speak. As he pulls open the door to leave, stopping to find my eyes.

"I won't change my mind." His eyes burn into mine with resolve. "And maybe you don't want to hear it right now. But I sure as hell won't change my heart, either."

And then I'm alone. Not Mackenzie. Not Seven. But something in between—a woman who isn't sure if she's the one getting left, or the one doing the leaving.

PART SIX

"Last"

chapter twenty-nine
MACKENZIE

It isn't the contract that has me in a bind anymore. It's the "compromise" the label made. The one that's a whole lot more of a threat.

If I perform in the showcase alone, they'll consider running with Mack & Sam. Which is to say, if I *don't* do it, any future for Mack & Sam is off the table.

In theory, the plan is simple. Go onstage and fill up as much of the billed time as I can by singing Mack & Sam songs alone. Even if I can't do them justice without Sam, the songs will speak for themselves—all of the hope and the joy and the depth that a Seven song could never capture on its own. The kind we had with "Play You by Heart." The audience will latch on to the new music the same way they did with that song back then, and the demand will force the label's hand.

In reality, I spend the whole day sweating like a geyser, trying not to upchuck my lunch.

It was daunting enough to debut my new voice in public with Sam by my side. It's another thing entirely to do it on my own. It may be overdue, but there's no escaping the truth everyone is bound to realize. I am not the woman who sang in Thunder Hearts, and I never will be again. There will be no reunion tours, no new recordings. The Mackenzie Waters they knew is gone.

It feels like I'm crashing my own funeral to bring something else back from the dead.

"You ready?"

Serena touches my arm gently, but I still startle. I haven't put the guitar down all day. My fingers are aching from rehearsing Sam's parts. My heart is aching even worse from missing him. I've still been holed up in Serena's apartment avoiding the cluster of people on my sidewalk, but that hasn't stopped me from checking the door every other minute as if Sam will magically walk through it.

I loosen my vice grip on the guitar, forcing myself to take a breath. It doesn't make a difference. My intestines are still playing hopscotch. My heart is still on the verge of cracking in two.

"As I'll ever be," I say.

When we get in the elevator, Serena reaches up and snaps the back of my bra. I let out a stunned laugh, turning to her to catch her familiar smirk. It's something we used to do back when one of us was nervous or in a funk before a show. Like shocking someone out of the hiccups.

It doesn't fix me, but it helps. Having Serena in my corner again helps. With all the work we've been doing trying to dig into Tick Tune's deal and salvage the one Sam and I already had, we've leaned on each other more in the past few days than we have in years.

Grayson and Hannah are waiting for us in the car Serena summoned to the curb. One look at the grim look on Grayson's face as I open the car door is enough to make me want to push it shut again.

"What is it?" I ask.

"The label owns all of Mack & Sam's content," he says.

Grayson has been acting as our lawyer, diligently poring over the contracts and contending label's legal team, working with Hannah to figure out what we can get away with tonight and working with Serena to see what we can do about Tick Tune in the long term.

But we've been over this. I knew that the label would legally own all of the Mack & Sam content we shared with them. They wasted no time filing copyrights on all four of the songs we sent.

As I slide into the car and Serena lets herself into the front, Hannah reaches over Grayson to put a hand on my knee. "The label's legal team is exercising their rights to them. If you sing any of them, it'll be a breach of contract."

The car pulls out into Park Avenue traffic.

"What about covers?" I ask.

Grayson shakes his head. "They had that baked into the showcase contract. No covers, either."

Serena lets out an undainty curse from the front seat. They would only have thought to cover their bases on that because it's the same loophole Serena's been using to let her openers perform without using songs that are tied up in contracts.

"So they're trying to force my hand," I say. "I don't have anything else I can fill the time with."

"The most important thing to remember here is that you've never admitted to being Seven," says Grayson. "They can stop you from singing Mack and Sam songs, but they can't make you sing Seven songs."

The thing is, I was willing to do just that. I have to be onstage for a full thirty minutes. Mack & Sam's songs couldn't hit that alone, so I would have sung some of Seven's songs, if it meant keeping the label happy. If it meant they were going to stay true to their word and consider Mack & Sam.

But they were never planning to consider anything. The revelation slides in like ice under my veins, but nobody else in the car seems surprised. I wanted us to have a chance so badly that I let myself believe.

I take a deep breath. It's too late for tears. I seam myself back up in a brutal instant, but when I turn back to Grayson, my eye catches on a stain by his lip.

"You've got a little—magenta," I tell him.

Grayson's cheeks nearly match it then. But not nearly as close as Hannah's lips do. I raise my eyebrows at her and she clears her throat pointedly. I make it clear with a pointed blink right back that I am filing this conversation away in "delayed, but not forgotten."

At least *one* thing isn't going to shit this week.

"Do you know what you're going to do?" Hannah asks.

For once, I'm drawing a blank. There's no winning or losing anymore. They have all the cards, and with Mack & Sam, my alter ego, and all these Tick Tune artists performing with me on the line, I'm the one with everything to lose.

When we arrive at Terminal 5, we drop off Hannah and Grayson, but Serena slides into the back and tells her driver to find somewhere to park a few blocks away.

She doesn't waste any time before handing me her phone. "I texted Sam to tell him what the label said about the Mack and Sam songs."

My eyes snap to hers. "Why?"

"I know you don't want to hear this. But Mack and Sam is over," she says, gentle but resolute. "Look at how much control the label has, and how they're using it. We can't trust them anymore. I know it might be hard to hear it from me, but he knows it, too. I thought it'd be easier to let it go if it came from him."

I swallow hard. It's nothing I don't already know deep down.

But it's still a tough pill to swallow, knowing that these people we've worked with our whole careers are so unfeeling that they'd rather use a contract to trap me than hear me out.

"It isn't," I say. "Sam already let it go. But I—I just can't."

Funny how working with Sam was my worst nightmare only a month ago. It's nothing compared to the nightmare of losing our shot.

Serena nods firmly. "Then we won't. After this is over, we'll find a work-around. Wait out the contract. Write new songs with Sam under a different duo name. I've heard what you did in a month. Don't try and tell me you two won't knock it out of the park again."

My throat is tight. Not at Serena's promises, but at the word *we*.

"What did Sam say?" I ask, looking down at her phone.

Serena takes her phone back, opening the thread. "He hasn't answered yet."

Dammit. I want to leave. But that's not fair to the artists who are opening, and doubly unfair to the ones coming after. This is their big shot, and I'm all too aware that it's the intrigue with Seven getting people in the door.

"I can't sing Seven's songs," I say.

"Then don't," says Serena.

I let out a breathy laugh. We both know that leaves me with nothing to sing, unless I sit in this car and come up with a whole album's worth of songs in an hour.

"Whatever happens tonight, we're doing a good thing for those Tick Tune artists. I wish I could do more to help with this part." She settles a hand on my wrist, squeezing tight. "But if I've learned one thing from watching you perform all these years, it's that nobody can roll with the punches like you can."

If that's true, it's only because I was never on my own. There was always the safety of being a part of Thunder Hearts, or of being

Sam's begrudging other half. My whole life I had felt so lonely that the stage wasn't just a place to perform. It was a place I shared with people I loved and would come to love. It was a place that felt like home.

It's easy to be wholly yourself when you're home. It's easy to take risks and push your limits when there's a soft place to land. But now it's just me.

"Can we just—sit here until we have to go in?" I ask.

"Of course," says Serena.

I regret it the moment after I ask. The car rolls to a stop at the curb, but my thoughts start to tailspin, and my stomach starts to twist. Just when I am on the verge of genuine panic, I'm startled by a little *knock, knock* at the window, and a muffled voice saying, "Ben! You don't even know if that's their car! Sorry, I—"

I roll the window down and sure enough, there's Ben, with a backstage pass slung over his tiny body. It's such a relief to see his big broad grin after the scare the other day that I almost forget the show entirely.

"Hey, you," I say. "How's the arm?"

Ben opens his mouth to say something, but his eyes balloon when he sees Serena. His jaw drops like he can't decide if he's going to use his next breath to speak or to scream, but thankfully Lizzie interrupts.

"Oh, hi," she says, breathless and surprised. "Sorry—Ben didn't want to miss the show. We had the taxi let us out here to go in through the back and he just marched right up before I could stop him."

"It doesn't hurt so bad anymore, but I basically got to *fly*," Ben brags, both for my sake and Serena's. "I was in the air for like, a whole minute before I crashed."

Serena lets out a stunned laugh. "He really is a tiny Sam."

"And you're *Serena*," says Ben, with a little jump. "This is *so cool*."

Lizzie sets her hands on Ben's shoulders to guide him away, but he shakes his head up at her.

"You said I could show her," he protests.

Lizzie shoots us apologetic glances. "I meant later, hon. Mackenzie's got a show to get ready for."

"It's okay," I laugh. "Show me what?"

Ben reaches his hand out for Lizzie's phone. "I've been listening to my dad's songs," he says, leaning his little head into the open window like a puppy. "You're right. They're good. But I like the new one he wrote best."

"Sam's been letting him listen to it," Lizzie explains. "He told Ben he wrote it based on one of your songs, but—I think he wrote it for you. I don't think he'd mind if you heard it."

Ben hits "play," but the song isn't new. The strumming pattern is too familiar. Almost identical to a song I've sung hundreds of times.

But another few beats and it is abruptly a song of its own. The chords aren't yearning and hopeful, but steady and bright. It only takes a few lines for me to understand what Sam has done, and it takes everything in me not to press a hand to my chest and cry.

"Golden," it's called. A play on the song "When I Was Green." Only this time instead of a song about someone trying to prove themselves, it's a song about someone who never had anything to prove. Someone who had what it takes all along, and only had to recognize it themselves.

If that first song I wrote was a call, this was the response. An uncertain melody that finally found its way to solid ground.

I blink before my eyes get misty in front of Ben. "Thank you."

Ben beams. I beam right back. Not just because of the song, but because of the reminder.

Whatever happens tonight doesn't matter, really. I have everything I need right here. Thunder Hearts by my side. Sam's love infused in every note of that song.

But most of all, I have myself. Whatever it takes to get through this night—whatever it takes to free myself of Seven, and rebuild Mack & Sam—I've had it in me from the beginning. I've come too far not to believe in myself now.

"You know what?" I say to Ben. "We're going to head in now, too."

Ben lights up, using one arm and his full body weight to yank the door open for us. We all laugh at his enthusiasm, which doesn't let up for the whole block it takes for us to get to the side entrance. He's still blasting "Golden" from Lizzie's phone even when security comes to meet us, refusing to leave with Lizzie until it's played all the way through.

We high-five Ben and hug Lizzie goodbye as the song starts up a third time, trailing off as they walk toward the front.

"It's damn catchy," says Serena. "It's too bad you can't sing that onstage."

"Yeah," I say, and then abruptly stop.

Maybe I can't sing that song, but "Golden" isn't the only gift Sam gave me. In fact, the other one may just be a secret weapon. I reach into my bag, a slow smile curling on my face.

It's been an entire lifetime of trying to spin my wheels for other people's sakes. Trying to make my parents care. Trying to make the wrong people stay. Trying to be the type of performer the label wanted, even if it meant letting them call the shots between me and Sam before we met.

Seven was my first chance to break away from expectations. But Seven only existed in the dark. Seven only existed because of the hurt other people caused. Now is my first chance to claim myself and do exactly what I want.

"You have a plan?" Serena asks.

"No," I say, laughing. "Maybe. Shit!"

Serena raises her eyebrows, amused and relieved. "Well, this ought to be good."

chapter thirty

MACKENZIE

The very first time Thunder Hearts performed live, we opened for a local band at a lounge downtown on a Tuesday night. It was so low stakes it was basement level, but just as the owner announced us, we froze. Hannah was shaking. Serena's cheeks were blazing red. I was sweating enough to pit out my sparkly dress.

We circled up. Squeezed each other's forearm's, *hard*, and nearly stumbled dragging each other to the stage, where we gave all twenty random people in that happy hour crowd the best damn debut they'd ever seen.

From then on, we did that before every show, and tonight is no exception. Just before I go onstage, Serena and Hannah circle up, giving my arms a quick pulse before letting me go.

That old magic buoys me. I take a last glance down at my old glittery boots, my faded denim jeans, my white top with its flowing, billowing sleeves. Then I hold my head high, throw my shoulders back, and blow a signature kiss out at the audience before heading toward the spotlit stool in the middle of the stage.

My heart is beating so loud between my ears that I can barely hear the applause. I've spent two years hiding from this place. Hiding from myself. No matter how tonight shakes out, it's too late to go back now.

I put my hands on the mic stand, steadying myself as I pull in a breath.

"Thank you all for joining us during what has been the . . . chillest, most uneventful week of my life."

The audience's laughter is a warm ripple. Like walking inside after a long day in the cold. The tension eases out of my bones as I adjust the mic stand and take a seat on the stool.

"I'll kick the night off with a fun fact," I say, lifting the guitar up from its stand to settle it in my lap. "This is the first time in my career I've ever performed onstage by myself."

The applause kicks up again in full force. I laugh and wave them off.

"Oh, don't clap for that," I say. "I haven't done jack shit yet."

More laughter. This is the Mackenzie they know. The one I was worried I lost two years ago, when I lost a part of myself I never thought I would.

If that's still a question, then the answer comes now.

"It's been a while. And to level with you, some of that is because my voice isn't the same as it was the last time I was up here."

I say it plainly. Not a confession. Not an apology. The audience is very still, unsure how to react.

"But neither are a lot of things about me," I say sincerely. "I'm pretty damn grateful for that."

I strum the guitar, easing into a slow version of a familiar chord progression. Before I open my mouth to sing, I aim a smile at the upper level of the venue, knowing full well it's where the label execs are standing.

They didn't bother to say anything about Thunder Hearts songs, knowing full well I couldn't sing them anymore. But the pages are crystal clear in my head—all of my words in Sam's handwriting. Old songs he helped me make new.

The label wanted this show to claim Seven. But it's my show now, and I'm reclaiming Mackenzie Waters, one song at a time.

The next twenty minutes are a time capsule pulled from the depths of my heart. The first song we debuted with as Thunder Hearts. Each of the songs I sang solo on our three albums. Songs I wrote about heartbreaks and triumphs that seem distant, now that they've been softened with time and by this new voice of mine.

After the applause dies down, I let my hand hover over the guitar strings, tilting my head toward the wings.

"I still have some time to fill, so I hope you don't mind if I welcome a few special guests up here."

If the applause was effusive before, it's deafening the instant Serena and Hannah walk out with handheld mics and stools of their own. We didn't have a second to spare to rehearse this backstage before I had to go on. But if there's one thing that hasn't changed about Thunder Hearts, it's that we know how to put on a damn show.

As soon as they settle on either side of me, we start to sing one of our old hits in unison. I'm so stunned I almost drop out to listen. I've never heard Serena's and Hannah's voices like this. They lower theirs to match mine, Hannah's sweet and light, Serena's rich and low. We were famous for our loud, striking harmonies, but now, hushed and quiet, they sound like something holy.

I don't even hear the roar of applause when the last chord comes to a stop. Serena grabs us both and yanks us in for a tight, haphazard Thunder Hearts hug. It feels like the farewell Thunder Hearts deserved, but never fully got. Not the end of something, but the beginning of so much else.

Hannah and Serena move their stools, settling behind me. The plan is that I'll sing one more song on my own. But first, I pull the mic off the stand again, addressing the audience one last time. I have the answer to my question, but they still need one for theirs.

"A lot of you came here tonight expecting to hear something from Seven," I say. "And this much I can tell you: She wrote those songs to let something go, and she did. Which is why I can honestly say that I'm not her."

The space is quiet enough to hear a pin drop. Everyone knows the truth about Seven already. But this is my truth.

And it still has plenty of power to speak for other people, even if it's done speaking for me.

"Tonight, you've heard a lot of other talented Tick Tune artists, and after this you'll hear more," I go on. "But while I've got the mic, I'd like to share that the three of us spent the past few days launching a website of our own. It's designed to let artists download and transfer their Tick Tune accounts, with their original stats, and claim the rights *without* making their identities public. It's in the beginning stages, but when we're finished, we'll also set up secure payments for all artists to get paid for their streams."

The applause is so loud that I barely get the last part out. I glance back at Serena and Hannah, whose grins match mine. Between Serena and Rocket's tech savvy, Hannah's eye for branding, and my inner knowledge of Tick Tune, we got the site up in record time. Turns out we make a good team onstage *and* off.

"Oh, shit." Serena laughs, and when I follow her gaze, I see that there's a light on in the back of the venue. The execs are moving. For the first time in our lives, we may get kicked off a stage.

I put my mouth up to the mic. No matter how I walk off this stage, it'll no doubt be without a label, without a duet, and possibly without a manager to boot. So I'm going to make every second count.

"Sorry to disappoint anyone who thought I was Seven," I say. And then I pause, letting a slow smirk curl on my face. "But if I were."

I play one singular chord. The chord that opens up the very last song that got uploaded to Tick Tune from my drafts and revealed my identity, and led us to this moment now. It is distinct enough that I hear several gasps before the cheering starts.

"If I were," I say, "this is the song I would have posted, instead of the one that went up. I'd like to play it for you. Not as Seven. But myself."

I close my eyes and strum the guitar.

"It's called 'Last.'"

And then I finally get to sing it. Sam's song, the way I rewrote it. Sam's song, the way it deserves to be heard.

Our song, the way I hope it always will be.

I sing it as if he's here. As if I can make every word of it fly through the air and reach him, wherever he is—not to tell him how much I love him. He already knows that. But to make him *feel* it.

As I play the last note, I sense shuffling in the wings. It's all right. Security can do whatever they want with me now—I've said my piece and then some.

But when I look up, it's Sam's eyes that meet mine.

chapter thirty-one
SAM

I pack a bag for New Jersey. I coordinate with Lizzie and Kara so they'll join me with Ben after the show. I schedule a car.

But I can't get in it. I have no way of knowing what will happen at that showcase. I couldn't stand it if something went wrong and I was a whole damn state away.

New plan: stay put until Lizzie and Ben get back so we can all head to Jersey together. I pull out my guitar to fill up the eerie quiet of Dad Side, ignoring the text from the unknown number on my phone for a good hour before opening it.

But the text isn't a nosy question from an entertainment journalist. The label's not letting her do your songs, it reads.

No context. It can only be Serena, who knows I don't need it. They'd only ban our songs to force Mackenzie's hand on Seven.

Stupid of them to underestimate Mackenzie, who no doubt has something up her sleeve. But I get myself to Terminal 5 within a half hour. Nobody is going to mess with her on my watch. The same way I'd step out of her way to do what's best for her, I'll step right into someone else's.

The show is well underway, so it's easy to slide in next to Lizzie and Ben unseen between acts. Lizzie's mouth pops open in enough shock that Ben frowns up at her.

"Mackenzie's about to go on and she's his girlfriend," he says, the *duh* implied.

I blink and Lizzie lets out a surprised laugh. Ben theatrically shushes us as the lights dim. None of us have had a chance yet to decide how to talk to Ben about the idea of me and Mackenzie, but as usual, this kid's a step ahead of us all.

And so is Mackenzie. She walks onstage looking like some kind of dream, damn near floating with wild hair sweeping with every step, with the glitter on her boots catching the light. She's timeless. The kind of star you only see once in a damn lifetime, if ever.

She's got the audience wrapped around her finger before she even starts to sing. It's one thing to hear that angelic rasp of her new voice. It's another to watch the awe on everyone else's faces when they hear it in real time. It's sweeter and bolder than the one she used as Seven, and just as unique as she is. It was worth every damn minute I spent messing with the keys of her old songs to hear them new.

By the time Thunder Hearts hits the stage, I'm not worried about a thing. Mackenzie's got this in the bag.

At least, until she announces the new website. That's when I hear murmurs from the execs a few rows behind us. They're drowned out fast by the cheers, but I'm not taking chances. I give Ben's head a quick squeeze and murmur to Lizzie that I'll be back, then slip for the door that leads backstage.

Maybe Mackenzie's never had to avoid getting hauled off by security before, but I'm happy to lend past experience to help.

I'm halfway there when she starts the song. The opening chords to "Last" nearly stop me in my tracks. She wouldn't play this. Not unless something went really, really wrong.

But she isn't. Once I open the backstage door, I can hear her. The melody may be the same, but nothing else is. The strumming pattern has a new momentum. Her voice is brighter and more unabashedly *Mackenzie*. And the lyrics are flipped on their head.

It's no longer a song of moments that will be "lasts." It's a song about all the moments she wants to last and last and last. It's clever and beautiful and so damn *us* that I can't help drifting into the wings. It's not enough to hear her sing it. I need the whole view.

And then I've got it, when her eyes unexpectedly meet mine and light up like a damn firework. She lets out a happy, disbelieving laugh and yells, "Come here!"

I shake my head. This is her moment. I'm lucky to be right back at the start of when I first laid eyes on Mackenzie, in a place I'll always want to be: watching her shine.

But Mackenzie starts playing chords, smiling at me until I recognize the progression. The opening chords to the song I wrote for her. One I've spent the past few days wishing I'd let her hear.

Please? she mouths.

As if I can deny this woman anything. She knows it, too. Her face splits into a grin before I take a damn step.

Mackenzie and I have shared the stage dozens of times. We've used them to tease and challenge and taunt. We've used them to pretend to hurt each other, and accidentally do it in the process.

But we've never done this. We've never shared this space the way we are now. Not rivals. Not duet partners. But something built to last after the curtain goes down and the crowd empties out. I walk to meet her slowly, savoring the hook of her smile and the gleam in her eyes, knowing that I'll spend my whole damn life trying to find the right words to capture her and never come close.

By the time we reach each other, the crowd is screaming. If all the little tension we created onstage over the years was meant to rile them up, then this is the impossible resolution they were waiting for.

One I've been waiting for so long that there's no helping it. The moment I've got her in my arms, I have to break one last rule of Mackenzie's, and go on breaking it the rest of my life.

"I love you," I say into her ear.

I'll have my whole life to say it when I have her eyes on mine. Tonight may be a performance, but this is just ours.

She knows it, too. She burrows her head into my neck, but somehow, I feel the smile. "I love you, too."

The words don't change a damn thing. The feeling has been there so long that I can't touch a single memory of Mackenzie where I didn't feel it.

Still. It's a hell of a feeling to get to say it out loud. To know that it doesn't matter what happens next—not on this stage or any other place we set foot on in this life. It won't change the part that actually counts. It won't change us.

Mackenzie presses her lips to the side of my neck before she pulls back, eyes wet and her smile wide. She grabs the mic off its stand, still close enough that the back of her shoulder is pressed against my chest. I wrap my hand into hers, steadying us. She beams up at me before looking back at the crowd.

"It's no secret that Sam and I have been writing songs all month. It's a damn shame we won't be able to sing my favorites for you to-night."

She talks like she's letting them in on a secret. The shift is quiet, but it's there. They may have come here to see Seven, but she's getting them in our corner.

"But Sam here—he started a song a few days ago." She squeezes my hand before she lets it go, then pulls her guitar off the stand. "If he's game, maybe we could sing it together for the first time."

She offers me the guitar. I take it, strumming the opening chords and leaning into the mic stand beside her.

"It's a song about a lot of things, really. About bad timing and better timing. About a man who saw all the wrong colors, and a woman who made everything golden." I turn my head to meet Mackenzie's eyes. "But most of all, it's a love song."

Judging from the look on Mackenzie's face, there's one thing that will never change: she may talk a big game, but nobody loves breaking a rule more than she does.

I can't even hear the chords when I start to play, the way the crowd is screaming. We both laugh, our faces so close that I'm half expecting the curtain to drop, cut off the way we were that very first time we kissed.

But the show goes on. I sing the first verse alone. A man in over his head, in love too soon. Mackenzie takes over the second verse; a woman in over her heart, in love too late.

We sing the bridge together, with a line I wrote and Mackenzie perfected: *Life is always changing colors, but what we have is golden.*

The song comes to a close. The audience has reached a fever pitch, and it's no wonder why. Mackenzie is so close that I can nearly taste her. So close that I can flash back to a hundred other times we were poised just like this onstage, inches apart.

I am stronger than the man I was, but right now I don't have to be. I don't have to resist this. I don't have to pretend. I don't have to be anything other than what I am: a man so in love and so damn lucky for it that I won't take it for granted as long as I live.

The audience finally gets their damn kiss, and I finally get Mackenzie Waters's heart.

epilogue
"GOLDEN"

Two Years Later: Mackenzie

"Hair down," Serena decides, pulling out the rose-gold claw clip.

Hannah catches my curls in a fist before they fall. "Up," she insists. "So we can see the earrings."

All I can see in the mirror of my apartment's bedroom are three best friends who are all perilously close to spilling rosé on my carpet.

"Half up, half down," I decide.

Serena considers my reflection in the mirror. "All right. But when we shoot the album cover next week, I think we should try it down."

I give a little spin, watching the fluttery tulle sleeves of my flowing, deep-V-cut ivory bridal gown swish in the reflection. Under ordinary circumstances, I wouldn't be wearing a full-on wedding dress to a birthday party in a bar, but Isla and Twyla never did back down from a theme—this year it's "Married in Vegas." Hannah leapt at the opportunity to have one of us photographed in the first dress in her new bridal line, and I drew the short straw.

Now I feel so frilly and light that I can't help but be glad I did. Especially when we're pregaming at my place, serving enough disco glam between the three of us that there's more glitter on my carpet than there was onstage after our shows.

Or rather, what used to be my place. I've been living on Dad Side, so these days the apartment is more of a multipurpose recording studio / crash pad / event-hosting space for Serena to put up new music talent while they're getting on their feet. Seven Records, the label Serena launched, is booming for both her public artists *and* the ones who have chosen to stay anonymous.

My phone buzzes with a text from Sam: Lizzie and Kara won't let me sneak a single pastry. I need reinforcements. ETA?

"Oh, shit," I say, noticing the time. "We're late to pick up the others."

"Wait—one last toast," says Hannah.

She snaps a quick picture of our reflection as we raise our glasses, Hannah and Serena flanking me in bright blue and yellow dresses from the Hannah Says summer line with their hair in massive updos with matching disco balls hanging from their ears.

Hannah blinks hard, her eyes misty. I give her a quizzical look, but Serena's already nudging my back toward the hallway.

"Car is here," she says.

When we reach Sugar Harmony, Rocket is already popping into a taxi with his guitar strapped around his shoulder. He's so busy as one of Serena's artists these days that I wouldn't be surprised if he's got a gig right on the heels of this.

He's got plenty of hits on his debut album, but I'll always have a soft spot for the only cover he has on it—an old song of Seven's. In the end, we gave each of the songs away to different Tick Tune artists in Serena's label who wanted to cover them with their own styles.

Seven was only ever meant to give me a new start. It means more to me than I can ever say, that people are using her to make theirs, too.

"Sam is in the back!" Rocket calls to me. "Also, you look very pretty!"

I stick my tongue out at him and let myself into the back kitchen of Sugar Harmony, where everyone is in a flurry. Sugar Harmony has expanded to the point of catering industry events, weddings, and parties all over the city, and any Twyla and Isla bash is no exception. Nobody spots me in the doorway at first, so I get to indulge in a long, lingering look at one Sam Blaze.

He's wearing a slim-cut white linen suit, leaning against the wall with his usual confident ease. It's a suit that might look unremarkable on any other man but looks borderline sinful on him, his shirt unbuttoned just enough to see the plane of his summer-tanned chest, his hair windswept in a way that's going to tempt my fingers all night.

A very naughty part of my brain reminds me that since the party is at Lightning Strike, we've got the best place in the city to hide. But at this rate I don't know if I can wait until we reach the Hole. I'm making designs on how to sneak Sam away for a few minutes when he nudges one of the cupcake boxes open.

"What flavors did they go with?" he asks Lizzie.

She grabs Sam's wrist instead of giving him her usual light smack. Sam blinks in confusion.

"It's a surprise. The, uh—the concept," says Lizzie, sweeping the box up. "You'll see. Anyway, we better get these over to Lightning Strike."

Sam frowns. "The flavors are a surprise, too?"

Kara slides past him to whisk away the other box. "You'll see!"

He opens his mouth to protest, but then he spots me in the

doorway. His lips curl into a grin, his eyes grazing me up and down, admiring every inch. By the time he reaches me, there's a gleam of mischief in his eyes that tells me he's not going to need any convincing.

"Beautiful," he says, sliding his hands onto my waist to pull me in. "Just goddamn beautiful."

I tilt my head up at him, beaming. "You clean up pretty well yourself."

He pulls me in tighter against him. "This dress is making me think we really *should* get married in Vegas. How else are we gonna show you off?"

Before I can answer, he dips his head to catch me in a breathless, heated kiss. I melt into it, the warmth of it pooling all over my body. Everyone has been inexplicably distracted and busy all day, but there's no peace in the universe like Sam's arms around me.

He pulls back slightly, squeezing the back of my neck. "I mean it," he says into my ear. "Ben's with my mom until tomorrow. We could get on a red-eye tonight."

"Mmm. I'm sure we'd be real subtle in this garb," I say wryly.

His hand slides to my jaw, holding me there. I realize he's waiting for an answer. That if I said okay, he'd be on the next flight with me without looking back.

But we talked about this. When we get married, we don't want a spectacle. The plan is to go to the courthouse in a week or so, before Ben's school year starts back up, and then come back to Sugar Harmony for cake. The last thing we need is some elaborate wedding that might get crashed by the press.

Besides, the real love story isn't in a wedding. It's in every beat of the songs Sam and I have written together under our new duet name, Golden. It took two damn years to get released from the label's contract and get the rights back to our songs, but when our debut album comes out with Seven Records, it will have been worth the wait. If there's one thing I never have to worry about with Sam, it's whether we have enough time.

"We'll renew our vows in Vegas when we're a hundred," I say.

Sam tweaks my jaw. "I'll be a hundred and three."

"And obnoxiously handsome as ever," I say, kissing him again.

We pile into the car, where Hannah pops open champagne. The night is already starting to take on a starry, shimmery quality, the memory pressing into my heart before it even gets to my head. I finish my glass, and Sam kisses the last few drops of it off my lips as we pull up to Lightning Strike.

When we open the door, I'm expecting more clamor and noise. Only the bar isn't packed to the gills with drunk, Vegas-themed revelers. It's lit up and sparkling from the disco ball on the ceiling and bursting with colorful wildflowers at every corner, with a slew of them lining the runway Hannah uses for her fashion launches.

And then, at the same time, Sam and I both blurt, "*Ben?*"

In fact, it's a whole mismatched group of people—Ben standing between Sam's mom, Anna, and Caspar. Grayson, who is dutifully waiting for Hannah the way he always does as the supportive boyfriend of the busiest woman in the world. Twyla and Isla, looking devilishly gleeful over two cocktails. And off to the side are Hannah's parents and, looking out of place but supportive, *mine*.

Ben runs up, slamming into us with a hug. I only stay steady on my heels because Hannah and Serena are right behind me.

"We weren't about to let you guys get married in some stuffy courthouse," says Hannah.

My eyes are already welling up before I fully realize what's happening. "Guys," I manage.

"Don't worry," says Serena. "We thought of everything. The place is completely secure."

But I'm not worried. I'm overwhelmed with the love in this room. I have never been more grateful for it, but right now it might just tip me over.

Ben runs off to his moms, and then Sam's hands are in mine, as he leans in close. "You're okay with this?" he asks quietly.

I nod, too overcome to speak. Sam smiles and squeezes my hands.

"Good," he says. "Because it's been too damn long for me to go another day without being able to call you my wife."

I let out a choked, happy laugh. "Better than Sparkles," I say.

He shakes his head. "You're always gonna shine," he says, kissing the top of my head.

I look up at this man who has been so many things to me. My most unexpected heartbreak. My toughest lesson. My past, my present, my future.

My best friend, and the love of my life.

We kiss, and the bar erupts in tipsy, happy applause before tossing into an ocean of hugs and kisses and desserts. My parents wait a few minutes to come over to embrace me, sheepish but pleased.

I know they love me. It's easier to understand some of it now that I have so much steady love in my life. I see it in the way they make an effort to get to know Sam better, in the way they ask after Ben. Things will never be perfect, but some of the gap has been bridged. It is just one more thing I won't take for granted in this new, unexpected life.

"Let's get these two hot people married!" Hannah declares.

The rest of the night is a sparkling blur. My dad comes to the start of the makeshift aisle with me to give me away, tearful and proud. Caspar waits at the other end of it, ordained and ready to officiate. Rocket plays an acoustic version of "Play You by Heart" on his guitar. Hannah uses one hand to stop her steady stream of tears while she films from her phone with the other. Serena beams with a pride that glows brighter than every neon light in the bar.

Sam walks down the aisle with Ben scampering proudly just behind him with the rings. Sam waits for him to catch up so they finish the last few steps together.

Then Rocket seamlessly shifts the song to the bright, sweet chords of "Golden." All eyes shift toward me, but I can only see one person in this room. He's already watching me, hazel eyes bright and welling with awe.

It is the slowest, sweetest walk of my life. I want to savor every moment of this, the way I savor them all. The warmth of Sam's chest against my back holds me in the middle of the night. The proud crow of his voice as we cheer Ben on from the soccer stands. The too-early mornings and the too-late nights, the whirlwind of music and family and laughter and tears and more happiness than I'll ever think I deserve.

"I love you," Sam tells me, the moment I can hear him. The words come out soft and reverent, like he still can't believe how lucky he is to get to say them.

I can't help it. I tilt my head up and kiss him. Everyone laughs as he sinks into it, grabbing me by the waist and theatrically dipping me, making me squeal with delight.

He sets me back on my heels with a breathless swoop. "I love you, too," I say. I'll never tire of saying it for as long as I live.

The ceremony begins. We don't bother with vows, because there is nothing left unsaid anymore. Nothing we can't already see reflected in each other's eyes, pressed into every touch, hummed into every melody.

Eventually Caspar must tell Sam he can kiss the bride, because he wraps his arms tight around me and does just that. Our friends and family break into cheers, but I can barely hear them over the happy beating of my heart. I am dizzy with happiness, more in my body and outside of it than I've ever been, like I am feeling not just the joy of this moment but the promise of all the joy yet to come.

We'll write a thousand songs trying to capture this, each one more beautiful than the last. But we'll never finish it. Even as my heart beats to the pulse of that song, I know this to be true. It swells and pitches, it tumbles and breathes, but it will never be written, because it will never, ever end.

Acknowledgments

Mom, Dad—I wish everyone had parents like mine. This book exists because you bought me my first Chicks and Linkin' Park CDs, because you supported every harebrained music dream I had from New York to Nashville, and because you filled our home with endless music and even more love.

A massive thank you to everyone who helped bring this book to life at Macmillan and beyond. To my editor Alex, whose brain I would like to nest and live in after all eight books (!!) of being in awe of it. To Cassidy and Ashley for their care and wonderful insights. To Lucienne for being such a phenomenal guiding force every step of the way. To Meghan and Kelly and Rivka and Lexi and Brant and everyone on the team for moving mountains behind the scenes that I only ever see the iceberg of—I am so lucky to work with such creative, amazing, kind people.

Thank you to all my beloved humans. This book was an odd one for me to write because some parts of it blurred reality in a way the others haven't, and it made me more grateful than ever for my family and friends who have been in my corner for all of it, including finding my own "Joyce" in my thyroid at twenty-five. I've lived like ten different lives over the last decade, and some of it should have been a whole lot more daunting than it was, but whenever I look back, the love is louder than everything else.

A thank you to my tiniest friends, in age order: Marcy and Henry and Stella and Noah and Teddy and Starling and Ben and Juliet, and my even tinier friends, Taylor, Nora Claire, Starling's little sister (!), and several other critters whose names I don't know yet. I love you all to the moon and to Saturn. Your parents are all too great for any of you to run away from home, but if you ever do, remember that I have the best snacks.

As always, the last and largest thank you is to my family. It is easy to write love stories when you're as loved as all of us are.

About the Author

Clinton B. Photography

Emma Lord is a digital media editor and writer living in New York City, where she spends whatever time she isn't writing either running or belting show tunes in community theater. She graduated from the University of Virginia with a major in psychology and a minor in how to tilt your computer screen so nobody will notice you updating your fan fiction from the back row. Her sun sign is Cancer and her moon sign is whatever Taylor Swift song is about to pop up on shuffle. She is the author of *Tweet Cute, You Have a Match, When You Get the Chance, Begin Again, The Getaway List, The Break-Up Pact,* and *The Rival*.